Praise for
Forgotten Reins

"I couldn't put it down! It felt like I was watching a movie; the descriptions were so vivid.

A Reader

"I found myself experiencing lots of emotions while reading this book. Pain, tears, happiness and love for the characters. Highly recommend this for all ages."

Robin

"Great characters and great ending! I couldn't put it down. A must read!"

Jennifer

"This was a great story about learning to forgive, trust, and love again. A story set in Kentucky, my home state, I really enjoyed it!"

Amanda

"Great read! This book has wonderful characters and great story line. You will not be disappointed! I can't wait to read the next books in the series!"

M.P.

"I really enjoyed reading this book. Good descriptions with a plot that made me want to keep on reading. This book is part of a series. I'll be on the lookout!"

Daleen

"I really enjoyed this story and wanted everything to turn out right with Sarah and Michael. As soon as you start the book you will be hooked. I look forward to more books in this series and by this author."

Donna

“Awesome read. I didn't want to put it down!”

R.H.

“A 5-star Christian romance. Wow! This is my first read by this author, but definitely not my last! From the first [page], you become so involved with the characters that it becomes a ‘can’t put down.’ Can hardly wait for book 2 in the series. Definitely recommend this book.”

Joy

“Wonderful Read! I was caught up in the lives of the characters from the first pages. It is [a book] I can definitely recommend to anyone who enjoys a good Christian romance and loves stories about horses and ranching.”

Ann

“If you like godly wholesome love stories with a bit of a modern day western twist, buy this book. You'll be glad you did. You'll be at the end of the book before you know it. The words and the characters propelled me forward to where I hated to put the book down.”

E.L.

“A good clean Christian romance. I loved the idea of a horse rescue farm as so many animals are abused and I am an animal lover. This was my first book by this author but I am looking forward to the next book in this series.”

JoAnn

“Loved It! This was a wonderful story. Once I started reading it I could not put it down! I am looking forward to the next book!”

Michelle

Forgotten Reins

Silver Wind Trilogy—Book One

SUSAN LOWER

Published in Williamsport, Pennsylvania by Time Glider Books. Time Glider Books is a trademark of Time Glider Books, LLC.

Time Glider Books, LLC, books may be purchased in bulk for educational, business, fund-raising, or sales promotional use. For information, please email bulkorders@timegliderbooks.com

ISBN: 0692372407
ISBN-13: 978-0692372401

3 4 5 6 7 8 9 10 11 12 22 21 20 19 18 17 16 15

DEDICATION

To my husband,
who handed me a pen
and encouraged me to write.

CHAPTER 1

Almost six years had passed since Sarah Colvert last attended a horse auction. There wasn't an auction barn in the whole state of Kentucky she hadn't seen or watched the sale go on inside.

Six years seemed like a long time.

The auctioneer's chant crackled over the loud speaker.

"We'd better get a seat," her friend Josh Anderson said. He lengthened his stride to catch up with her.

Sarah hesitated in front of a lone pen in the far corner.

How many times had she followed her father through an auction barn like this one while he checked out the livestock? Even though he was no longer here, his memory filled her heart.

She heard something rustle inside the pen. It was too dark to see inside, so she reached for the gate.

"Don't go in there."

Startled, her hand flew back. Josh's sharp tone had jolted her. She took a deep breath and looked over her shoulder at him. "I'll just peek."

"They put animals in there for a reason." He stood between her and the gate.

Overhead, the auctioneer called for the first bid.

"They're starting without us."

Sarah bit her lip with indecision. She couldn't see in the shadows of the corner pen what was in there. The auctioneer called off his chant of numbers and grim lines formed on Josh's face. She sighed and headed toward the sound of the auctioneer.

She and Josh stepped inside the auditorium-style room of the auction house, and the potent smell of cigars clogged her nose and made her cough. Josh stepped aside and allowed her to choose their seats on the wooden bleachers that wrapped around three sides of the ring. He and his twin, Jenny were her two best friends. She'd met them years ago, when they spent the summer working together at Kingsley's Estate. Her heart stopped as she remembered, Michael had been there, too.

She took the thought from her mind. For some reason, tonight brought about thoughts of the past that were best kept behind her.

Six years ago, there would have been a bounce to her step and a hummed tune to her lips, for she loved bringing home new prospects.

But time had changed everything.

She'd waited all those years for this moment, when she could restore her family's name and fill the stables once more with horses. Her father always did the bidding at auctions. He could recognize a champion even in the roughest condition. She prayed for his eyes to guide her tonight.

She looked over at Josh, his red-brimmed cap only a shade brighter than his hair. Freckles ran across the bridge of his nose and gathered on his cheeks. His intense green eyes fixed on the first horse in the ring, but he flashed a white-toothed grin when he caught her looking at him.

"See anything you like?" he teased.

"What's not to like?" She ignored his flirtation and redirected her gaze to the horse in the ring, with its powerful ripple of muscles across its shoulders. Did Josh think by bringing her here, they were on a date? How long would he wait, knowing her heart belonged to another? She knew he loved her. He'd even offered to marry her a time or two. Yet, she couldn't bring herself to love him in that way, not the way she'd loved Michael. She'd made a promise all those years ago, after the summer they'd first met.

A promise she intended to keep.

Three more horses stumbled out, and Sarah rubbed her eyes. She'd run off on a fool's errand and couldn't remember now why she'd agreed to come. She was ready to give up and go home, when the ring crew whipped a thoroughbred mare into the ring.

Josh started to rise, "Let's go."

"No, wait." Sarah grabbed his arm as the horse collapsed in a heap of skin and bones. It's once chestnut hair smeared with manure and rubbed off at the hip. Sarah tightened her grip on Josh.

The horse didn't attempt to rise.

Was it dead? *Oh Lord, please don't have let this poor horse die in the ring.*

"We've seen all there is," Josh said.

The auctioneer rambled off a number, then a lower number, but nobody made a motion to bid. On the edge of her seat, she watched as the scrawny horse scrambled its long legs in all directions in the attempt to find equilibrium.

"Let's go," Josh repeated.

Inside her pocket, she carried hope along with the two hundred dollars she had been saving for this very occasion. Her gaze locked on the horse. "I want that one."

Three times the auctioneer dropped his starting bid, but nobody called out the traditional "Yep." Sarah looked around at the remaining few buyers who sat tallying up their cards or heading off towards the office to pay their bill. No one, but Sarah, paid attention to the horse in the ring.

"*That* one." She pointed to make certain he understood.

"Put your hand down." Josh grabbed her arm and pulled it down. "Charlie will think you're bidding."

"I am." She raised her hand again.

"You're crazy!"

"Yep," the auctioneer said.

Josh glanced between Sarah and the auctioneer.

"Seven, did he say seven dollars or seven hundred?" Sarah looked over at Josh.

"Dollars, seven dollars."

She waved her hand at the auctioneer and turned toward Josh. "I'll meet you at the ramp with the trailer."

He stomped off. "Of all the horses ..."

At the edge of the loading ramp, Sarah watched as two workers, along with Josh, pushed and dragged the mare through the chute. The mare stumbled on knees and hooves to keep up with the men prodding and pushing her along.

Sarah lurched forward. "Stop!"

All three men halted.

The mare collapsed.

"Now, we'll have to drag her up again," one of the men said. She heard him speak earlier to a man waiting ahead of them to load. He called himself, Ed.

Now, Sarah walked over to the mare. It flinched, as she bent down and petted the horse's head. "Josh, get a halter out of the truck."

"We ain't got all night, lady."

Josh jogged past Sarah, and she heard the truck door squeak and slam shut. A few minutes later, Josh produced a halter.

She crooned softly to the horse as Josh handed her the halter.

"We've got other animals to load," Ed complained.

Sarah looked up at Ed. "Then they'll just have to wait."

Another man scuffed his foot.

"I wouldn't do that if I were you, Billy," Josh warned. "You kick that horse and she's liable to kick you."

Billy scowled and Ed chuckled. "Well, let's get on with it."

"Come on, girl. Just a few steps and you'll be headed home." She didn't know if the horse understood her, but the animal's eyes tugged at Sarah's soul. "You don't want to stay here with them."

Josh nudged Sarah. "Ready?"

She gave the horse one last look, and then glanced up at Josh and nodded.

They grabbed the mare's halter from both sides. Josh nodded to the other two men, and on the count of three, they pulled. Josh nudged the horse's sides. Billy and Ed lifted the horse's rear end.

The horse groaned as the men pushed. Sarah pulled. Her arms ached with the strain. Slowly, the horse scooted forward onto front knees. Half crawling, half dragging and kicking, they managed to get the mare onto the end of the trailer.

Exhausted, Sarah leaned back against the cold metal gate.

"Be dead by morning," Billy grumbled.

Sarah glared at Billy.

"Don't pay him any mind Sarah. He's just sore he got stuck in the stocks tonight."

She hopped off the loading ramp, heading for the truck's cab. At least for seven dollars, the horse would have a thread of hope, unlike at a slaughterhouse, its only other option.

"Thanks, Josh." She settled into the truck seat beside him.

"For what?"

She watched him secure his seat belt. "I know you gave up working tonight so you could bring me."

Josh shrugged, "It's not like Ed and Billy can't get along for a night without me."

At home, Josh backed the trailer to the stable's entrance. Sarah slid from the seat of the truck and flipped on the walkway lights, flooding out the night.

"I say we roll her off. She's not going anywhere."

The animal didn't balk at the drop to the ground, air exhaled sharply from its lungs. Sarah ran her hand over its rail track chest to feel the slight movement of breathing.

"If she's alive in the morning, I'll call the vet." Josh clamped the trailer door shut with a loud bang.

Sarah watched him walk into the darkness.

She brought a bucket of water and placed it in front of the horse. The mare looked at her with mournful black eyes. She slipped down on the ground, sitting beside the mare. Stroking the horse's neck, she drifted off to sleep and dreamt of not so long ago.

Sarah sneaked past the stalls with only the dim lights from the walkway to guide her. Heart pounding, she drew closer to the stall door. Her long hair flowed down her back and swung gracefully at her waist.

She took a deep breath and inhaled the sweet aroma of alfalfa.

Sounds of stomping and scraping as horses dozed broke the stillness of the night.

She glanced behind her. She knew Ron, the security guard here at Kingsley's estate, had already made his rounds. But she looked back just the same.

From within the next stall, a hand reached out and grabbed her arm, yanking her inside, while another covered her mouth before she could make a sound. Slowly, the hands released her as she looked around.

Several blankets lay spread over a bed of straw and from behind her, the stall door slid shut. For a brief instant, she willed the quiver in her stomach to ease.

"I was beginning to wonder if you'd show up." He drew her toward him. Dark locks of hair fell across his wide forehead, and his pale blue eyes held her captive. She looked up at him and traced the tip of her finger across the line of his square jaw.

He bent down close, rubbing his nose against hers.

"Michael," she whispered.

"Umm." He nuzzled her neck.

She pressed her hands to his chest. "I don't think we should be doing this."

He laughed softly, tilting her head back to look at him. Sarah bit her lip and looked away.

He wove his hands through her long hair and she sighed. He eased her body down and pushed her back into the layers of blankets and straw. The fragrance of fresh sawdust and alfalfa mingled around her, and a thousand butterflies took flight inside her stomach.

"You're so beautiful," he murmured.

"What if we get caught?"

He chuckled into her neck and pulled her closer.

"I don't want to ever have to leave this place."

"I doubt the stall owner is willing to share," Michael said, his breath warm against her neck.

Sarah inched closer. "I'll bribe him with a few sugar cubes."

He pulled away. His face sobered in the shadows. "As long as it's the horses you give sugar to, and no one else."

"Jealous?" She giggled.

"Maybe."

"Only maybe?" She leaned over him with her elbows on his chest. Her unbound hair spilled down around her face. A movement in the walkway caused her to tense. The horse in the next stall shifted, and another horse further down nickered. Michael's hand slid up her arm and gently pushed her away.

He motioned for her to lie down and stay still. He pressed his fingers to her lips. Sarah's heart thudded in her chest. Quickly, she rolled herself up in the blankets, covering herself from head to toe. She heard a rustle of movement in the stall, and a few horses nickered again, announcing an intruder.

At the sound of the stall gate sliding open, she froze. Afraid to breathe, she took small, quick gulps of air. Michael's voice muffled along with someone else's from the other side of the gate.

Strands of hay scratched patches of her exposed skin.

She flinched at the sound of the door latch click.

Why was Michael taking so long?

Sweat trickled down the side of her face and neck, and the rough texture of the blanket stuck to her flesh.

Her leg twitched. She bit her lip, avoiding the temptation to reach down and rub her shin.

A prickling sensation engulfed spots all over her body, and she squeezed her eyes shut, trying to ignore it. Her heart pounded so loudly, she feared whoever was out there would hear it.

The voices faded a few moments later. Unable to resist any

longer, she rolled and scratched as the blanket spun itself around her like a cocoon. She tried to struggle free …

The sudden jerk of her "cocoon" sent her spinning.

She blinked, awake, spitting out dirt and sawdust smeared on her mouth. Rolling onto her side, Sarah became aware of the pair of black boots a few feet from where she lay.

"Sarah?"

She looked up into his pale blue eyes and her heart skipped a beat. "Michael." His name escaped in a rush of air.

He dropped the end of the blanket. His face paled. "Are you okay? I didn't mean to … I thought you were a bunch of barn cats …"

Cats … She stumbled forward, tripping over her sluggish feet.

"Here let me help you?"

Disoriented, she felt as if she awakened only to have stepped back into a dream. "What are you doing here?"

"Tending my first patient, it would seem." He reached out attempting to steady her. His touch was real, as real as the horse next to her.

Six years! She coughed. This had been the man she'd fallen in love with all those years ago. The man who never said he loved her. And, the man who gave her back the joy in her life while crushing her heart at the same time.

She felt her heart cracking like the shell of a nut.

He frowned as Sarah dodged him and glanced around to the fallen horse. A deep seated ache radiated from her heart.

"I'm surprised she's not dead," he said.

His voice sounded as shaky as her legs felt as she walked past him to the horse. She attempted to find some composure, but her pulse became erratic.

What was he doing here?

After all these years, he'd chosen now to show up. A sudden chill ran down her arms.

Unless ... no, she pushed the thought away, now was not the time.

"I bought her last night at an auction."

Michael hunched down on his heels beside the horse. He was silent. Deep lines formed across his forehead.

Sarah kneeled in front of the mare's head. At least the poor horse was still lying on her belly—a good sign.

"I hope you didn't pay much."

"Seven dollars."

Michael shook his head.

"It was better than the slaughter house," Sarah said, with the sudden urge to defend herself.

"I'll be back in a moment." He headed outside to his truck.

Sarah raced into the stable's office, grabbed the phone off her desk, and made a call. On the other end of the line, Jenny yawned.

"Jenny! Keep Ethan in the house!"

"Why? Is the horse contagious?" Jenny asked.

"You saw her?"

"Yeah, I sneaked down a couple hours ago and checked her out. Where did you think the blanket came from?"

Sarah looked out the small office window. A red diesel truck sat parked outside, with a cap full of compartments, and the short aluminum stock trailer hooked behind it cast a glare in her direction.

"Sarah?"

"I'll explain as soon as I get there."

"Josh said he called Dr. Miller, but some new guy, Wolfe, I think, is on his way. Is that him?"

Leave it to Jenny to have her nose pressed to the kitchen window.

Now that Gran passed away, Jenny had moved in the old farmhouse with her and Josh had taken up residence in the cottage across the bridge.

"I have to go." Sarah spied Michael.

She returned to the horse, and lifted its muzzle to slide her bent legs underneath. She brushed the forelock aside and massaged the horse's ears. The mare sighed and watched her with those same mournful-looking eyes, and Sarah willed herself to relax, not wanting Michael to discover he was the reason for her flustered behavior.

"Seven dollars." Michael hunched down beside her. His face had relaxed a little, she thought, his features were still the same as she remembered him.

He ran his hand down over the horse's rib cage, keeping his focus on the mare. "I don't suppose she can stand?"

Sarah shook her head. "Why are you here, Michael?" All these years and not once did he ever tried to contact her. So, why was he here now?

"I believe you called me." The mare flinched as he pulled the skin of its rump to slide a needle in. He popped open the case and extracted necessary supplies.

She frowned, confused. "You're Dr. Wolfe?"

"At your service." He mocked a bow.

"What happened to Doc Miller?"

Swiftly, the mare turned its head to nip him. "He's retiring." He clenched a tube between his teeth and in seconds an intravenous line was running into a vein in the horse's neck.

"Of course." She held onto the mare's halter as it jerked. So, Michael was the new hot shot veterinarian from Louisville, creating buzz by everyone in town.

"That's all I can do for now. I think she'll be fine here until she can stand. Just a bit of an inconvenience to work around is all." He cleaned up his litter before gripping his medical case. "I'll need to unload Clyde before I head out."

Alarmed, Sarah followed him from the barn, ignoring the gray clouds and the gentle rumbles of the sky. "Hold on!" she cried as he headed towards the back of the trailer. "Who's Clyde?"

If Michael heard her, he gave no indication. The trailer gate swung open and he stepped inside. Sarah braced herself.

A moment later, he emerged with a tall black horse at the end of a lead rope.

The black was a good seventeen hands. Its muscular shoulders reminded her of a thoroughbred, though the body type was chunky.

"Meet Clyde." He passed her, heading into the barn. The mare squealed lightly at the black, and the cogs in Sarah's brain turned as she followed Michael.

"Hold on a minute!" She jogged in front to halt his march. "What do you think you're doing?"

"I'm boarding my horse in your stables, unless I misunderstood the guy I spoke with last week."

"Josh!" Suddenly, she recalled a conversation with Josh about a temporary boarder at the stables.

Sarah took a deep breath.

"You can have the stall on the end." She pointed down between the rows.

"What's wrong with this one?"

When Sarah didn't reply, Michael flung open the nearest stall gate and led Clyde inside. She opened her mouth then closed it, that stall was for her rescued horse.

He patted the horse's neck and stepped out, latching the gate.

What little composure she held on to, snapped like a rubber band. "I don't know what kind of arrangements you made with Josh, but let's get a few things straight." She huffed as Michael leaned back against the bars of the stall. "This is not a boarding stable. This is an equine rescue facility."

"Then it looks like I came to the right place."

Sarah fought to regain composure. She wasn't about to let Michael get beneath her skin, not when the shock of his appearance still clung to her like a wet rag.

"We only board horses in need of a home until a more suitable one can be found."

"I think I got the idea." Michael crossed his arms. "You should talk to your foreman. It looks like we're going to see a lot of each other from now on." He pushed away from the stall, his height only a few inches above hers.

Sarah stepped back. "What is that supposed to mean?"

"Ask Josh. I believe that was his name?" He hooked his finger under her chin. "Just be sure you keep to the agreement."

She jerked her chin from his grasp. "Make sure you send me the bill for the horse."

Quickly, she turned away. Her heart squeezed in her chest until it ached and tears burned in her eyes, but she refused to release them. She lengthened her strides heading toward the house as the first drops of rain fell from the bleak sky.

CHAPTER 2

A flash of lightning split the sky.

Michael slid into the cab of his truck as rain splashed the windshield, blurring his view of the large stone house, as Sarah's hasty form, a smudge of purple, disappeared within. Hearing the engine purr to life, he turned the steering wheel, heading back down the lane with his empty trailer still attached.

How could he have known, when yanking the blanket free from the struggling form that Sarah would come rolling out at his feet? Her dark hazel eyes were wide when she saw his face, and her shock, mirrored his own. He'd never thought he'd see her again.

"Six years." He glanced in either direction before pulling out of the lane and onto the road, where he turned right, towards the farm he'd purchased a few months ago. The wiper blades screeched across the windshield, while the rain pelted noisily against the cab roof.

He still couldn't believe his eyes. He placed Clyde in the nearest stall not wanting to walk past her. He had been afraid Clyde might strike out at the sick mare in the walkway. But more so, he'd feared turning around to find she was only a mirage.

What happened to the Sarah he remembered, the one who'd

stand and challenge the world on a whim? For a split second, he imagined he saw her again, with pieces of straw and sawdust speckled through her hair. That sweet seventeen-year-old girl, replaced with a mature woman—her oval face unchanged. Yet, once the initial shock passed, she hadn't seemed able to look him in the eye.

He pulled into the lane of his property, and parked in front of the house. This farm never reached the market, as his realtor swooped down on the place before the owner could have second thoughts about the sale. The shabby old plantation, since the day he bought it, was coming back to life.

Through the advice of his realtor, he'd hired a construction outfit to remodel the house. Once a single-family dwelling, it was now transformed so his veterinary practice was on the first floor and his living quarters on the second. It was the perfect location for his new equine clinic, close to the road, yet far enough out of town for privacy—when he felt like being alone.

Less than half a mile down the road was the only farm near him; joining his property on two sides. Yet, he had plenty of room to roam without crossing the road.

Michael climbed out of the truck, dashing through the rain to the house. He kicked off his boots and glanced around the room. All throughout his second-story apartment were his belongings, still stacked in piles of boxes. His mother arranged for them to be shipped down from Louisville, but unpacking was far from his mind right now.

What had he done to make Sarah so distant? When two old friends saw each other, they usually embraced. But not Sarah. Yet, he couldn't blame her. Only she'd been the one to run out on him. So why was she still running?

Michael hadn't been a saint in his youth. He was one of those boys a momma warned her daughters to stay away from, but it was the warning—the daring—, the excitement that kept girls chasing him through college. None but Sarah had ever made him chase back. But then she disappeared without a goodbye.

"Smooth move, Ace." He fell back onto the plush gray couch,

misplaced near the dining room table, and tried to concentrate on something other than Sarah.

His new second-story apartment sported two bedrooms, a bath, and the addition of a study. His mother would have a field day with the standard beige walls and the cherry-stained floors. All his life she fussed about details, designs, coordinating her house, but she'd never found time to tuck him in at night. Marie, his brother's nanny, had seen to that, but more often than not, his father relieved her of the chore. Yes, Harold Kingsley always treated him fair, allowed Michael to call him father, and treated him like his own son.

Harold Kingsley was the only father he'd ever known—until he discovered his Heavenly Father.

Michael knew he should unpack, but as he crossed his arms behind his head and mused, Sarah popped into his mind. He could hardly wait to see her again, now that the shock had eased from his system. How could the sight of a pretty face elicit such strong emotions? Michael always prided himself on being attentive to women, and liked that he could sweet-talk them, make them laugh, and cause them to smile with a wink. His mother taught him how to be polite; she wouldn't expect him to be any less.

His mother did, however, expect him to be a doctor.

He hadn't failed her, though his patients were of the four-legged kind. His family didn't seem to mind. Harold encouraged him, set him up with contacts, and believed in his ideas.

His clinic would change the number of horses destroyed or permanently disabled from injury.

If only the expert from Indiana would hightail it down here to build his horse clinic.

Thirst parched his lips. He rose, walked into the kitchen, and pulled a bottle of spring water from the fridge. Twisting off the cap, he took a long swig from the bottle, and then halted mid-tilt.

His plans were coming together as expected.

Only Sarah Colvert as a neighbor hadn't been in the plans. When he purchased the farm a few months back, Sarah wasn't drawn into the blueprints. He'd tried to forget about her when he went to college—then spent his internship on the other side of the state.

Now, with Sarah so near, he wasn't quite sure what he'd do about her. All he needed to do, he told himself, was focus on the business at hand.

Like all he needed to do one chilly winter night at the campus chapel, years ago, was place his life in God's hands. The hardest thing he ever did was admit that God, not Michael Wolfe, was in charge.

"By grace ..." he muttered over the lip of his bottle, finishing the swig. His father, Harold, taught him that, or at least tried. As a youth, Michael had been too stubborn to listen, and turned a deaf ear to the teachings his father shared with him even into his teenage years.

It took an error in his training, and a Christian lab partner, to redeem him.

So Michael found God, and God welcomed him in this life. Now, Michael Wolfe was a man renewed, determined to change the reckless reputation of his youth.

Michael finished off the contents of the bottle in one long gulp. He'd noticed the way Sarah stumbled from the ground like a foal gaining legs for the first time. Her jeans were caked with dust and thin at the knees, and her lavender blouse was wrinkled and stained from the leaking drool of the horse's mouth.

He replayed in his mind the flare of her eyes, the parting of her lips, and the tint of pink across her cheeks. There had been no smile, no warm welcoming, only the chill of surprise.

"Surprise, Sarah." He tossed the empty bottle in a box on the counter. "You can't run from me this time."

Sarah searched for a pan. *Thanks Josh*! Pans scattered across the floor and crashed around her, much like her life. One by one, she slammed each of them back into the bottom drawer of the stove.

"What's the big deal? I thought we were all in this together,"

Jenny said.

Sarah's head snapped up. "That's not the point."

"Then what is?"

"Michael's here."

Jenny's eyes grew wide, "As in Kingsley's Michael?"

"None other." Sarah turned her head to look at Jenny, and paused from pouring batter into a baking dish. "The man ruins my life and shows up on my doorstep six years later, but it's no big deal."

"Wow. Is that really how you feel?"

"Yes ... No ... I don't know." She placed the batter-filled pan in the oven. She really didn't know how she felt about the appearance of Michael in her stables. Scared? Shocked? Excited? It all swirled in her chest and built up into the anxiety she now faced.

Six years ago, she'd been in love with him, and maybe deep down inside, those feelings were still there. But things had changed; she wasn't that lonely teenage girl who yearned to be loved. Now she had responsibilities.

Placing the mixing bowl on the table between them, Sarah paused to dip a finger into it. "He looked as surprised as I did this morning." She licked her finger while Jenny sampled the spoon.

"You don't think he knew you were here?" Jenny asked.

"How could he?"

Jenny laid down the spoon. "You make it sound as if you're hard to find."

"Of all places, I can't believe he's here."

"Believe it," Jenny said. "If Michael bought the Sherman place, then he's not going anywhere. You'd better get used to it."

Sarah paused. She listened to the sounds of a television floating in from another room.

Jenny slid from her chair. "You'll figure something out. You always do."

But somehow, Sarah didn't feel encouraged.

"I hate to chat and run, but I'm going to the office. I thought I'd surf the web and keep the horses company. Besides, smelling chocolate makes me gain five pounds." Jenny ran her hands down her generous hips. A smudge of chocolate still graced the corner of her lips.

"As if five pounds would hurt. That would be the least of my problems," Sarah turned on the water in the sink.

Jenny grinned. "You never know. Maybe Michael coming here is God's way of setting things right."

"You've obviously forgotten I've committed a sin." Sarah dipped her hands into the soapy water.

"Pastor Johnson isn't around anymore."

"Yeah, but he was right." Sarah whispered as Jenny walked out of the kitchen.

She finished cleaning up the dishes and sat watching television with Ethan while she waited for the oven timer to buzz. Jenny's words echoed in her mind as she looked over at her son. *What would Michael think when he saw Ethan*?

"Mom?" Ethan leaned against her and finished his half of the brownie she'd split with him. "Can we go see the horses now?"

"Not now, maybe when it's not raining so hard."

Ethan scowled. "Can I go jump in the puddles?"

"Maybe later …"

After supper, Sarah helped Ethan dress in an old pair of jeans and a long-sleeve shirt. He donned a rain poncho and slipped on a pair of rubber boots.

Sarah sat on the front porch watching Ethan jump in puddles down the lane as the rain changed into a mist on the warm May evening. Jenny came out of the house from cleaning up the supper dishes and sat down beside her.

"So, have you decided if you're going to let him keep his horse here?"

"We need the money," Sarah admitted. Getting the equine rescue up and running would take more financial support than what Sarah, Jenny, and Josh could currently provide.

The reality of their situation sank deeply within her. Michael lived down the road. Out of all the farms in the county, why did he have to choose a neighboring property?

She jumped to her feet, heading for the barn. She needed to check on the mare, and this seemed like a good time.

"Where are you going?" Jenny called after her.

"Watch Ethan; I'll be right back!"

The mare had scooted down a few feet from her original position, so Sarah gathered up the hay and water and pushed them closer to the animal. The intravenous tubing remained in place, and the animal's eyes seemed more alert.

"We'll get you into a stall as soon as you can stand," Sarah told the mare as she walked down to the stall where Michael housed his black gelding. Clyde laid his ears back as he tossed his silky mane.

"Clearly nobody thought to inform you that you're not a stallion anymore," she told the horse.

"He'll get used to the idea."

Startled, Sarah turned in the direction of Michael's voice. "Your handiwork?"

"He'll settle down soon," Michael said, reaching for the gate. As Sarah turned away from him, he reached toward her. "Sarah." But she shook her head and walked away.

She didn't look back to risk seeing the expression on his face. "If you're worried about tending to your horse, don't be. It's included in your board."

How long would it be before he moved the horse to his own place? She wanted it to be soon—but what would she do then?

Outside the barn, she called for Ethan. He paused in front of a large mud puddle. Looking at her, he jumped. Water and mud splashed up his legs. He glanced over his shoulder at her and grinned. Sarah laughed.

"You've had your fun now. It's time to come in." The sooner, the better. She took one last look at the barn before herding her son back to the house.

Ethan stomped his feet the whole way. Sarah took his poncho and pulled off his boots once they were inside.

"No bed," he mumbled as the sun was starting to set, but Sarah guided his small body up the stairs.

"Bath first." She ran the water in the tub.

"Ah, Mom." He shrugged out of his wet clothes while climbing into the old claw-foot tub with Sarah's help. "Can I have bubbles?" He splashed around while Sarah sat on the tile floor beside him. She let him play until his fingers and toes became shriveled and pink.

"*Two* books," he demanded. She tucked him in after three.

"Stay please, Mom." He held on to her hand. Sarah squished herself beside him on the small bed and held him close while he fell asleep.

As she gazed out his bedroom window at the stars dotting the blank sky, Michael arrived. In the faint glow of the pole light, she watched him step out of the barn and pull up the hood of his jacket.

CHAPTER 3

Sarah piled her long locks of hair on top of her head—spiral curls draped down her slender neck.

"You're definitely gonna turn some heads," Jenny said.

"I think you'll be the one with a trail of boys." Sarah turned so Jenny could zip her gown. "I'm not sure if I should go. What if I don't fit in?"

"Like I do?" Jenny managed a small laugh.

"Don't we look stunning?" a voice said when the door was pushed opened.

"Josh!" Sarah gasped.

"Get out of here! Can't you see we're not ready yet?" Jenny snapped as she attempted to push her twin out of the doorway, but Josh eluded her by stepping inside.

"I'll be your date tonight, Sarah," he offered with a grin.

"Why aren't you dressed?" Jenny asked.

"I'm not a girl. It doesn't take me all afternoon to get ready. All I need is two seconds."

Jenny's eyes narrowed. "If you say so ..."

"I suggest you hurry up."

"Why?" Jenny tugged at the short spikes of her auburn hair, molding them to stay in place.

"You've only got a half hour," Josh said with a tap on his watch.

Jenny rolled her eyes. "Look who's talking. Not even dressed yet."

"I can fix that. I'll be right back."

Sarah turned and gazed at herself in the tall mirror mounted on the closet door. She ran her hand down the black silk gown, remembering the day she bought it. She'd searched the mall and every dress shop in Louisville to find this gown. Timothy Gowan asked her to the prom, but Sarah didn't take advantage of the opportunity. The prom hadn't seemed important the day she stood by her parents' freshly-covered graves.

Sarah blinked away the moisture, so her mascara wouldn't run. Jenny had been so patient in applying it; she didn't want to ruin the effort.

Jenny picked up their fringed shawls, handing one to Sarah.

"Hey," Jenny said in a soft voice. "It's just a party."

Sarah tried to laugh, but the huge droplets of tears left a black trail down her cheeks. "I know. It's just that ..."

The image of her mother standing behind her when she first tried on the gown came to mind.

"Give it some time," Jenny told her, laying a hand on her friend's shoulder.

For a moment Jenny looked as if she would say more, needed to say more, but plastered on a cheerful smile instead. "Now let's get those eyes repaired and find Josh. We can't have Michael seeing you this way, can we?"

Josh returned in his black suit to escort them, and Sarah stood outside the entrance of the colonial, four-column mansion. She gawked at the guests milling around the front porch before she entered. The door greeter nodded at her, stacking her invitation on top of the pile.

Sarah wandered in, awed with the splendor of it all. Inside the foyer, shawls rustled as they were shed. High heels clipped across the black marble floor, while giggles, hearty laughs, and low murmurs buzzed around her. She looked at the sleek wooden banister of the staircase, and thought of Cinderella. *Had she felt this way, too*? Sarah ran her hands down her hips, smoothing any invisible wrinkles of the clinging fabric. There were so many people milling about, she wondered how she'd ever be able to find him.

Aimlessly, she wondered from room to room, found the ballroom on the second floor, and squeezed through the crowds to enter. Her heart raced, watching the couples dance across the polished floor. Jenny was among them, swept up in the arms of another coworker Sarah recognized, named Todd.

Tall windows from floor to ceiling held their golden draperies open to view the evening sky. Several entrances stood open, leading to curved balconies, and the crystal chandeliers sparkled in the cathedral domes above her. A large orchestra played from the far corner.

"Miss Colvert!"

Sarah jumped at the sound of her name.

"Mr. Kingsley."

Her spine stiffened at the sight of her employer—Michael's father.

"Sarah Colvert." Harold Kingsley smiled. "I'm glad you came."

She forced herself to relax. "Thank you." She wished she hadn't left her shawl downstairs. Despite the warmth of the night, she yearned to have something wrapped around her like a hug.

"You look very lovely tonight." Her cheeks warm at his compliment. "May I have this dance?" Mr. Kingsley held his hand out toward her.

He led her out amongst other couples onto the dance floor, and for a fleeting second Sarah forgot how to waltz. She glanced into his eyes, which captured her with their kindness. Soft hints of grey wove into the sides of his dark hair. The light laugh lines barely crinkled the corners of his eyes, but he seemed the type to use them often. Like every man attending the gala, he wore a black tux tailored to fit his thin frame.

His eyes fixed on her face. "You look like your mother."

"You are the first to think so." She rested her hand on his shoulder. She felt her cheeks flush as his hand warmed the small of her back while they danced. *Would this have been what it was like to dance with her father*? She looked away, afraid Harold Kingsley would see the pain etched there.

"Perhaps it is your father's features that strike them first."

She followed his lead to the music. "Perhaps."

Fresh grief formed a lump in her throat.

When the music ended, he stepped back from her. "Thank you for the dance, Sarah."

She smiled, a small curve of her lips, and glanced down at the floor.

"I hope you enjoy your evening." Mr. Kingsley slipped into the crowds of guests.

Sarah retreated to the corner of the ballroom, admiring the gowns of the ladies in attendance. Josh stepped in to claim a dance with Jenny, and the two of them smiled and laughed. Why she thought she could fit in here amongst these people was beyond her, and a chill of goose bumps swept up her arms.

The room sizzled with the rising heat of bodies jammed close together, and Sarah headed downstairs for her shawl, but in the midst of her retreat, her eyes found *him*.

Her lungs screamed for air and her body forced her to suck in oxygen. His eyes were locked on her over the head of a petite blonde, and the room darkened. Sarah's knees buckled, as she noticed the displeasure of his posture—as if he longed to be with her rather than the blonde on his arm. His eyes seemed to brand her with their intensity, and he flinched as the blonde ran her hand through his jet black hair.

Sarah tore her eyes away from his stinging gaze. She stepped backwards, bumping into another woman, and whirled around to flee. The woman stepped aside. Sarah tried to smile and excuse herself, but tears threatened to burst forth. The hot rush of embarrassment flooded her cheeks, and she fled toward the entrance.

She ran across the lawn—the slim heels of her sandals sank

into the soft turf. Sarah stopped, bent over, and then headed towards the stables in her stocking feet with sandals dangling from her hand.

Sarah sat beneath the large oak tree with her knees hugged close to her chest and her chin rested on the rough denim of her jeans. Smears of damp grass stained across both her knees. Her favorite gray sweatshirt clung damp with perspiration.

She'd worked all morning alongside Josh, mending wire and replacing rotted posts in the overgrown pasture. She didn't know what she'd do without Jenny to watch Ethan, and Josh to help get the equine rescue on its feet.

At one point in her life, this place represented her father's dreams and his father's ambitions. But the horses her father raised had been sold years ago. Not one single halter hung in the barn.

Now that Gran had passed away, Sarah worked hard, determined to carry on one man's dream to the generation of another. Jenny insisted on moving in the old farmhouse with Sarah, and Josh took up residence in the old cottage across the creek. Together, they formed Silver Wind Equine Rescue.

Only now, with Michael here, she wondered if her dream would succeed.

She'd managed to avoid him for several days, but sooner or later she would have to face him, face their past ...

A gentle morning breeze captured the spiraled tresses of her hair—cool and refreshing. She'd slept little at night, with dreams of the past plaguing her.

She tilted her face towards the sun and closed her eyes. *Why did he have to come here*? Of all the places Michael could have chosen, why here? Why now?

She yawned. Ethan wasn't the only one who needed a nap. But Josh arrived soon with more fence posts.

Strong hands touched her, then reached over and massaged her stiff shoulders. "I thought you'd be gone longer," she said.

"I'm sorry I disappointed you."

Sarah jerked her head up, surprised. "I thought you were Josh."

"Apparently."

Michael pressed his thumbs into the center of her shoulder blades.

"What do you want, Michael?"

"Have I done something?" he asked.

Her shoulders tensed.

"If this is about ..."

"I've got a lot of things on my mind right now," she said.

"And I'm one of them."

"Yes," Sarah admitted.

Relief flooded her eyes as she spotted an old green pickup bouncing through the field in their direction. Michael eased down beside her from his crouched position, and he leaned back against the trunk of the tree a few inches from touching her. He gave her a long sideways glance, "I could sit here all day."

Sarah ignored his remark. Tilting her face away from him, she shielded her eyes with her hand. Josh waved his hand from where he parked a few feet from the fencerow. Sarah jumped to her feet and wiped at the stains of grass on her pants, while Michael pulled his long frame up beside her.

"Forget something?" He held out her work gloves.

"Thanks." She snatched them from his hand.

"How many do you figure you got left?" They walked through the field in the direction of the truck. Josh slammed the truck door as he got out.

"Too many, but we plan to string wire for this field tomorrow."

"Anything I can do to help?" He stuck his hands in his pockets as he walked alongside her.

Sarah shook her head.

Michael took a shovel from Josh's outstretched hand as Sarah reached for it.

"Got some time, if you don't mind," Michael told Josh.

"Be my guest," Josh said.

Sarah stalked behind the pick-up truck and yanked on the tailgate. She glared at Josh as he and Michael came around the side of the truck bed.

Michael gave her a lopsided grin and she grabbed a post, shoving it into his chest.

They worked until noon. Josh and Michael dug and pounded posts while Sarah strung new wire. By Sarah's estimation, the new fence would be finished in a few days. She planned to labor all afternoon, determined not to allow Michael to get in the way of her plans. Whatever the reason he had for finding her, she suspected it had to do with Ethan. Surely, by now he noticed the little boy running around the farm.

Jenny leaned against the wall, while Sarah spread sawdust through the empty box stall.

"You ladies have been busy, haven't you?"

Josh whistled low at the clean stalls Sarah and Jenny had spent all afternoon preparing. Sarah looked up from her rake, her mouth transformed by a long, lazy smile. Jenny dumped another load of sawdust. "All we need is a few more horses."

Sarah rested her chin on the end of the rake, and the sound of Ethan's laughter made her heart ache. Inside a freshly cleaned stall, he flopped down into the sawdust to play.

"I'm building a castle." He descended on his mission with hands full of sawdust. "Uncle Josh, come help!"

Josh fetched a bucket near the wall and joined Ethan in the stall.

"You could still marry him, you know," Jenny said, her voice low as they walked out of the stall.

"And make him give up that date with the sassy blonde tonight?"

"You can't deny you love him."

"You know I love Josh." Sarah strolled toward the stable's office. "Like a brother."

Jenny rolled her eyes. "To think we could have truly been sisters."

"So, what else is on our agenda for today?" Sarah tried to redirect Jenny back to their daily tasks.

Jenny shrugged. "I don't know, I guess as long as we're done before supper."

"Don't tell me you've got a hot date tonight, too?" Sarah teased.

Josh slapped sawdust from his clothes. It even trickled out of his plaid shirt pocket.

"Who?" He leaned against the door jam.

Jenny gave Josh a slight shove, "We already know you do."

Sarah tried to peer around the doorway.

"I locked him in a stall," Josh said.

Sarah narrowed her gaze on Josh.

"But he can get out," Josh added quickly.

Sarah sat at an old office desk. Her chair, along with the dented filing cabinet, and the bookcase with the bottom shelf scraped were donated from the local high school.

A swell of ownership congested her chest. Every day for the past month they cleaned and repaired the stables in preparation for boarding horses again.

Jenny sat on the corner of the desk and stretched out her legs.

"What's this?" She picked up the pieces of mail piled atop the scuffed-up desk.

Josh snatched the top letter from her hand to read the return address. He waved it in front of them like he had a million bucks in his hand. "This, my dear sister, is a copy of the registration papers for Sarah's seven dollar deal, or shall we call her Bonnie."

"Give me that." Jenny snatched it from Josh's hand and passed it on to Sarah. Jenny huffed as Sarah tore open the envelope.

"Bonnie?" Sarah asked.

"Yep, I called the Thoroughbred Association. I know a guy working there. Anyway, it appears our girl's got a record. Not a good one, mind you, but she'd been on the track."

"That's probably why someone ditched her," Jenny said.

Josh shot a dark glance at his sister. "As I was saying, horse's name is Blue Bonnet."

"Great, we've got Bonnie and Clyde in the barn," Sarah said.

Josh and Jenny grinned at each other, and he tapped the paper in Sarah's hand. "You need to fill that one out, and put a copy of the bill of sale with it. Then the association will research it, and you can get the papers for the horse in your name."

Sarah opened the form, scanning the lines. "By the looks of it, we could also report Bonnie's condition when we found her."

Jenny looked at Josh. "I don't know, Sarah. I mean—it could cause a lot of trouble."

Sarah's jaw clenched. "So Bonnie lost a few races. Does that give someone the right to starve her? Abuse her? Abandon her?"

"Sarah ..." Josh stepped behind her. He placed his hand on her shoulders as she took a shaky breath. "Let's take it one step at a time." He gave her shoulder a light squeeze. "You have to fill out the form first."

Josh lowered his chin on Sarah's shoulder. "There's an auction next week."

Sarah laughed. "Are you offering?"

"Sure."

Josh winked at Sarah as he headed out of the room.

Jenny handed Sarah a pen and together they filled out the papers.

CHAPTER 4

"Got a minute?"

Josh stopped long enough from clearing the breakfast dishes to get Sarah's attention. Jenny snapped a towel at Ethan, who ducked behind his mother for protection at the same time Sarah stepped back.

"What's up?" Sarah placed a hand back around Ethan to keep herself from tripping over him.

"There's something I want to show you." Josh stacked dirty plates in front of her by the sink.

Sarah looked around at each of their faces, each one smiling. The scent of a secret lingered in the kitchen amongst them, and it didn't smell of maple syrup.

"What are you three up to now?" Sarah asked, apprehension lacing her voice.

"I got this, you go on." Jenny told Josh as she winked at Ethan, flexing her dishtowel.

"I can't wait to see this," Ethan said.

"As soon as you eat the rest of that pancake." Sarah pointed towards the half-eaten food on his plate.

Ethan pressed his lips together like he was closing the gate tight.

"Two bites." Josh instructed Ethan. He took Sarah by the hand and led her out of the house.

"Where are we going?" Sarah asked, halfway down the lane.

"We're almost there." Josh slowed his pace and allowed her to walk ahead of him. At the end of the drive he reached up and covered her eyes with his hands.

"Josh!" Sarah exclaimed. "I can't see!"

She stumbled forward.

"It's just a few more steps," he said.

Sarah reached up and grabbed his hands, trying to pry them away from her eyes.

"You're almost there."

Sarah held onto his hands. "This better not be another one of those times where you push me in the creek so you can rescue me."

"Now, do you honestly think I would do that to you ... again?"

"I'm not going for a swim," Sarah warned. She tried to peek below his fingers but she only saw her feet—nothing to give a clue to the secret about to be revealed.

Josh laughed. "I seem to remember us both getting wet that day."

She recalled the stern look on Gran's face as she stomped up the stairs to her room soaking wet. She received a good hour's lecture on adultery while Ethan slept in his crib.

Josh turned her head. "Now turn. Turn. There you are. Ready?"

"As I'll ever be ..."

As his hands fell away, Sarah gasped. A large wooden farm sign stood at the end of the lane. Its fresh coat of paint gleamed in the morning sunlight. The silhouette of a running horse appeared life-like painted in black. Large elegant print scrolled SILVER WIND EQUINE RESCUE across the bottom of the sign.

Her hand clutched her chest, as her heart struggled to keep up with the adrenalin rush.

"Did you make this?"

Josh grinned from ear to ear. "Do you like it?"

Sarah walked up to the sign and ran her hand across the curved top of the post.

Silver Wind, the name was chosen in memory of her mother's horse. The beautiful mare hadn't survived in the same accident as her parents.

Josh, with an expression of hope on his face, stood back from the sign. "You do like it don't you?"

"Oh, Josh, I love it!" She flung her arms around his neck. She felt him pick her up, twirling her around before setting her back on her feet.

Slowly, he released her from his hold. Clearing his throat, he stepped back. "I had Sally Mason from over in Mulberry paint it. She came by yesterday, while you were working in the field and took a few pictures. I guess she used it for some community project for school before she could graduate. You know the ones they make you do your senior year?"

"How many hours did she need?" Sarah rested her hand atop the sign. She thought back for a moment to her own community service in order to graduate high school. She'd been pregnant with Ethan.

She remembered Gran's oatmeal raisin cookies and her class project with local retirement community. No matter how many times she tried, none of the residents would accept a cookie from her tray.

"Six, maybe seven." Josh shrugged.

Sarah's attention drifted back to the sign. "It took that many?"

"Maybe half, the other half she had to plan what she was doing, right?" Josh asked.

Sarah laughed; leave it to Josh to help a soul out of a jam.

"We can always have it redone."

"Don't you dare! It's perfect." More than perfect.

It renewed her hope and brightened the dream she held for this place. Only what kind of dream would it be if Michael captured her shooting star?

The sight of a child poised in the dugout cove of a sawdust pile made Michael shake his head as he walked around the corner of the barn. He supposed, for a child, it was as good as any sandbox.

In the afternoon light, the blue streaks of the child's ebony hair glinted. The small boy loaded the back of a large metal toy truck with sawdust and imitated the sound of the loudest diesel engine he'd ever heard.

Where was the child's mother? He was looking at the same kid he'd spotted jumping mud puddles the day before, wasn't he? The boy appeared school age, but kids weren't anything he specialized in or had experience with.

But then Michael thought of his own childhood, and it brought a sour taste in his mouth. His biological father never knew he existed.

He heard a loud thud from inside the barn. His head jerked from the boy to the sound. Michael quickened his pace.

Inside, the mare struggled to rise. From behind the horse, Michael gripped each side of the mare's severely indented rear-end and gave the horse a boost.

The sound he'd heard came from a wobbly behind bumping the wall. It was a wonder, thought Michael, that the old thoroughbred hadn't broken a hip in the collision.

Standing on the other end of the horse, beside the wall, he spotted Sarah. She bit her lip and tugged on the horse's halter while her weight shifted to keep the horse's front end from falling. By the way the horse's body swayed and its swollen knees threatened to give out, he couldn't take a chance of letting go of its rump.

Slowly, the mare managed to place all four hooves into the dusty sod, and stand. Sarah held on tight, waiting for the mare to find sturdy legs. Her face grew pale as she peered down the side of the horse's protruding ribs and spotted Michael holding the two curved hipbones at the mare's flank.

He smiled and shrugged, but she frowned. One foot in front of the other, they managed to escort the mare into a nearby stall, where the horse groaned and fell into a heap of bones inside the threshold. Michael brushed his hands on his pants, while keeping his eyes on Sarah.

She wore a pair of jeans ripped at the knee, a faded old t-shirt, and a pair of scuffed brown leather boots. Her hair hung loose at her shoulders, and she flung it back from her face. He almost thought he saw a flicker of amber in her eyes, but with a blink it disappeared.

Michael checked the intravenous tubing in the base of the horse's neck. He picked up the bag of fluid and secured it inside the stall. In a few days, he'd be able to remove the line.

When he first came upon the fallen horse in Sarah's stables a few weeks ago, he doubted he could save her. Now, the mare's progress became an encouragement to him and to those who lived at Silver Wind.

He saw the way Sarah's face glowed a bit more each time she came in the stables since he arrived. It was the horse, not him, that brought light into her eyes. Each time he drew near her a dark cloud seemed to roll over both of them.

Sarah glanced through the doorway, avoiding his gaze.

Stepping out of the stall, he slid the door closed, and at the sound of it banging shut, Sarah leapt at the door, her hazel eyes wide with apparent fright.

"Don't you dare lock me in!" Her knuckles turned white gripping the bars of the door. "You can't do this to me again, Michael. Let me out!"

Michael leaned in against the door. "Again? I don't recall ever locking you in a stall."

"Then your memory serves you wrong."

"By all means, enlighten me."

Sarah's cheeks puckered, then blew out air. She curled her finger more tightly around the unyielding bars, and her words came out jumbled and fast. "The night we—the last night—in the stables..."

The past drudged itself up from inside his mind, and he almost released his hold on the door.

"I didn't lock you in," he said, his voice hoarse.

"*Someone* did." She jerked the door, but he held it strong. "Let me out, Michael." Her eyes searched around the stall, down the hall, and landed back on him. Darts of amber formed around the center of her eyes.

He refused to let go of this opportunity. *Finally*, he thought, *after all these years I'll know the truth*. "If you were locked in, how did you get out?"

He kept her cornered, trapped. Her eyes darted around like a spooked horse.

"Josh found me." She jerked at the door again.

"Ron didn't catch you?" He wouldn't let her go so easily this time.

"Of course he did, why else would your mother fire me and send me home?" She blew at a strand of hair dangling in her face.

"Fire you? Mother?" Why didn't Mother ever tell him?

"Mother never fires *any*one."

"Well she did." Sarah huffed.

"I find it very hard to believe," Michael said.

"Ron told Josh he was young once, but couldn't overlook the situation because we broke the rules. Your mother suspected Josh and I were having a rendezvous in the barn."

"Josh?" Had Sarah been two-timing him that summer?

"He came looking for me when Jenny discovered I hadn't slept in my bunk for the night."

He bit the inside of his cheek. "So Ron assumed when he found you, Josh was the one you'd been with?"

She would have been bounced off the estate within the hour, if what she said were true.

He slid open the door for her to step out. As his hand brushed her hair, sputtered sounds of an engine along with a child's laughter drifted down the aisle.

He wished he could walk through a portal and take them back

to that moment in time, where he'd clear up the past and change their future. But he didn't really want to, for it would mean giving up the course his life took after that point, the work he accomplished, and the difference his newfound relationship with God made in him.

She turned her gaze away from him. She appeared like a lost child. Did she recall another time, another place, and another man? How would Sarah react if she knew he were a different person now?

"You don't believe me." She looked at him.

"Mother usually doesn't fire anyone."

"Ron gave me twenty minutes to pack before reporting to the main house. Your father wasn't home, so Mrs. Kingsley handled the situation," she said.

He leaned forward, their foreheads touching. "Please believe me when I tell you I didn't lock you in. I tried keeping Ron occupied so you could escape back to the bunk house."

"You ... never came back." Her voice trembled.

"I saw a figure run towards the summer house, and I assumed it was you." Michael's hand cupped the side of her face. "I didn't know until the next day that you were gone. I went with Dad and Drew to inspect some horses for sale." He paused. "As a matter of fact, I was here."

"You were *here*?" Sarah clutched him tightly by the arm.

"Yeah, I'm pretty sure Dad bought a few horses out of this very barn, now that I think about it. I didn't really recognize the place at first." Like he hadn't recognized she was gone until the day after, when she didn't appear in the stables for their morning ride.

"Irish Rose," she blurted. "Was one of the horses, a sorrel mare with a flaxen mane and tail? She had a small dab of black on her right hind sock."

A fire lit in her eyes, only to be extinguished by his words. "I don't know."

"But you could ask?"

"I can check." Anything to keep that spark of hope he saw in her eyes.

He tilted his head slightly towards her, a whisper held between their lips. Her quick puffs of breath warmed his skin.

"Hey that's my mom!"

Abruptly, Sarah jumped back. Michael glanced over at the boy who glared up at him. For the longest minute of his life, Michael felt his world spin backward. He looked nothing like his mother. Thick masses of black hair fell over the boy's forehead. His small oval face dominated by intense blue eyes, narrowed on Michael. It was those eyes that caught him by the throat. Shaken, he stepped back another foot from Sarah and the boy.

His gaze never left the boy's face. "I wondered who she belonged to."

"She's *mine*." The boy wedged himself between Michael and Sarah, despite the distance Michael put between them.

Sarah reached over and locked the stall door behind her.

"I'm glad to know it. Next time she looks lost, I'll be sure to bring her back to you." He half expected the boy to smile at his jest, but instead the scowl deepened.

"I'm Michael." He offered his hand, but the boy's glare assessed him, assessed his hand, and then glanced over at Sarah. Her eyes, like a scared rabbit, jumped from him to the boy.

He waited, silence stretched between them. All the while, something hot burned in the pit of his stomach. He could have sworn he heard the mare shift and Clyde's hooves clatter against the door.

So, this is where Sarah went after she'd left him. This was the last thing he expected to discover—Sarah had a son!

Her hand swept across her cheek and settled on her mouth. Sarah gave the boy a simple nod, as a warm flush crept over her face.

"Ethan." He hit his chest with the rap of Tarzan. "I'm five," he held up five fingers.

Did he and Sarah? Did they? His chest congested with a swirl of emotion. He glanced up at Sarah. She stood looking at him, her back straight, and her eyes narrowed. Like mother like son.

His gaze dropped back down to the boy.

"Glad to meet you, Ethan." Michael extended his hand further, but Ethan didn't budge or lift a finger toward him, so Michael let his hand fall back to his side. Sarah stepped closer and laid her hands on Ethan's slim shoulders. She shook her hair back and tilted her chin as she aimed her stare in Michael's direction once more.

Ethan looked up at her. "I'm hungry. Can we have lunch now?"

Sarah ruffled his hair, brushing out the sawdust. "You can join us if you like," she said.

One look at Ethan's face gave Michael his answer. "Maybe some other time. I've got rounds to make with Doc Miller today."

"I thought he was retiring."

"So did I." Michael shrugged, unable to remember why he'd come to the stables before seeing Sarah.

Ethan led his mother away. He glanced back over his shoulder to make sure Michael didn't follow them. Michael waved before they disappeared out of sight.

Sarah had a son.

CHAPTER 5

Michael leaned back against his truck, watching the remnants of the old barn crumble into a pile of rubble.

Steam rose from his mug, and the strong liquid scorched his throat. Sounds of production rang in his ears, but the face of Sarah Colvert haunted him.

Sarah's son was five years old. Michael held his hand out in front of his face—five fingers. A dark, rippling chill crawled over his flesh as he stuck his hand in the front pocket of his hooded sweatshirt.

Michael couldn't stop this feeling of remorse, even while he watched the construction crew finish demolishing his property. Wood splintering, cracking, moaning first thing in the morning caused him to think about the future. A new barn, a new clinic—and now Sarah and her son were drawn into the picture—and now, he didn't know where she fit into his plans.

Their paths hadn't crossed in days, but he hadn't made an effort to step into it either. What if Sarah was married? There had been no ring on her left finger. Yet, she'd seemed upset in the barn after he'd been about to kiss her.

If not for the boy, would she have kissed him back?

All the times he ever pictured Sarah, motherhood never

crossed his mind. But, it suited her. Sarah always loved horses, loved caring for them, and tending to them. Horses were like babies in many ways. She always helped the other grooms on his father's estate when she found a minute, and never took a second for herself.

He'd been selfish. He saw something he wanted and took it. He'd always been the one to walk away. Never a second thought to those he left behind. He could have written the love-them-and-leave-them rule, only this time he got burned. Sarah left him.

A bitter taste lingered in his mouth. He stared down at his coffee.

"This is the old Sherman place, is it not?"

A tall man walked toward him.

"So I'm told." He dumped the contents of his cup on the ground.

"We're cleaning up the mess now. Be a few days before the foundation can be laid. Seems a shame we had to knock it down. The first good gust of wind would have done it for us."

Michael chuckled.

"You were smart tearing it down and starting from scratch. Foundation was starting to crumble."

"Did you get the plans I faxed to your office last week?"

The man hitched a thumb back over his shoulder. "Got 'em in my truck."

"I appreciate you dropping your other projects to come out here." Michael clasped Jack Dougal's shoulder.

"This is big stuff. Fancy, too."

"We're going to be busy around here," Michael said. He rested his empty mug on the truck's hood and rubbed his hands together. He blew hot breath into the cup of his palms.

"You bring the boy with you?"

A spasm hit his chest like a punch in the gut, and Michael struggled to regain his breath, "Boy?" he wheezed.

"You still got that black beast, don't you?"

"Clyde," Michael let the air out of his lungs. He had to get Ethan out of his mind.

"He's down the road." Michael jerked his head in the direction of Sarah's place.

"Silver Wind. I passed it on the way here."

"Silver Wind?" The name stuck in Michael's throat like a chunk of dry cake. The large wooden sign at the entrance of the farm would have said as much, if he ever paid attention.

"It's the old Colvert place, the girl …" Jack snapped his fingers. "Sarah, I think. She's running the place now, isn't she? It's hard to say anymore, with the old woman passing on a few months back."

Sarah's grandmother passed away? Michael found there were more things about Sarah he didn't know, and some he needed to find out. Like, for instance, did Sarah believe in God? Or was this the reason she'd been brought back into his life?

Then there was the matter of Sarah's son, Ethan. A whirlwind of questions stormed around him. He would have to get his answers soon before this tornado of uncertainty blew him and his chances with Sarah away.

He cleared his throat. "I'm sure her husband is a great help."

"I don't know about a husband. It seems to me the place went empty years ago—sold off every horse in the barn and closed up shop. Then Sarah showed up with that kid of hers, and it's a wonder the girl's grandmother didn't take to her grave sooner."

Michael shook his head. Sarah had a child out of wedlock, but teenage pregnancies weren't uncommon. Not like, when his own mother conceived him and was forced to marry, but deep down inside the lowest pit of his soul he felt as if this were his fault too.

What would he have done if she stayed that summer? He would have blown her a kiss goodbye, and moved on. Or, so he wanted to think. Truth was, when Sarah left, she took a part of him with her. One of the few slivers of goodness he carried before he became acquainted with God.

"You alright there, Mike?" Jack gripped his arm.

"Fine." Michael coughed. "You were saying?"

Jack snickered. "You need to switch to caffeinated in the

mornings."

Sounds of bulldozers and machinery operating muffled their voices. Men sorted stray pieces of wood and scrap metal from the fallen building.

"Maybe that's the problem, too much caffeine and not enough sleep," Michael grumbled, rubbing the back of his neck.

"You want to look over the blueprints one final time?"

Michael shook his head. He should have paid more attention to Sarah's son. Had he changed her, turned a sweet girl into what he had been—or had Ethan? Nevertheless, the question he yearned to ask most was, "who was young Ethan's father?"

Josh ...

"It doesn't make sense," he muttered as Jack joined his crew of workers across the driveway. If Josh was Ethan's father, why didn't Sarah marry Josh?

Maybe she needed time to grieve the loss of her grandmother, but Ethan was five. Maybe she wanted to marry for love. Or maybe, just maybe, Josh wasn't the father of Sarah's child, after all.

He lifted his face to the hazy sky and prayed for guidance.

Sarah plodded alongside Ethan on their evening walk after supper. They crossed the cobblestone bridge, built from the same quarry rock as the house. Blood, sweat, and tears went into the labor of her ancestors to build her home. It was one of the last remaining houses to survive the civil war. A few bullet holes told the history.

She could almost hear her ancestors' moans of disappointment in her.

Ethan plucked bright yellow buttercup blossoms from amongst the sheltering grass, and he handed each one to her. Someday this farm would belong to him.

She would leave him several hundred acres, but unlike Gran, she would restore her family's pride despite the smear of her reputation. She couldn't afford to buy big fancy bloodlines and raise Thoroughbreds like her father, but *could* fill each stall and give horses like Bonnie a home.

She spotted Josh pounding in a loose board. As if he sensed her eyes upon him, he paused and looked over the wooden fence at them. He waved, rubbed his stomach and held up two thumbs towards her.

Ethan handed her another flower as they continued to walk in the field behind the barn. She didn't need to look back to know Josh continued to watch them as he fixed the outdoor ring in the middle of the U-shaped stables.

"Hey, mom," Ethan said.

"Hmm?"

"Can I go over there?" He pointed his finger toward the knoll slightly off their path.

"Stay where I can see you, no wondering into the woods."

She watched as he went his separate way. She never let him stray far. Josh called her overprotective. But wasn't that what he did now, watching her walk through the field with a hammer resting on the rail?

A long thin piece of a weed jutted out the corner of Ethan's mouth, and his small steps turned confident. *My little peacock*, she mused. The impersonation Ethan created of Josh made her chuckle, and someday she would tell him that men don't really strut around like roosters walking on glass.

Her skin prickled. Josh made a good father stand-in. But, Ethan had a father. Although, her son never questioned his parentage, she couldn't tell him.

If Ethan found out he had a father who didn't want him, it would crush him. It would crush *her*.

Sarah's gaze darted to Ethan. Behind him, she spotted Michael astride his black horse. He urged Clyde into a fast-paced trot across the field in her direction. Michael's tan breeches stood stark against his dark mount. The horse's neck arched, and lean powerful muscles flexed beneath the saddle.

Tears sprang to her eyes as she opened the gate into the small family cemetery at the edge of the woods. She stood at the foot of her parents' graves, as she did on the day she'd watched their caskets lowered into the ground.

Grief swelled up in its gentle tide, a reminder that it would forever cling to this place.

She cried a zillion times, but it didn't bring her parents back. She wanted them to see the woman she'd become. Meet their grandson. Would their eyes have seen what Gran saw, shame?

Her parents loved her. They nurtured her and trained her as an equestrian rider. She hoped one day she would become like her mother.

If only she could turn back time.

At least God had been merciful to her. The God her parents raised her to believe in, to trust, to have faith in, and to love bestowed upon her a great gift. God gave her a son when she had no one left to love. Lost and alone, Gran sent her off to Kingsley's Estate to work for the summer.

She'd been alone.

"You knew him before he was born. You created him inside me. You made me his mother. How can I deny him the identity of his birth? But then, how can I not?"

She looked up at the hazy blue sky. Large fluffs of white clouds floated across the horizon, like they did on the day of her parents' funeral.

She stood amongst the crowd. Friends and acquaintances came from all over the state to pay their last respects to Hannah and Robert Colvert.

She could still hear the droned words of the pastor in prayer. Gran stood front and center of those who attended, sobbing loudest. She remembered those anguished cries more so than her own.

She'd been alone then too.

Lost in a whirlwind of grief, she fell to her knees. Long after her parents' caskets were buried, she clutched a handful of dirt.

No one came to comfort her, not even Gran. Left alone, choking over her own tears, she clung to the last piece of earth her parents touched. In the days that followed her parents' death, she had nobody to cling to. No one to help her understand what happened in the hours past her parents' departure.

They promised they'd come back.

Then, they were gone.

Now, she stood amongst past generations of her family. Her son would carry on their name, and restore their family reputation to the grandeur it had once known. She would bring it all back—the horses, the name, the recognition—all in her parents' honor.

"For you." Ethan thrust a bouquet of dogwoods and weeds under her nose, and raced back into the field as she called out her thanks to him. Michael and his horse drew closer. She turned back to her mother's headstone, hoping if she ignored Michael, he would ride away.

Gently, she placed the flowers on the ground.

She saw her mother's face. Warm hues of brown eyes swept under dark lashes, ignited by the kindness of a smile. That was her mother. Along with soft-spoken words and forever laughter, those were the memories she held onto most.

They rode every morning, while Father tended to the horses. At fifteen, she became one of the top riders in the state. She yearned to follow her mother's footsteps: a wife, mother, national-ranking champion. She still did, but she jumbled the order.

A soft sigh escaped her lips.

Sarah came here often, seeking tranquility and peace. Only this time, turmoil twisted around her. Memories long stashed away in her heart resurfaced all because of one man.

She no longer could find a firm stance on the ground, and it scared her. She'd always been the "calm one," the one who made everything right, but with both her mother and Gran gone, who would kiss her scratches and make them better? There was no Band Aid big enough to cover all her hurts.

From behind her, she heard the sound of a twig snap.

CHAPTER 6

Michael slid out of the saddle and gave Clyde a pat on the neck before tying the horse's reins loosely to the cemetery gate. He would have kept on riding, except he spotted Ethan's bright red shirt. The tall grasses in the field rubbed Clyde's underside and came to the boy's shoulders.

Ethan's eyes grew large as he spotted the big black horse. Michael lifted his hand in greeting, but Ethan's stare remained fixed on the horse.

"What have you got there?"

"Flowers." Ethan turned his gaze on Michael.

"For your mom?"

"Yep."

"Mind if I deliver them?"

Ethan tilted his head, one hand shielding his eyes from the afternoon glare, while the other rose, offering the bunched up stems to Michael.

"Thanks pal."

Ethan walked past Michael in Clyde's direction. "Can I ride him?"

"I don't know if your mom will permit that. I'll have to ask her first."

He pointed to the far corner of the gravesites. "She's over there."

"You keep an eye on Clyde, while I ask your mom."

Ethan nodded, eagerly. Then, as if to catch himself before showing too much excitement, he shrugged.

Michael smiled despite himself. "Clyde's not fond of kids, so don't go near him. You stay right here. I don't want either of us getting in trouble from your mom, you hear?"

Michael glanced over at the graves and spotted Sarah's back. Any moment, he figured, she would turn to check on the boy.

"Sure." Ethan grin revealed his crooked white baby teeth.

"I'll see what I can do about your mom." Michael patted Ethan on the head.

"That wasn't so bad." He walked into the cemetery.

Sarah flinched as he came up and stood behind her. Kitchen scents of leftover supper fumes clung to her clothes, making his mouth water. He wanted to lick his lips and taste her delicious aroma—pot roast and a hint of apple pie.

He reached around her, and Sarah looked at the weed-infested arrangement in his hand. Hesitant, she accepted them as he waited, without a word, for her to take them. Her fingertips brushed velvet-soft heat across his knuckles. A faint smile formed on her lips and lifted the gloom that hovered on her face.

"Thank you." She glanced over her shoulder to check on Ethan. He sat in the grass not far from them. Clyde stood, tied, tossing his long mane to ward off flies. Sarah turned back and stared at her parents' graves.

"How did it happen?"

For a moment, he didn't think she would answer him, but then she spoke so soft, close to a whisper. "They were traveling to the state competition. An eighteen-wheeler skidded out of control."

"You were only seventeen." He remembered. It happened the summer they met.

"Sixteen," she corrected. She wrung her hands around the stems of the bouquet.

Sorrow stirred between them, and he couldn't find the words to express his thoughts.

"Gran passed away about two months ago." She buried her damp cheeks in the petals.

"I'm sorry, Sarah."

"You don't know what it's like to lose your entire family," she said.

"Maybe not, but you haven't lost them all," he said. "You have a son. One who's itching for a ride on Clyde—right now."

Sarah laughed and swiped away the tears beneath her eyes. "So that is why he's been sitting still all this time?"

Michael looked over at the boy, who sat in the same spot as he left him.

"How do you do that?"

"What?" she asked. "Have eyes in the back of my head?"

"Yeah, something like that."

"Motherly instincts, they send them home with you at the hospital."

"Do they come with instruction manuals too?"

She drew herself up straight. Her features darkened and the gloom returned. It lingered around them.

"What do you want Michael?"

"Get acquainted with an old friend. Give a kid a ride on my horse."

"Still haven't scratched my name out of your little black book?"

"There never was a book," he said, quietly.

"I'm not interested in being your *friend* Michael, not anymore."

"Good, because I'm not looking for that kind of friendship, *not anymore*."

His temper warmed the blood in his veins. She stared up at him. Her hazel eyes widened. He saw a flash flood of hurt, surprise, and anger wash over her face as she marched away from him with the bouquet clutched in her hand.

"Time to go, Ethan."

Michael fell into step behind her.

"I thought you were gonna ask her?" Ethan scowled at Michael.

"She didn't give me an answer, Sport," Michael replied.

"Can I, Mom?"

Sarah peered over at the horse. Clyde pawed and snorted at their approach.

A deep frown and rigid brow marred the beauty of her face.

"Maybe some other time." She took Ethan by the hand.

"Why *not*?" Ethan jerked his hand away. He stood, fist planted on his hips, and glared up at her.

"The horse is still green, it's not safe."

"I want to ride!" Ethan yelled.

"Don't shout at your mom. It's not her fault she's probably right."

Ethan's lip trembled and fists clenched.

"Fine, but if this horse so much as sidesteps in another direction you're both dog food," Sarah warned.

"You heard the woman," Michael said to Clyde.

Clyde snorted as Michael gave Sarah the reins and lifted Ethan into the saddle. Clyde stood for the burden of his small passenger. Ethan took a large hunk of thick black mane in his hands. Michael took hold of Clyde's reins and Sarah walked beside Ethan's dangling leg as they walked through the field toward the stables.

Josh's head lifted from his task to watch them.

"Have you told him?"

Jenny curled her legs up on the creaking porch swing, and a deep frown etched across her round doll face. Sarah lounged back against the porch post with one leg drawn up to her chest and her arm draped over her knee.

"No." She kept an eye on Ethan playing in the yard.

"He's been here almost three weeks."

Sarah rested her head back. "I haven't had time." Loose

strands of hair fell out of her braid and a bead of sweat ran down the back of her neck.

From dawn to dusk, she strung wire across fence posts alongside Josh. Michael's absence increased as the construction crew broke ground at his place.

Jenny inspected the new coat of pink polish on her nails. "Seems to me ..." She blew on a nail. "You got plenty of time for other things."

"It hasn't been that long."

"Eighteen days."

"I'll tell him when I know for sure the time is right." Sarah looked at Jenny, her auburn hair curling in the June heat, and the glimmer in her green eyes twinkling with the curiosity of a cat.

"When Ethan's eighteen?" Jenny set the swing in motion.

"It's not like it's your business, anyhow." Sarah straightened her leg.

"If you don't tell him, Sarah, I will."

Sarah's blood ran cold. Her gaze flew to Jenny, the one person she could always count on. "Why would you do that?"

"All I'm saying is, if you can't tell him, I will."

A donkey could be sweet-talked faster than Jenny. "Thanks, but I think I can handle this." Only now, she needed to figure out how.

Michael's words, that day at her parents' grave, ebbed her aching sorrow. Reacquaint with an old friend, he said. Had he ever felt anything more for her than lust? Could Gran have been right all these years?

She refused to believe she'd been the object of a young man's desires. But what if she was? The teenage girl inside cringed.

Jenny blew on another nail. "Uh-huh."

"I'll handle it." Sarah stood.

"You sound like Josh now." Jenny planted her bare feet down on the porch.

"Your point?"

"Ethan needs a father."

"He has Josh."

"Josh isn't his father, Sarah! He isn't always going to be around."

Sarah clamped her mouth shut.

"What about Michael?" Jenny's voice raised an octave.

"What about him?"

"You can't deny him."

"Who says I'm denying him? What if he doesn't want my son? Have you thought about that?" Sarah took a deep breath.

Jenny lifted a shoulder.

"You want me to tell my little boy who his daddy is and have Ethan running into the arms of a man who doesn't want him?"

"I didn't say that," Jenny replied.

"I can't do that. Don't you understand? It would crush his heart."

Jenny set the swing into motion with the ball of her foot. "Are you sure it's Ethan's heart you're trying to protect? If I didn't know better, I'd think you're afraid."

Sarah arched a brow and crossed her arms over her stomach. "Afraid? I'm not afraid."

Jenny stopped the swing. "You're afraid Michael will take Ethan away, and you'll be all alone."

Sarah shook her head. She looked across the yard to where Ethan kicked a soccer ball in the grass. A bird flew across the bloomed azaleas caught her attention, and its hum vibrated through her heart as she inhaled the weak scent of the flowers drifting lazily in the air.

"You love him, don't you?"

Sarah took a step closer to Jenny. "He's all I've got."

"You've got to stop dwelling on the past." Jenny got up. She reached out and touched Sarah's arm.

How could she not? A lump formed in her throat and made it hard to speak. "You wouldn't understand. You still have your father."

"Your father didn't abandon you, Sarah." Jenny's voice softened. "You have so many wonderful memories of him in your heart. Doesn't Ethan deserve a chance to know *his* father, to make memories *he* can hold onto?"

She turned her head and watched Ethan.

"You love him."

A dam of tears built in the pools of her eyes. She tried to blink them away. The one thing she held most dear in her life floated across a river of indecision with no sight of hope within reach. She grabbed hold of Jenny. "I can't lose my son."

Briefly, she closed her eyes. A wave of nausea rose over her. *I can't lose one more person, Lord. Don't take my son away.*

"Then make him a part of your life."

"I can't." She waved her arms. "I can't deal with this now." She jumped down from the porch and stomped off down the lane as she shook her head in the effort to clear it.

"Hey, Ethan, you want some ice cream?" Jenny called out. Ethan ran towards the house.

Sarah walked, brisk at first, and then slower as aggression melted from her system. Jenny would tell Michael about Ethan, and she couldn't afford for that to happen right now. Silver Wind was starting to take shape, Bonnie's intravenous tube was out, and almost all the fields were fenced. But the truth would knock it all down, and without Ethan she was no better off than Bonnie when she first found that pitiful horse, abandoned and unwanted.

Even as she carried her precious child in the womb, Sarah clung to her love for Michael. Gran tried to convince her it was a schoolgirl's fantasy, a young man's lust, and nothing more. Only every time she thought of Michael, her heart betrayed her. He chose his path in the world, while she chose to raise their son.

She stood on the old stone bridge. She'd never intended to come this way. For a moment, she watched the waterwheel turn slowly into the creek. Her grandfather's father built this wheel right after the civil war. The carriage house, her parents' house, now Josh's bachelor pad, blended into the scenery.

Sadness crept over her. As a child, she would run across the bridge, to the house, where Gran would sit and tell her stories over chocolate cookies and milk. She heard them so often she knew them by heart. Many a night she shared these with Ethan. Nothing, to her, was more important, than for Ethan to know his family history.

Except, he didn't.

To Ethan, Michael was a stranger. He saw Michael as a threat. Although, since the day she allowed Ethan to ride on Michael's horse, boy and man had formed a bond. Whenever Ethan spotted Michael near the stables, Ethan followed behind him. Complete hero worship for the knight on the black horse, she thought, with a shake of her head.

She walked down the road until she came to the front of Michael's house. A large bay window had been added and a new pane glass door.

On the porch, she stepped back to allow a woman with a Persian cat tucked under her arm to push open the door and glide by her. Inside, she found the waiting area empty.

Slowly, she turned around, admiring the dark wood paneling and matching wood benches. On the far wall, wooden shed doors from the old barn hung on a track as part of the wall beyond the receptionist desk.

Piled receipts and scattered invoices cluttered the top of a desk. Underneath the mess, she spied an appointment book, a folded laptop, and a cordless phone absent from its base.

Her breath hitched in her throat. She picked up a discarded invoice and read the heading. *For by grace you have been saved through faith, and that not of yourselves, it is the gift of God, not of works, lest anyone should boast.*

She dug through the invoices. Scanned each top line. Every invoice in her hand contained the line of scripture written from Ephesians. *What did this mean?*

Had Michael become a Christian?

Surely not. Not the Michael she knew. But if she had changed, why couldn't Michael?

He still had those same piercing blue eyes, and that same charming grin. His voice was still rich and smooth, like velvet. People change. She changed. Why couldn't Michael change too?

She managed an unsteady breath. If Michael changed, then she really didn't know him anymore. The man she fell in love with so many years ago no longer existed.

She clutched the invoices to her heart.

Michael gazed out the window of his examining room and spotted Sarah at same time a patient arrived. He saw the Persian cat, asked the necessary questions, and politely avoided the personal ones from the cat's owner. It didn't escape his attention that every single woman in town brought in their cat or dog since he arrived. If he didn't know better, he'd think Doc Miller and his mother were in correspondence with each other.

Michael gave the cat a routine examination. He took great care in handling the agitated feline.

"When Doc Miller announced his retirement, we were all so sad. But now that I've met his replacement, I can't find one complaint."

Michael tried avoiding sharp claws.

"Thanks." He handed the feline back. "He's all good to go, Ms. Davis."

"Please, call me *Beth*." She batted her lashes and stroked her protesting cat.

"Right—Beth. I'll see you again in six months."

"The Jubilee is coming up in a few weeks," she hinted. "I sure hope you'll attend." She left him heading for the door with a sway in her hips.

She hadn't been as forthright as the last woman who came in with Jack Russell. Doc Miller owed him big time for this favor. It wasn't exactly hard for him to find a date when he wanted one. Not that he wanted one. Not since he'd seen Sarah again.

Something shuffled on the other side of the door and outside in the parking lot gravel crunched beneath car tires.

He walked down the hall and discovered Sarah bent over the reception area.

Her braid hung loose down her neck, and the frayed cut-off denims she wore revealed slender legs. He leaned back against the wall and admired the view.

"Looking for something?"

Sarah spun around. She tossed the invoices on the desk behind her. "Not in this mess."

"As you can see, my receptionist is invisible right now."

"You don't say." She crossed her arms.

"Want to apply for the position?"

"No thanks."

"I could really use the help." He hoped Sarah would take him up on the offer.

She tilted her head, her eyes narrowed. "I can send Jenny over to help you."

"Great, I think I lost my sanity in the clutter."

"I'm sure she'll be grateful for the job, and keep you in good order."

She was still as confident as he remembered.

"Jenny's the one living with you?"

"Do you have a problem with that?" Sarah held her chin high.

He doubted it would matter if he did. Sarah had a mind of her own, he discovered.

Seconds ticked by into a minute of silence. Sarah opened her mouth to speak, but closed it again. She turned and headed for the door.

"Sarah." He jogged around her and blocked the exit.

"I shouldn't have come here. I need to go."

He stayed rooted in her way. "Did you need something?"

Sarah shook her head, and strands of loose hair curled around the sides of her face.

"I thought since you walked over here, you might." He wanted to believe that she came to see him. He searched her face.

She fidgeted under his gaze. "I thought I'd stop in and see the improvements you made. It definitely is a change from when the

Sherman's lived here. I'll just be going now." She attempted to step around him.

"Would you like a tour?" he asked. "You did come the whole way over here to see the place, right?"

"No," Sarah said, as she dodged to the right.

Michael blocked her path. "Perhaps you came to see me, then?"

"Why would I do that?" She glanced at her watch and made yet another attempt to leave.

"I don't know, maybe you missed me?"

Sarah's slim brows rose. "Hardly."

"It's been a long time, Sarah."

She crossed her arms and stared at him.

He decided to try a new tactic. "Saw the new farm sign. Looks good."

"Don't try to interfere with what I'm doing, Michael." Her voice became cool as an October breeze. "I'm not going to interfere with your business. Stay out of mine."

Michael's hands went up in defense. "Whoa! I only thought, since we are neighbors, you might be interested in working together. With the rescue right across the road from the clinic, we could be partners, to save the horses, of course."

"You stay on your side of the road and I'll stay on mine." She brushed past him, the jingle of the bell sounding at her exit.

Michael watched her depart, his heart heavier than before. *Join the clinic and the rescue*? He laughed. It was a good idea, even if it came to him in the heat of the moment. Then again, if Sarah and he were partners then she couldn't run from him anymore.

He made a mental note to schedule daily encounters with Sarah and her son. A dark shrouded cloud of mystery hovered above him.

CHAPTER 7

The same dark cloud followed Sarah into the house.

She heard the phone ring, but left it for Jenny to answer. She dragged her feet up the stairs. Her Encounter with Michael in his office only scratched the surface of her scars.

At first, she missed Michael every hour of every day, when she last saw him those many years ago. After months of false hope, she finally accepted his absence from her life. Gradually, her heartache subsided, replaced by a mother's love.

Ethan slept on her bed, his soft cheeks smeared with ice cream. Quietly, Sarah trod into her room.

She sat on the corner of the bed and gazed at the photos on her bedside table of her parents, Gran, and little Ethan, an hour old.

He stirred, curling in a ball. She laid her hand on his back and rubbed it like she did when he got fussy as an infant.

She could still envision Gran's face that frightful day when she revealed her pregnancy.

"Which one?" Gran demanded, her face reddened and her cheeks puffed out, as she sputtered like a pressure cooker.

"His name is Michael, and we're in love."

"Love? Ha! You're just a girl! What do you know about love? Lust! That's what young boys are after."

"No! It wasn't like that! He loves me and I love him," Sarah cried.

"Love? What were you thinking getting involved with a boy like that?"

Sarah bit her lip. It would do her no good to argue.

Gran turned away. She clenched her fist and ranted, "After all I've done. After all I've been through. This—this is what I'm left with?"

Sarah listened, blinked back tears, and took deep breaths to calm the swell of queasiness in her belly.

She wrapped her arms around herself and huddled on the bed. Deep inside her, new life blossomed, but what if Gran forced her to give up this baby like everything else she'd lost?

She squeezed her eyes shut. Small broken sobs escaped her raspy throat. She cradled her abdomen and held onto the small piece of life seeded inside her womb while she prayed, silently.

"Seventeen." Gran clucked her tongue as she swung back around to face Sarah.

"I'm sorry," Sarah whimpered.

"Sorry won't fix this, Child." Gran held up a hand as Sarah parted her trembling lips in response.

"Now what to do about it."

"What do you mean?" Sarah hugged her abdomen tighter.

"He's older than you. College, I believe. If it's the young man, I'm thinking of. Kingsley's boy, am I right?"

Sarah nodded; tears spilled down her cheeks.

"This will ruin your reputation, and mine. You've disgraced our family name." Gran bristled.

Sarah hung her head and sobbed.

Gran made a disgusted sound in her throat, and her expression turned grim as Sarah looked up, her vision blurred. She swiped away tears with the heel of her hand. Gran's hardened stare forced her to look down again.

The old floorboards creaked as Gran paced the room. Sarah

struggled to regain her breath between sobs and hiccups. She heard Gran mutter, as if she spoke to people who were no longer here.

Sarah yearned for her mother. *She always knew best.*

Gran sighed and sat down beside her.

For a long moment, Sarah didn't move.

She didn't breathe.

She didn't dare look.

She heard a long rattled exhale from Gran and knew she prayed. For several beats of her heart, Sarah waited. She sniffled and tears soaked her lashes.

"No sense in crying yourself sick," Gran said. "What's done is done."

Sarah hiccupped again, unsure what to say.

"We won't be able to keep this a secret for long," Gran said.

Sarah's head snapped up. Desperation washed over her. "Please don't send me away again."

Hesitantly, Gran reached out and ran her hand down over Sarah's long hair. "No, I suppose that is what started this in the first place." Gran's expression softened.

"Gran?" Sarah whispered. Gran continued to pet Sarah on the back of the head.

"Don't you worry. Everything is going to be alright."

"But what about Michael?"

"What about him?" Gran asked.

"I have to tell him."

Grief and loss took its toll on Gran; Sarah could see it in the pained expression of Gran's eyes. Their once vibrant color had faded in the weeks of Sarah's absence from the farm. Her father's horses, including Irish Rose, were gone. She had nothing but this baby to call her own.

"You're not to say a word about the father, you hear?" Gran said sternly. She notched her chin and stared straight ahead for a moment before she looked at Sarah.

"It doesn't seem fair." She sniffled.

"You'd be better off forgetting about him."

She shivered as the memory of Gran's voice faded. Stretching out beside Ethan on her bed she tried to push that moment of the past out of her mind.

If only then, she had listened to Gran and forgotten about Michael. Bitterness swelled in her heart.

Even now, she felt Gran's presence. Sweet fragrance of dried up roses from vases on the dresser wafted through her room. It was Gran's scent. How long would it linger before it, too, disappeared from her life?

"Mom, are you sad?"

"Come here." She held her arms open and Ethan crawled onto her lap.

"I love you," she whispered in his ear.

Two little arms wrapped around her neck. "Mom?" Ethan wedged himself into the curves of her body.

"Hmm?" She stroked his hair.

"Are you mad at Jenny?"

"Why do you ask?"

"I don't know. She gave one scoop instead of two." Ethan's blue eyes, like his father's, looked up at her.

"You know how I get upset at you sometimes because you're about to do something bad?"

Ethan nodded.

"It can be the same way with adults, too."

"Oh," Ethan said.

If only it were so simple to explain everything to him, but he wouldn't understand. Why did Jenny have to go putting her foot inside doors that were better off kept shut?

"What if she said she was sorry?"

"Not likely. But, we'll go talk to her anyway. I have something I want to tell her."

Ethan hopped off the bed and she stood, taking him by the hand. The worst was yet to come.

"What a mess!"

"It's really not that bad." Michael questioned Jenny, "Is it?"

She smiled wearily. Stacks of papers were ready to topple. Beneath all those papers lay a phone, a laptop, a calendar, and a natural wood-varnished desktop. Somewhere.

He'd let the place get a little out of hand since he moved in last month.

When he agreed to work with old Doc Miller, he naturally assumed Doc's secretary, his wife, would come with the deal, but when she put her foot down she stuck to her word.

"Sarah said you needed help." Jenny took a seat in the cushioned roller chair on the other side of the desk. She glanced over the mess again, grim.

Her red Capri pants and striped shirt made her appear like an over-ripe strawberry, but as long as she could do the job, why should he care what she wore.

"Should I ask to see a resume?" he said.

"If you want, I can supply one."

"You still interested?" He spread his hands across the desk.

"A girl's got to make a living somehow." Jenny picked up a stray invoice teetering on the edge of the desk. "The rescue isn't exactly booming these days, but I have faith things will turn around for all of us." Invoice in hand, her eyes scanned the top lines of the document. Looking at him, she grinned. "How true!"

Michael lived by those lines.

"I didn't figure you for a man of faith." Jenny laid down the paper.

Michael scratched the stubble of growth on his chin. After a restless night, he forgot to shave this morning. "I became a Christian years ago." Michael explained about his lab partner and how he'd come to know Christ.

Jenny sat back in the chair. "I'm glad you found your faith."

"Seems to me, we all have faith in something, it's *believing* that people find the hardest." He thought of Sarah, sweating over building a dream, but for whom? Her son's future?

"Not of ourselves, not of works, but a gift from God brought us to reach the gates of heaven." Did Sarah think by rebuilding the farm, changing it into a rescue for abandoned and abused horses, her labors would redeem her in the eyes of God?

He didn't realize he'd said those words aloud, until Jenny replied, "Nothing is ever easy."

"No, but heaven is a gift." He sat on the corner of the desk. It took him almost twenty-five years to figure that out, and his life was a blur from that moment on, or it *had* been until Sarah tumbled in.

"Try telling that to Sarah."

"She hasn't accepted Christ?"

"She has, or at least says she has," Jenny said, a mournful note in her voice, as she shook her head.

A stone cast deep in the pit of his belly hit the bottom hard. He pinched the bridge of his nose and took a deep breath. He did this. He'd stripped a young girl of her innocence. Now she lived in a world full of hurt with only her son as a beacon of hope through the darkness. God forgave Sarah. But had Sarah forgiven Michael?

"Try fixing this one," Michael muttered.

"Oh, I can handle it. We'll have this straightened out in a day or two, tops," Jenny said.

"What? Oh, yeah, great." He ran his hand through his hair. He forced himself to focus on the task laid out.

"You would have preferred Sarah?" Jenny tilted her head to the side.

"I offered her the job first, if that's what you mean. I thought she might need one." Unable to admit he wanted her near him each day.

Jenny narrowed her gaze. "She doesn't. Her parents left her an inheritance. Grace kept most of it squirreled away, but after the funeral Sarah took possession of everything."

"You mean Grace's funeral?"

"Of course it would have been after Grace passed. You didn't think Grace would have allowed Sarah to have the run of the farm while *she* was alive, do you?"

"Grace Colvert was a woman set in her ways."

Jenny snorted. "To say the least."

Michael stood up; a kick in the pants would have felt better than this. Who else's arms had Sarah run to when his no longer held her? He didn't know why he ever let her go. A mistake he wouldn't ever make again.

"Besides, Sarah's busy getting the rescue running, taking care of Ethan, and come fall she wants to go back to college," Jenny said, as if he missed half of the conversation.

Sarah never went to college?

Jenny picked up a pen and flipped it through her fingers. "I can start today, if you want."

Michael stared. She looked at him oddly. "Uh, yeah." *Pull yourself together Wolfe*. "I'm out on calls in the morning and in the office on afternoons. Doc Miller is here most mornings and occasionally an afternoon or two during the week."

Jenny's eyebrows shot up. "He hasn't retired yet?"

Michael shrugged. "You know how it goes, you can lead a horse to water, but you can't make him retire."

Jenny laughed.

"He still wants to handle office visits, and I don't mind. I think more or less the old coot just wanted a partner to take over the farm visits and large animals. If you have any questions on scheduling or billing, you can ask him. He'll be the best one to help you."

"I think I got it." She saluted him.

"Try not to let the workers distract you." He winked. "The crew arrives every morning around nine and leaves at dusk."

"I'll do my best," she said, in a stern voice.

Michael headed across the room to the door, with Sarah on his mind. He paused, weighed the wisdom of his next question, a question which he had tossed and turned in bed each night for the past few weeks. "About Sarah …"

"I don't play middle man," Jenny said.

"I was going to ask about Ethan." He watched her lips twitch. She tilted her head and eyed him curiously.

"I would think that it is obvious."

Her wisecrack tone irritated him. "The boy's father ..."

"You need to ask Sarah that question."

Asking Sarah was precisely what he planned to do. The idea of her having a child shocked him at first, but the boy's age haunted him more. "I'll do that."

Jenny leaned forward. "Sarah gave up everything so she could raise her son. The rescue has been a long awaited dream for her."

"I get that."

"Do you?" Jenny rested her elbows on the desk.

"Yeah, I got it. Sarah's out saving the world, one horse at a time. But who's saving Sarah?"

Jenny flinched and her lips parted.

"What happened to Sarah's horse?" Michael changed the subject. He needed to know more in order to link the past to the present. "She seems to think my father may have bought her mare."

"Her grandmother sold all the horses after Sarah's parents died. When she came back home from working at your father's stables, she found them gone, including Irish Rose. Grace forbid any horses to step foot on the farm again while she was alive, claiming they were the death of her children."

"She hasn't ridden since, has she?" A pain far worse than getting kicked by a horse, tormented him. The loss, sacrifice, and hardship Sarah endured registered inside his heart. Her lack of faith gnawed at his gut.

"She got accepted on the equestrian team in Louisville. They offered her a full scholarship to go to college, but her grandmother fell ill. You're a bright man. You can figure out the rest."

He should have known better than to enter into a game of twenty questions with Jenny.

"Which leaves the boy's father where?" Michael asked.

The sound of the bell distracted him. Doc Miller shuffled across the wooden-planked floor.

"Late start?" Doc Miller asked. Long white hairs combed in a deep left-sided part on his head tried to hide the shine of his crown.

"Doc, this is Jenny. She's our new receptionist."

Doc Miller sized her up with a satisfied grunt and then turned to Michael. "You'd best be off, got a schedule to keep."

"I'll see you later." He turned, headed for the door.

"Tell me, Doc Miller." Jenny paused and then continued, "If a foal is born in the spring, say oh—April, when would the mare have conceived?"

Michael reached for the door. His hand hung mid-reach. His ears tuned in on each word Jenny spoke. His spine stiffened as he pulled open the door. He waited for Doc Miller's reply.

"Oh, I'd say somewhere in the ball park of July, maybe August."

Michael glanced over his shoulder. He met Jenny's deliberate stare. A twitch formed at the corner of her mouth.

CHAPTER 8

Ethan's laughter echoed through the barn.

Jenny stuck her head around the corner of the office door while Ethan raced down the empty aisle. Sarah stood on the other side of the doorway holding her hands over her eyes and counting to twenty. Ethan's giggles floated out from inside a stall and gave away his location.

Clyde snorted and kicked the wall.

"Ready or not, here I come," Sarah called as Jenny whistled her way back to the house.

Sarah walked down the aisle. She peered through the bars of each stall door. She heard hay rustle, while Bonnie chomped her meal. A small burst of giggles erupted beside Clyde.

Clyde's head bobbed up and down, almost as if to point out the hiding boy, as she approached. As the stall door slid open, Ethan dashed under his mother's arm and rounded the corner of the walkway and collided with Michael.

"Whoa there." Michael reached out to steady him. Ethan jerked back, and fell on his backside. Hunched down, Michael offered Ethan his hand. Sarah skidded to a halt behind him, peeling away hair flung in her face during the chase.

"Where's the fire, Sport?"

Ethan pulled himself to his feet. "We're playing hide and seek. Do you want to play?"

Sarah's heart fluttered. Ethan's eager face lifted in anticipation of an answer.

"I think Michael's a little old to play games with us." She tucked a piece of hair behind her ear.

"*You* play with me, and you're just as old, Mom."

"Ethan—Ethan Colvert!" Sarah said flustered. Michael was definitely older.

"That's some name you got there. Which one is your middle name?" Michael winked.

"Ethan."

"Got another name besides Ethan?"

Sarah held her breath.

"Ethan Colvert."

"I think it's time for us to go now," Sarah said.

Michael glanced at her as he straightened.

"Oh, Mom, not yet." Ethan grabbed Michael by the hand. "You have to see Bonnie."

Sarah stayed back. Ethan pulled Michael the length of the stable's walkway. He stepped up on a turned-down bucket outside Bonnie's stall and peered in.

"She's skinny."

"You and your mom are doing a good job fattening her up," Michael said.

"I give her hay all the time." Ethan grinned.

"Oh, yeah?"

Ethan nodded.

Sarah's throat constricted and she fought the wave of grief rising from the pit of her soul. She felt her cheeks turn cold.

Together Ethan and Michael shifted the bucket across the aisle to Clyde's stall.

"Can we ride him today?" Ethan asked, while Michael refilled an empty water bucket.

"Maybe some other time, Sport."

Ethan frowned as Michael helped him down off the bucket.

"The south pasture is ready now, I told Josh to start putting Clyde down there during the day," Sarah said.

"What about Bonnie?" asked Ethan. "She never gets to go out."

"She will soon," Sarah promised.

"If you need me to lend a hand ..." Michael offered.

"I've got Josh." The words left a hollow tone in her throat. "Come along now, Ethan. It's Jenny's night to cook dinner."

Ethan scuffed his toes in the sawdust. "Can Michael come too?"

Ethan's anxious face beamed up at her like a pair of pale blue headlights. She could hardly say no. Just this once, she told herself, what harm could it do? "Sure."

"Let's go!" Ethan looked at Michael.

Michael shrugged. "Why not?"

In a family fashion, they walked together to the house. Sarah's feet became heavier with every step along the path they traveled. She hoped Jenny wouldn't mind one more mouth at the table tonight. It was Wednesday, so Josh was at an auction. However, Jenny for a hostess at dinner ... Sarah's imagination ran frantic with the possibilities. Maybe this wasn't a good idea, after all.

Ethan led them inside the house, and single file, they entered the kitchen. Jenny was nowhere in sight. A small note left on the table caught Sarah's eye. She reached for the note. Her arm brushed Michael's waist and her face grew warm. As she stepped back, she bumped into the counter.

"It looks like the cook ran off," Michael said.

Sarah read the note. "She's gone off with some guy named Brad for the evening." She tossed the note on the counter. Jenny couldn't have planned a timelier exit to put her alone with Michael. Well, not *entirely* alone, she had Ethan. But whose side would he be on?

"One of the builders over at the clinic would be my guess."

Ethan rubbed his tummy. "Can we go there to eat?"

"I can cook," Sarah said.

"We could order out," Michael suggested. "Or go out?"

Sarah glanced around the kitchen. The old stove was marked with age, and the refrigerator hummed, plastered with Ethan's latest artwork. Tan linoleum rolled out beneath their feet dinged and nicked. Heat rose up her neck.

"Out, Mom!" Ethan cried with enthusiasm. "Pizza!"

Two pairs of blue eyes pleaded with her.

"Let me get my bag." She headed down the hall. Ethan skipped behind her while she grabbed her purse off the end of the banister, checked for her wallet, and found her keys.

Ethan raced Michael to the car, but as soon as Michael saw her beat-up little Ford, he paused. He would have to twist his long legs like a pretzel inside her dinky little Escort. Politely, he offered to take them in his car.

They waited while Michael jogged over to his place. She assumed they'd ride in his truck, but then she spotted the shiny two-door black sports car. Ethan's jaw dropped and he pointed. Sarah pushed his arm down and waited for Michael to park in the driveway.

Fancy cars didn't impress her. Not the way they did Ethan. It was just a car.

She secured Ethan in his booster seat, and they drove into Shelbyville to the local pizza joint. Buttery-soft leather seats made her want to melt in them, but the cool blast of the air from the dashboard kept her from dissolving.

Ethan chose a corner booth near the arcade in the back, and inhaled his food in record time. Sarah allowed Michael to indulge him with a few quarters to play games. Ethan chose race-cars.

"He's a good kid."

"Wait until you get a chance to know him." Sarah bit into a slice pizza. Cheese oozed and grease ran down her fingers.

"Is that an offer?" He wiped his fingers on a paper napkin. Sounds of race cars zoomed behind his head from the arcade.

Sarah took a sip of cola. She watched Ethan beyond Michael's head. More sounds of screeched brakes and crashed cars interrupted the chatter around them. Three other booths held occupants.

The owner, Tony, flung a piece of dough in the air. He stretched it, turned it, and worked it out into a large round form.

Her gaze fell to the red brick floor of Tony's establishment. Each rectangular stone mortared and placed as a part of the restaurants foundation. She'd built a solid foundation for her son. If she left Michael into their lives now, would it crack?

"Sarah?" Michael placed his hand over her cold, fragile one. His touch thawed the chill. A small hitch caught in her breath as she looked into his eyes. He squeezed her hand, and traced his thumb over her tender flesh. Her head spun, not from the fresh aroma of oregano and grease, or Tony's dough, but from Michael's touch. She needed to finish her pizza and get out of here. The booth was closing in on her.

"I think we should go now." She pulled her hand from his grasp. Her flesh tingled from his touch.

"You haven't finished your slice."

She took a huge bite, chewed, and swallowed. "There!" She put on her sweetest smile. "Time to go, Ethan."

"Five more minutes," Ethan held up his hand.

"Take your time, Sport." Michael piled their paper plates together.

"Some of us have to be in bed by eight o'clock." Sarah looked at her watch, sucked on her straw and drained her soft drink.

"It must be tough raising a kid on your own." Michael tossed a napkin on top of the pile.

"Some of us don't have a choice." Sarah searched through her bag for her wallet. She pulled it onto her lap as she spilled out the contents. A pack of tissues, keys, pen, notepad, Tylenol, and a ponytail holder, then, finally her denim wallet.

"I got it." Michael flicked out bills from his wallet. Sarah froze and stared at her emptied purse contents.

"Thank you." She bit her lip and put her wallet back inside her purse.

"I lost." Ethan rounded the corner of the booth.

"Can't win them all, Sport." Michael tussled Ethan's hair as they walked out of Tony's.

Ethan fell asleep halfway out of town. Michael glanced in her direction many times, but not a word broke the unforgiving silence of the night.

Michael opened his door, reaching back to flick his seat up as he got out. "I've got him, you get the door."

Sarah watched him maneuver Ethan from the car. Ethan snuggled against Michael while he pushed the door shut with his foot and followed her into the house.

Sarah dropped her bag on the first stair. She led him upstairs and clicked on Ethan's dresser lamp. As she pulled down the quilt, her pulse raced like the cars Ethan drove at the arcade. This felt like a family moment. Why did God make her to go it alone in life?

In the soft glow of light, Michael laid Ethan in his bed, and Sarah pulled off his shoes. As Michael reached for the top of the quilt, she grabbed it, their eyes locked, and he backed quietly out of the room.

She brushed her hand over Ethan's hair, kissed his forehead, and tucked his quilt around him. Content, she left the room.

At the bottom of the stairs, Michael leaned against the door. Sarah took a deep breath. This wasn't a date. She reached for the doorknob, and he stepped out of her way. "Thank you," he said, stepping out onto the porch.

Sarah blinked. Was that what someone said at the end of a date?

"I had a good time."

"You make it sound like a date." She leaned on the door.

"Are you saying it wasn't?" He appeared wounded.

She almost laughed, but smiled instead. "Goodnight, Michael." She started to push the door shut.

Michael thrust his foot in the doorway. "What? No kiss?"

"Why would I want to kiss you?" She clung to the door, her knees threatened to buckle and she hoped he would go before it happened.

"I remember a time when you welcomed my kiss." His voice deepened. He smoothed back a lock of her hair.

She ducked her head away. This couldn't happen. She knew that. Like she knew, one look into his eyes would lead her astray.

He hooked a finger beneath her chin, and tilted her face up. She refused to look at him.

Sounds of crickets filled the muggy air. There wasn't a star in sight, but Sarah feared it would take more than a wish to mend the broken fence between them. "That was a long time ago."

"What about now?" He pulled her into his embrace, wedging himself into the doorway. Sarah stiffened.

She squeezed her eyes shut. His lips pressed gently against hers in a sweet kiss. Slowly, he increased the pressure until she kissed him back. A small whimper balled up in her throat, and her resistance weakened as the kiss ended.

Michael stepped back and released her. Sensations of suppressed emotions surfaced. She raised her hand as if she would slap him, but he took that hand and kissed each knuckle tenderly. She sucked in her breath, any resolve inside her wilted.

She stepped back into the house, shut the door, and bolted the lock. She reached up and touched her lips. Outside, she heard the car engine roar to life. She waited—waited, until she heard his car engine fade before climbing the stairs. She stopped in front of Ethan's door. Her forehead rested against the wood, she prayed. She needed all the strength she could get.

"Be still my heart," she crooned.

The teenage girl inside her bubbled with giddiness, leaving the mother inside her to fret.

CHAPTER 9

Sarah ran the thick bristled brush down the horse's sleek sorrel coat. A whisper of a breeze swept down the stable aisle. She lifted her face to catch its faint chill across her cheek. Long braided hair hung down the middle of her back as she worked. Sweat dampened her shirt, and her leather-clad calves felt as if they would bake by midday from the sweltering July heat.

Sarah dropped the brush into a tack bucket at her feet and patted the horse's neck. "Here you are," she fetched a small white sugar cube from her front shirt pocket and held it out. She rubbed the horse's ear as its soft muzzle pressed to her palm.

From the stall beside her, an anxious whine called out. Her heart ached for her horse, Irish Rose.

Who would help Gran tend to her father's stables while she was away?

She returned one horse to its stall and slid open the door to another.

"Watch!" A hand reached out and jerked her back. Equine teeth darted towards her and the stall door slammed shut.

Her hand flew to her chest. She turned, about to thank the person who'd saved her, but the man who stood behind her wasn't a groom. He was the owner's son—Michael.

She bumped against him.

She'd never been this close to him, having only viewed him from a far. She sucked in her breath. His ebony hair glinted blue in the bright morning sunlight. He stood a few inches taller, and he held a black leather crop in one hand.

Her stomach quivered and she took a deep breath, unable to hold it any longer.

"You may want to be careful with that one, you're more than likely to get bitten a time or two," he said.

She stared into his eyes, startled by their unusual color. They were like a pair of robin's eggs, soft blue like a cloudless sky. Her heart jumped—a hard swift yank like an old lawnmower that wouldn't start. She reached back and held onto the stall door.

Her heart pounded. He slid the end of his crop down into his polished leather boot. She swallowed. Suddenly, her throat went dry.

As she lifted her gaze, Michael crossed his arms and leaned his broad shoulder back against the black iron bars.

From the other side of those bars, the horse snorted, and Sarah remembered her task. *Steady girl, steady now*. She slid open the stall door again. The horse jutted its head forward. Michael grabbed hold of her at the same time the horse's teeth encountered her arm. He yanked her back against him with one hand and slid the stall door shut with the other.

The horse whinnied and scuffled within the stall's closure. Sarah stumbled, pressed against his chest, while she clutched her arm.

"You okay?" he asked.

She nodded. Her cheeks burned as she rubbed her arm from the pinch of the horse's teeth. She knew better than to swing open stall doors to strange horses. Her father had taught her that from the time she could walk.

"Warned you, didn't I?" Michael said.

"Should've listened after the first time, right?"

Dark brows arched and soft creases spread out from the corner of his eyes when he grinned. "I haven't seen you around here before. Newbie, uh?"

Sarah flushed, "Is it that obvious?"

He held out his hand. "I'm Michael."

"Sarah." She placed her hand in his. Warmth from his fingers spread up her arm.

"No wonder she doesn't like you." His eyes danced with amusement. "The horse's name is Hagar." Even as he spoke, he held her hand, and Sarah tightened her grip.

"I guess that explains it." Her gaze fell to his hand. It was the first time someone reached out to her since the day of her parents' tragic accident. The heat reflected in both his eyes and his touch caused her sweaty palms to grow cold.

Michael released his hold, placed his hand on the stall gate, and leaned toward her. "I thought I was the only one who got up this early to ride."

Pull yourself together. Sarah forced a smile. "It seems you are mistaken." She reached across his arm for the leather bridle that hung on the front of the stall door.

"Apparently," Michael muttered. His hand reached for the stall latch at the same time she did. Quickly Sarah snatched her hand away. Michael eased the stall door open, while Sarah stepped into the stall's threshold and quickly dodged the horse's next attempt to nip her. "Keep it up," she told the horse, "And I won't give you any sugar when we're done."

Michael's eyebrows lifted. "You want some company?"

Sarah caught hold of the horse's halter. If Hagar hadn't bitten her, she would have thought she was dreaming. She fumbled with the clasp as she juggled the bridle in her other hand.

Michael stepped in on the other side of the horse's head to help slide the bit into its mouth. Hagar revealed her teeth. Sarah gave the bridle a quick tug and Michael shoved the bit in the horse's mouth.

"Ornery one, this one, tries to bite just about everyone. Most of the grooms always try to saddle her off on some unexpected newcomer."

Hagar stepped back as Sarah managed to slip the bridle over

the mare's ears.

She frowned. So that is why Jenny, her roommate, offered to trade her one horse for two of Sarah's horses for the summer.

"I've dealt with worse." Sarah thought of the roan stud she'd left back at her family's stables. She often wondered who would take care of the horses while she was gone. Gran never had a fondness for horses, not since one kicked Grandpa squarely in the chest and caused him to have a heart attack.

Horses were the cause of death for both the men in Gran's life. According to Gran, it was her mother's horse. Silver Wind, that caused the accident which took her parents' lives—nothing would convince Gran otherwise.

"Hagar here is about the nastiest of the bunch."

"So why do they keep her?" Sarah pushed back her thoughts and focusing on buckling the bridle's throatlatch.

"Are you kidding? Hagar is my mother's prize mare." Michael patted Hagar's neck and the horse flicked its muzzle towards him. He stepped out of range from Hagar's menacing teeth. "I'll grab your saddle. You don't mind do you, if I ride along? That is, unless you *wanted* to ride alone?"

Alone? An ache spread down to the pit of her stomach. These past few weeks were like an eternity, and she didn't care to be alone anymore. Especially when she lay awake in the darkness of the night, God—like her parents—felt lost to her.

Where was God when her parents had their accident? Where was the God her mother promised would always comfort her sorrows?

There had been no one to hold her in the days after her parents' deaths. Her own grandmother didn't even want her. That's why she was here, wasn't she? Gran didn't need her space to mourn; she simply hadn't wanted Sarah around.

Sarah led the horse out of the stall and into the aisle.

What was it her mother had always told her? "He comforts us in all our troubles so we can comfort others." But why should she? Her mother was gone.

Sorrow stabbed her chest as she watched Michael toss a blanket and saddle across the horse's wither. Did someone like Michael know what it was like to be alone?

How could he? Guys like Michael got everything they wanted.

Sarah's heart whispered something her mother once taught her from the family Bible. "As you share in suffering you will also share God's comfort."

There was no comfort in death, Sarah decided grimly—only deep-saturated grief. She was doomed to carry its burden in her heart for the rest of her life. Yet, no matter how much she hurt from the losses she'd endured, the fact was, her parents had left her behind. Life, however, constantly pushed forward.

"I still have one more horse to ride after Hagar." She watched him buckle the cinch.

"Which one?" he asked.

Sarah indicated the stall behind him. "No problem, I'll ride this one and you take the other."

She tried to ignore the flutter in her stomach. She dismissed it and tried to brush off the little voice in her head that taunted the fact she was going horseback riding with her employer's son.

Outside the stables, she put one foot in the stirrup and held onto the reins. Heat rose up her neck and spread into a blush. Behind her, she could sense Michael's eyes traveling the length of her backside.

They rode around the oval track with thick-branched trees to shade them from the sun. Kingsley Estate wasn't at all like her family's stable. Here every board around the track gleamed with a fresh coat of white paint. Track horses, show horses, and breeding horses where all kept in different stables across the property.

She looked over at Michael. He sat straight as a pole. His thumbs pointed in towards one another on the reins, as her mother always taught her. She frowned, her mount switched leads, and she gave the animal a nudge with her heel.

Somewhere in the trees above them, she heard a bird sing.

"What brings you here for the summer?" He leaned forward allowing the horse a looser rein to keep pace with Sarah's horse.

"My grandmother didn't give me a choice. You?" Sarah stared

out over the horse's head, her hips thrusted forward in a customary English post while the horse trotted.

"Summer vacation, then back to college." He reined in closer, the toes of their boots bumped.

"At least you know where you're going after the summer," Sarah replied, wistfully.

Michael laughed, "Yeah, another year of having my nose in a book and then off to Veterinarian school." He grinned, wide. "Why don't you say we have a little fun?'

"Fun?"

"Race you, first one to complete a lap around the estate and come back to the barn wins!"

They weren't supposed to race the horses off the track, nor was she to take any horse out of the designated areas of the estate. She bit her lip. Inside her, adrenaline pumped like water rushing down a stream through a broken dam.

"What do I get if I win?" she asked.

Michael tilted his head back and laughed. His horse sidestepped beneath him as they both slowed to a walk. Then he looked over at her, sober. "You'll have to beat me to the barn to find out. Considering you're on my mother's nag, I'd say I have a good chance of getting there first."

His eyes gleamed with the challenge.

Her blood hummed with the thrill.

She could be kicked off the estate and sent home if she got caught. A slow smile spread across her face. Gran couldn't ignore her if they sent her home. Then there was Michael. He leaned down low on the saddle and prepared to race.

She leaned forward, her gaze locked with his, and her heart sped, even though the prize remained unnamed. It was worth the risk to live in this moment.

"Ready?" he asked.

"Set."

"Go!" he shouted.

Sarah laid her heels into the horse's flanks and Hagar leapt forward. Turf flew from behind them. Adrenaline rushed through her veins as the wind blew her hair back. Michael's horse stretched to take the lead. He pulled his crop and tapped the horse on the front shoulder, urging his mount to pass her and Hagar.

She leaned up over Hagar's neck and gave the horse free rein. It was just her, the horse, and no one else as she raced around the estate following Michael's lead.

She waited. *Not yet ... Not yet ...*

Then the stables came into sight.

She squeezed with her thighs, pressed in her calves, and soon she and Hagar raced past Michael and his mount. She glanced back over her shoulder as she entered the stable yard ahead of him.

She pulled back the reins, leaned back in the saddle and made Hagar circle in front of the stable yard. Slowed to a walk, Michael did the same.

From inside the doorway, Josh Anderson watched from the morning shadows. He paused, mid-push of a wheelbarrow full of sawdust. His sister Jenny walked up beside him clad in her breeches and waved to Sarah.

Beneath her, Hagar heaved for breath. The horse's coat turned sleek with sweat. Sarah kept the horse walking in circles in the opposite direction of Michael.

They both slid out of their saddles at the same time, and Josh left his wheelbarrow behind to approach Sarah. She, like the horse, gasped for breath.

"Are you crazy?" Josh asked.

Sarah laughed. "It was fun."

"Give me that horse, both of you need to go cool down." Josh scowled.

Michael handed Josh another set of reins. "Thanks, man." He placed his arm around Sarah's shoulders and walked towards the cool shade of the barn. They passed Jenny, who gave Sarah a half-smile as she jogged towards Josh.

Sarah looked back at the Anderson twins, as they both led exhausted horses to cool down. With the adrenaline of the ride dissipated from her veins, Sarah frowned. She should have never run the horse like that, and now she'd handed off her duties to someone else. Before she could dwell on it any further, Michael took her by the chin and directed her gaze toward him.

"I never thought I'd say this, but you won. So what will it be?" he asked.

Her heart beat faster. She licked her lips, looked around him at Jenny and Josh, and back at Michael.

She couldn't help but notice his windblown hair—and wanted to run her fingers through it. Neither one bothered to wear their riding helmets. He slipped his crop back in his boot. Sweat ran down his forehead, as if he'd run a foot race.

She'd won. She'd beaten Michael. As he stood with his eyes assessing her, shamelessly, she could only think of one thing she wanted. Her cheeks flamed.

She twisted her hands together, looked into the depth of his eyes, and said, "Could we do it again? Not today, but you know, another day. If you're too busy …" she blabbered like an idiot.

"Is that all?" He chuckled. "No gifts or favors? I am Harold Kingsley's step-son you know."

Sarah shook her head. She didn't want gifts or favors. She simply didn't want it to end—this alive feeling Michael jolted through her heart.

"Sure," Michael agreed. "How about we make it the first ride in the morning, so we won't have an audience watching when we hit the finish line?"

Sarah nodded, breathless.

"Tomorrow then, bright and early." He reached down and took her hand and kissed it. Sarah's breath caught in her throat. He let his fingers brush against her palm as he released her hand and strode away.

"Tomorrow …"

CHAPTER 10

Shortly after two o'clock, Michael returned to the clinic from his morning rounds. Buzzing saws, splintering hammers, and shouting men greeted him. A skeletal frame of his equine clinic stood in the hot sweltering July sun.

He was late for his appointments, and Doc Miller shuffled out promptly at noon. Jenny sat at the desk; her fingers worked the keyboard of a laptop. Neat piles of invoices were stacked beside her, keyed into the system, and slid into envelopes. Wrapped up in her work, she ignored him when the bell above the door rang.

Michael greeted his patients with a pat on the golden retriever's head and waved at the little girl suffocating the yelping pup in her arms. He walked down the hallway to the back part of the old house where a small kitchen was tucked around the corner. As he poured himself a cup of coffee, He rolled back the stress on his shoulders. The strong scent of over-brewed dark coffee beans stung his eyes.

"Looks like someone was out late last night." Jenny tapped a folder in her hand. He noticed her lime green blouse and tan shorts, even more vivid than the red outfit she wore that first day. All he ever saw Sarah wear was faded blue jeans or cut offs.

"I wasn't the only one out last night." He held out the cup of coffee. Jenny shook her head.

"Decaf." She smiled. "Miller brought it in this morning, grumbling something about his wife."

The delight of a good stiff cup of coffee went stale in his mouth.

"Your first appointment is Chester, who needs his shots updated, and his little cousin Hiccup cut his paw on some broken glass." Jenny read the file.

"I'll be there in a minute." He sagged into a chair.

Jenny laid the folder on chair arm beside him and walked out.

Sarah's spooked expression flashed in his mind, and the sweetness of her kiss lingered on his lips. Even though she kept running from him, the spark was there. He'd proved it to himself when he stole that kiss.

Son or no son, Michael wanted Sarah back in his life. However, the obstacle of the boy's father remained a hurdle he needed to jump. Jenny said she wouldn't play middleman, but she gave him more information in one morning than Sarah had in a month. Perhaps the next time he got Sarah alone, he'd ask her.

She loved him once. His gut twisted with thoughts of all the other girls who proclaimed their love. Sarah was different. Sarah came to him vulnerable and alone. No other woman could make his blood pump like Sarah.

Maybe her life would be different if he hadn't interfered, or maybe his life wouldn't have changed at all. Who was he to question the works of God?

He picked up the folder and stood. On his way out, he set his cup of coffee on the counter.

The golden retriever thumped his tail when Michael opened the door.

Later that afternoon, Sarah sat on a bale of hay in the barn loft with shafts of orange and goldenrod sunlight streamed across her face. Dust motes floated across the bands of light, settling on her bent head as she buried her face in her hands.

Ethan plopped down beside her, his small hands cradling his chin. He tilted his head to look over at his mother.

Both doors at the end of the hayloft stood open. Stacked formations of hay clustered around them like Swiss cheese with large gaping holes.

Jenny stood beside the bale of hay where Sarah sat and made a face that reminded Sarah of the one Ethan expressed when vegetables appeared on his plate. A few feet away, Josh stood with his arms crossed in front of a large opening in the floor.

A mixture of rotted wood and moldy alfalfa baked in the sweltering heat wafted through the air.

"Is there anything left up here to salvage?" Sarah asked.

Josh lifted his hat and wiped the sweat dripping down his brow. "Only what I tossed down this morning. We'll have new hay coming in soon, but the back corner of the roof needs repaired."

"I was afraid of that," Sarah said.

Jenny looked over at Josh. "Can you do it?"

"Not alone I can't. We're talking climbing up on the pitch of the roof. Who knows what I'll find up there."

"How long before we're out of hay?" Jenny asked.

"A week, maybe two if we stretch it." Josh scuffed his boot through the hay shaft on the floor.

"Then we'll have to stretch it." Sarah reached over and pulled Ethan close. He wrapped his arms around his mother's waist and gave her a bear hug. "We can do it, Mom."

"It'll be weeks yet before our cut of the hay crop is ripe," Josh warned.

Sarah grimaced. She could almost see Gran smiling down on her from heaven, as if the old woman planned this, even in death. What would her father have done if he were here?

"We might have to buy a bale here and there and keep it stacked below," Jenny said.

"It's not possible. What little we saved to get this place running is gone. I spent it all on fence post and we're …"

"We still have two fields yet to mend," Josh interrupted Sarah as he walked across the dusty planks to the back of the loft to inspect the worst section.

"You spent your savings, Sarah, but Josh and I haven't contributed much." Jenny put her hands on her hips.

Josh turned, his brows shot up. "Speak for yourself, Sis."

Sarah patted Ethan's back and stood. "Josh is right. This is my problem and I'll figure it out, somehow."

Jenny moved closer to Josh and punched him in the arm. He scowled. "What'd you do that for?"

"Because we're all in this together, remember?"

Josh rubbed his arm. "You know, now that I think about it. I don't believe I've ever had any say in the matter. Seems to me you two are always dragging me along for the ride."

"Nobody forced you to move here, you know," Jenny quipped.

Sarah walked over and placed her hand on Josh's arm. "Thank you."

His gaze softened and the ridged lines of his face relaxed. He placed his hand over Sarah's. "I'm here for you, Sarah."

Jenny grinned and winked over at Ethan. "Well, when you two love birds get done cooing up here with the pigeons, Ethan and I'll be waiting down below where it's not so hot."

Jenny extended her hand to Ethan.

Sarah's face flushed. Josh's eyes turned a darker shade of green as he stared at Jenny for a long moment. Jenny bit her lip in attempt to hold in the laughter Sarah saw in her emerald eyes. Josh's gaze returned to Sarah. "We can throw a tarp over this for now."

"I'll help!" Ethan bounced with excitement.

"Oh no, you don't." Sarah wagged her finger.

"Go on with Jenny, before she melts." Josh ruffled Ethan's hair as he walked past a bit slower and without the bounce.

"Why can't I help?" Ethan pouted.

"You can," Sarah took him by the shoulders and turned him so she may lower herself to his height. "You're a great help around here, my best helper, and when the hay starts coming I'm going to need you to keep count of all the bales for Uncle Josh to stuff up here."

"You help feed the horses and clean the stalls too." Jenny pointed out.

Ethan's lower lip protruded. "It's not fair."

No, Sarah thought, life never is.

She looked at Josh. A beam of sunlight touched the bill of his cap and cascaded down over his face. He hunched down beside her. "There's plenty to do around here, we all have different jobs. Besides, we can't do it all."

"Like feed the horses," Ethan asked.

"Yep," Josh grinned.

"But I'm still your right hand man even though I can't go up there, right?" Ethan pointed up to the damaged roof.

"Always," Josh assured him. "Now run along with your Aunt Jenny. I think I see a puddle forming at her feet."

Ethan giggled and followed Jenny down the ladder. Sarah watched Ethan's head disappear. She walked toward the back opening of the loft, where, like a large painting, it gave her a bird's eye view of the landscape. Josh came up beside her and wrapped his arm around her shoulders. She leaned into him and rested her head on his chest as he drew her close.

She watched white drifts of clouds float lazily in the sky. Below, the landscape was mixed with green fields and golden streaks of crops in the late afternoon sun. Above them, a pigeon flew out from the rafters through the opening, and out into the sky.

Sarah lifted her gaze to Josh—his jaw taunt as he stared out the opening. Perhaps she should marry Josh. It wasn't as if he'd never proposed. That made her smile. How many times had Josh offered to marry her? A dozen or more, she recollected. Each time she hadn't taken him seriously. She wondered if he suggested it because, like Jenny hinted, Josh loved her, or because he was just being there for her.

Josh had always been there for her. Not like Michael …

In her heart, she was unable to break the promise she'd made to Gran. Josh looked down at her, their gazes met.

Gran was dead and buried. Had the promise she'd made as a pregnant teenage mother died with Gran too?

As Sarah looked at Josh, her heartbeat remained steady. She took a deep rattled breath of stagnate hot air and mold-laced hay, and sneezed.

"Bless you," Josh said.

Sarah wiped her nose with the back of her hand. Josh reached in his back pocket and pulled out a hankie for her. "I'll get the rest of this out of here by tomorrow. We'll have a bonfire down in the lower field by the swamp. Not much good for anything else."

Sarah nodded, and then sneezed again. "Thanks."

"Don't worry, Sarah, we'll find a way to take care of this."

She frowned. Why couldn't Josh make her heart flutter like Michael? She'd always known that love between two different people was never the same, *so why, Lord, can't I bring myself to accept Josh's offer to be my husband*?

Why, indeed.

"You're a good man, Josh."

"Yeah, well like Jenny said, it's getting hot in here and I've got to find a tarp to cover this roof before the next rain until we can get it repaired."

"Let me know how much you think it'll cost," she said, relieved for the distraction from her thoughts. She followed Josh to the loft opening and he motioned for her to go down the ladder first.

Michael heard a murmur of voices overhead and scuffs of boots walking across the planks over the stables. Shafts of hay fell through the board cracks from above, and the dust made his nose twitch.

He went over to check Clyde's stall, not surprised to find both Clyde and Bonnie were gone. He looked up at the aged planks and headed toward the stable's loft ladder, but before he could investigate, Jenny and Ethan approached from the far end of the aisle.

"Hey Mike!" Ethan ran with Jenny behind him.

"What's up?"

Ethan wrinkled his nose as flecks of dust trickled down over his head. "Josh says the hay is bad and the roof is broken."

Michael looked up at the planked boards then back down at Ethan. "Your mom and Josh up there now?"

Ethan nodded. "Uncle Josh can fix anything."

Michael tilted his head and listened. Any sound from above faded from earshot. "Is that so?" He contemplated what Sarah and Josh were doing up there as their muffled voices no longer carried down below.

"I'm gonna help because I'm Uncle Josh's right-hand man." Ethan jabbed a thumb in his chest. "Isn't that right, Aunt Jenny?"

Jenny walked up behind Ethan. She fanned herself with her hands. "Yep. What he says." She took a deep breath. "Lord, it's hot up there." She puckered her flushed cheeks and blew out air.

"Anything I can do to help cool things down?" Michael asked.

"Like a fan?" Ethan asked.

Jenny laughed, "Yeah a big fan that spins hay."

Ethan's eyes grew large, "Like Rumpelstiltskin!"

Michael smirked. He liked this kid, especially his sloppy crooked-tooth grin and blue eyes. Didn't all kids have blue eyes until they reached a certain age?

"Not likely," Jenny replied, "Although, if Rumpelstiltskin should want to appear and spin our moldy hay into gold, I doubt anyone would object." She smiled.

"Hay shortage?" Michael guessed money was on short supply too. He could imagine the bills added up around this place. Too much, he assessed, for Sarah to sustain on what little inheritance she would have received from her family.

Jenny wiped her sweaty palms down her torn jeans. "Josh has to throw out all the hay from the back corner of the loft. The roof has a leak and with all this heat …"

Michael got the idea. Wet hay and humid temperatures made for an unhealthy situation.

Above the voices resumed.

"I don't know about you, but I could use a cool drink." Jenny told Ethan.

"Can I have ice cubes?" Ethan took Jenny's hand.

"As many as you want. I might need a few myself."

"See you later." Michael waved them off and headed towards the stable loft's ladder. As his hand touched the first rung, Sarah's backside came into view.

He reached out and grasped her by the waist. Startled, she released her hold on the ladder and Michael lifted her down the rest of the way.

Sarah turned in his arms.

"Hello there," he breathed in the rank scents of alfalfa and leaned closer trying to identify the other—rose perhaps?

She ducked her head. Above her, Josh jumped down midway off the ladder beside them.

His brows drew together. Without a word, he nodded at Michael.

Sarah pulled out of Michael's embrace and stepped away.

"I was helping the lady down." Michael grinned.

Josh tore his gaze from Michael and looked at Sarah. "I'll head into town, see what I can do."

Sarah nodded. Josh turned his head and kept an eye on both of them as he walked out of the stables and into the yard. Michael felt the heat of Josh's stare bore into his back.

"I hear you have a hay shortage," he tried to ignore the discomfort of Josh's gaze.

"Josh is taking care of it. Now that the fence is around one of the fields, we can let the horses out to graze more."

"What happens when you take on more horses?"

"I'll deal with that as it comes. Right now, I've got a barn roof needing repaired, two more fields needing fenced, and empty stalls needing filled." She started to walk away.

Michael took her by the arm. "Have you thought about my proposal?"

He noticed her hair graced her shoulders rather than its usual restrained ponytail. Her eyes were hazel, darted with slivers of blue hues and green. Not at all like her son's. Where joy and curiosity sparked in the young boy's eyes, he saw only deep-seated sorrow swirled in a mixture of hope and longing.

His gaze seemed to penetrate her soul. She hoped he wouldn't notice the small tremor of her chest. "I told you once, and I'll tell you again. Stay out of my business, Michael. Jenny and Josh are as much a part of this place now as I ever have been. We're a team."

"Every team has its players, Sarah. Think of how a basketball team runs plays by using different members of the team's talents to their best advantages. You've got the ball coming down the court and Jenny and Josh are your points, but who's standing guard?"

"This isn't basketball."

"I became a veterinarian because I wanted to save lives. I wanted to help all types of animals, mostly horses, because like you—I grew up around them too. Shouldn't you have someone on your team, Sarah, who can help save the lives of these horses that you bring here to rescue? Do you think Josh can fix them like the barn roof?" the veins in his neck throbbed, and his jaw drew taunt. Why was she so afraid to let him help her?

"I don't need your help," she told him.

There it was, feisty Sarah ready to take on the world, alone. When Lord, he asked, would Sarah learn to accept she was never alone?

And we know that all things work together for the good of them that love God, to them that are the called according to His purpose. He recalled a piece of scripture from the book of Romans.

"At least let me give you an advance on Clyde's board." Michael pulled out his wallet. Payment would guarantee him at least another month in Sarah's presence.

She bit her lip, tried to decide one way or the other. Her gaze watched his hand pull out the money from his wallet. She pressed her lips in a firm line and her gaze met his. For a moment, he held his breath, prayed she wouldn't refuse his offer.

"Only because it's almost the end of the month." She held out her hand.

Michael folded her fingers around the cash. "Looks like I'm locked in for another month."

CHAPTER 11

Sarah hung up the phone and covered her face with her hands. She wasn't going to accept that her cause was hopeless. That familiar itch made her reach for the keys of the computer, refusing to write off the day as a blunder.

She called all over the state, looking for orphan foals or yearlings from nursing mare farms to raise. She crossed her fingers. She crossed her heart. They were out there somewhere. She would find them.

When the computer didn't cooperate, she spent another hour on the phone. After dialing every listing in the phonebook for horse farms, she tried auction houses next, and hit the jackpot! Excitement bubbled like a brook through her veins.

Mayfield was having their auction tonight, so she started to make plans to leave. She wasn't a fan of evening auctions, and this time she'd have to bring Ethan along. The prospect of sharing this with her son outweighed the downside of taking him on a road trip late at night.

She left the office in pursuit of Josh, and it didn't take long to find him near the barn. "Whatcha doin'?" She cocked a hip against the fender of the old faded-green truck. Josh backed away from underneath the hood. Ethan hung over the side with his feet dangling in an effort to watch.

"Giving her a tune-up." Josh wiped his hands on a rag and grinned at her.

"You up for a road trip?" She rubbed her hand across the fender.

"Yep, I'm pulling out in a few hours."

"What?" Sarah's hand paused, "Where are you going?"

"Where are *you* going?" he tossed the rag. Ethan snatched it in midair, grinning from ear to ear.

"I asked first."

"You find some foals?" He reached over and helped Ethan hop down to the ground.

"The season's over, but a few said they had a couple of late breeders, and would call if they decided to sell."

Josh hooked his thumbs in the pockets of his faded jeans. "So where are you going?"

"Mayfield. The auction starts at six, and the phone recording said there's a herd of sixty coming in."

Josh whistled. "Somebody sold out."

Ethan scooted away from the adults to collect the bicycle leaning against the side of the barn. He rode down the lane away from them, towards the house, but she knew he would turn back at the porch.

Sarah crossed her arms. "I want to go, Josh."

"Take this with you." He reached in his back pocket for his wallet, and pulled out his business card.

Her eyes narrowed, she took the card from his hand. "Since when do you have a hauling business?"

"I've got to make a steady income somehow, Sarah. Working over at the auction barn once a week might be steady, but it don't support a man. This will." He tapped the card.

"Is this where you're running off to tonight?" As she held up the card, dark clouds of frustration rolled in over her. She counted on Josh being there when she needed him. Since when did he get it in his mind to go off on his own?

"I told Fred Dodson I'd deliver a horse for him. You never

know, Sarah I could put in a few good words at some places, and get the word out. You know, word-of-mouth kind of thing."

"What about Mayfield?"

She felt the bubble of excitement fizzle under her skin. She was the one to set Jenny up with the job over Michael's clinic, and now Josh started a business of his own. But where did that leave her? Who would be left to help her with the rescue?

"Why don't you ask the good doctor? I'm sure he'll jump at the chance to take you." Josh's voice matched the sharp cut of his gaze.

"What's your problem?" She planted her hands on her hips, and her cheeks flushed.

"I'm not the one with the problem." He slammed the hood of the truck down. "Seems to me you're the one without a truck and trailer."

Sarah bit the inside of her lip. What had gotten his goat? She cocked her head to the side.

Ethan peddled past them. His bicycle tire skidded across gravel and he fell over.

He picked up his bicycle, brushed himself off, and grinned at Sarah. Ethan got back on his bicycle to do it over again.

"I thought we were together."

"So did I." He leaned back against the chrome bumper.

Ethan rode way towards the house.

"I need to go tonight, Josh. With that many horses, there's bound to be foals."

Josh reached to the back of his head, scratching a tuft of thick red locks curling at the edge of his cap. He puffed his cheeks full of air and exhaled. "How much cash you got?"

"I can afford the price of a newborn foal."

"Two fifty won't get you much. Here." He shuffled through a handful of bills, he handed them to her.

I can't take your money." She stared at the wad of cash in his hand.

"Take it. There's plenty more where it came from." He held out the money to her.

She looked at the bills, then at Josh. “I can’t.”

Taking money from him didn’t settle right in her stomach. She didn’t have the means to pay him back anytime soon. What was left of her inheritance after she paid off all Gran’s debts only left her treading the pond. A foolish person might try raising a son on an empty bank account and a dream, but she was not a fool, or even a dreamer. She would scrape by in her own way.

“I thought we were together.” He rubbed the money beneath her nose. The smell of opportunity was heady, like a cheap perfume.

“I’ll pay you back.” She grabbed the bills from his hand and counted them. “There’s almost a grand here!” She counted the bills again, making sure she’d been right the first time. He blushed under her stare.

“Consider it a donation.” He walked around the fender of the truck.

“This hauling business of yours must be off to a good start.”

A trickle of sweat ran down his neck, and Josh coughed. He reached through the open window for a half-empty bottle of water. Unscrewing the cap, he guzzled the liquid down to the last drop.

“There’s enough here we can fix the barn roof,” she said.

Josh shook his head. “You take that and buy some foals.” He tapped the money in her hand. “Don’t you worry about the roof. It’ll get taken care of.”

“Taken care of?” Sarah asked, “By whom?”

Josh gave her that look. The look that appeared as if he knew something she wasn’t supposed to know. “I’ve got to get over to Dodson’s to load. I’d offer to spring for pizza, but I heard you already went out for supper last night.”

Sarah’s brows shot up. She folded the wad of bills and stuffed them deep into her front jean pocket.

“So that’s what’s bothering you?” His wince showed she’d hit the bull’s eye.

“Spending a lot of time with the guy is all.” The fat lower lip of his mouth puckered out. Ethan , no doubt, had been giving him lessons.

"You really know how to put me between a rock and a hard place."

"Sooner or later you'll yield," Josh said.

She studied his face. Tight-lipped, twinkle-eyed, freckled-nose Josh. She knew he was keeping a secret from her. "I've got to find a truck and a trailer."

Construction stopped. Quiet stillness surrounded Michael as he stood near the hollow structure of his new clinic. For the past few weeks, workers laid the foundation and raised the frame.

Everything was coming along—until now.

Jack walked up beside him. Under a cluster of spruce trees at the far edge of the clinic's structure, a group of workers sat in the shade. Jack took out a stained white hankie and wiped the back of his neck as they stood beneath the hot sun.

"Framework's set, but I figure the boys and I will be taking some time off until the lumberyard catches up with our order."

"How long are we talking?" Michael couldn't afford to have his clinic opening delayed. Clients were calling and waiting for the clinic's services. A setback like this could cost him those clients.

He thought about the bank loans, the research grants, and shook his head.

Jack shrugged. "Hard to say. Could be a few days, could be a month. That's some fancy cargo you've got ordered for a horse stable, if you know what I'm saying."

Michael did. His clinic was going to have the best technology in horse medicine available, not only in the state, but in the country. He'd been blessed by research grants, investors, and his family to support his dream.

But Sarah didn't have that. He looked over at Silver Wind's stable. The sun glinted off a silver tarp on the stable's roof like a taped bandage.

Michael only half listened to Jack's ramblings as he spotted

Jenny step out onto the porch along with an elderly woman with an orange striped cat stuffed in her oversized bag.

Jack followed him across the gravel parking lot.

Two workers sat under the shade of an old elm tree. Jenny smiled and waved. Two men ribbed each other with an elbow. The taller of the two men got up and walked in Jenny's direction. Michael took a few more steps down the gravel lane as the elderly woman drove past with her cat curled in the passenger seat next to her.

He stared down the road at the stables across the way. Sarah didn't want him in her life. Hadn't she made that clear time and time again? Deep down inside him, he didn't believe her. She was hiding something. Something that brought fear to her eyes every time she looked at him, like a spooked filly.

He'd seen too, a longing, much like his own.

And, when he'd pulled her in his arms for that kiss, he'd felt it. So had she. Why else was she so upset?

He turned and faced Jack. "I need you to do me a favor."

"Whatever you need, you're the boss."

Michael grinned, clasped Jack on the shoulder. They headed for the shade of the trees. While they walked, Michael filled in Jack on his plans.

It would take a lot of nerve, and all the willpower she could muster to face Michael, but Sarah was willing to come to terms with that in order to get where she needed to go.

Last night had been a test, and she'd failed miserably. She told herself she wasn't going to let Michael affect her that way again. It was a lie. The moment he put his foot through the door, she lost before the battle started.

Where's your dignity, girl? She heard Gran's voice as Ethan peddled his bike beside her. She would march right up to Michael and request his cooperation. Josh didn't think she would do it, otherwise he wouldn't have suggested it. She'd show him!

Michael's coming back not only affected her, but all of them.

She saw anger and fear flare in Josh's green eyes. She would have to find a way to assure him their friendship was secure, and that things wouldn't change between them. However, the fact still remained to be seen.

As a teenager, Sarah would have given anything for public recognition as Michael's girl, but at the pizza joint she was rude, defensive, and protective. She hadn't been very appreciative when he'd paid his board, either. Instead, she'd stood there while her mind wandered back to the night he kissed her.

A thrill shot up her spine, and goose bumps prickled her arms. How much longer could she avoid his curiosities? She needed to explore her own, starting with that kiss. She swiped the tip of her tongue across her dry lips. Sooner or later she'd find herself trapped in another stall with no one to let her out.

It wasn't a date, but like long ago, it all started with a simple kiss. No, Sarah thought, it started with a locked door. But who had shut her in and slid the bolt across the door? Things didn't add up. Not that she would ever find out, and maybe it was best she didn't. Yet, one fact remained—Michael didn't do it.

Sarah tracked down Michael at the clinic. Ethan left his bicycle at the bottom of the clinic's porch ramp, and as they entered, the cool interior swept over her perspiring skin.

"Howdy," Jenny pulled out a desk drawer and dug inside. She held out a lollipop in Ethan's direction. "Am I the only one who got any sleep last night?"

"Why is everybody saying that?"

Ethan rolled the sweet hard candy around in his mouth by the stick and shrugged.

"Have you seen yourself lately?" Jenny reached back in the desk drawer for her purse, and shuffled around in her bag for a mirror. Sarah stared at the woman in the small circle in Jenny's palm. Dark circles hung beneath her bloodshot eyes. How could she face Michael looking like this? She peered down at her old scuffed-up brown boots, and her black tank top soaked in sweat from the heat of the day. She lifted her arm to smell. Not exactly roses.

"Great," she muttered. Now she'd have to go over to the house, take a shower, change into fresh clothes, and come back to face Michael. Talk about all the excuses to turn and run—but wait. Michael wouldn't try kissing her in this smelly, sweaty state.

"How'd you make out?" Jenny sat down as a woman waddled alongside a golden retriever. A young girl went down the hall at Jenny's signal.

"There's an auction over in Mayfield tonight. Only problem is, Josh took off on some new hauling business he started." Sarah sat down on the edge of the desk.

Ethan peered at the posters on the far wall.

"Did you know about it?"

"Nope, didn't say a word." Jenny waved to the woman with the dog as they left. "Not a bad idea. Granted, he probably can pick up good business working at the auction barn on Thursday nights."

But Sarah didn't want him traipsing all over the state, hauling animals. She wanted him *here*. But Josh was a man, he needed cash, and she didn't have it to spare. If the money he gave her was any indication of the profits he could bring in, then she had no right to stop him.

"He gave me cash this morning," Sarah stressed. "A lot of cash."

Jenny sat back in her chair. "See? Things are working out."

"I don't have a good feeling about this." The thought of this much cash burning a hole in her pocket chewed at the lining of her stomach.

"All done." Michael walked the girl out into the reception area. Jenny swiveled around in their direction.

"Now that didn't take long," she told the girl. "Your aunt's out at the car getting Chester settled. She already took care of the paperwork. You go on now. Have a nice day."

The young girl scurried out the door with the puppy licking her face. Ethan sat on a bench with his lollipop.

"So who's next?" Michael gave Jenny back one of her folders.

Sarah looked around. "I am." She met the warm stare of his intense blue eyes. An electric crackle shot through the air between them. Seconds ticked by. Jenny cleared her throat. Sarah diverted her gaze. Warmth swept across her cheeks.

"That was your last appointment." Jenny clasped her hands together. Ethan jumped off the bench and walk up to Michael.

He smiled at Ethan. "I've got the rest of the day, so what shall we do?"

Sarah spoke up, "I need to ask you a favor."

"We're going on a trip," Ethan said.

Inside, Sarah groaned. She hoped to be the one to tell him.

"You are?" Michael asked.

"Josh has plans tonight and I need to get to Mayfield." *Oh boy, here we go.* "I need a truck and trailer." She spit the words out fast.

Michael scratched his chin. Sarah shifted from one foot to the other, and Jenny pretended to work at her computer. Ethan crunched the last bit of candy off the stick.

Sarah waited for his response. Like an anxious child, she couldn't hold still. If she didn't want to go to Mayfield so bad she would slap the silly smirk forming on his face.

"Mayfield is a long drive from here. What time did you want to leave?"

"It starts at six, and I'd like to get there to see the foals."

He flipped the small case of his cell phone up from his hip and pulled out his phone to check the time. "We'd have to leave now." He shrugged out of the white coat covering his blue plaid short-sleeve shirt.

"Does that mean we can go?" Ethan asked.

Sarah hoped.

"Make sure you close up no sooner than five. Any emergencies call Miller and tell him I had to go out on call." Michael slipped his phone back in its case.

"No problem," Jenny said.

"What about you, Sport?"

"He's coming with us." Sarah wrapped her arm around

Ethan's shoulder. It had seemed like a good idea at the time.

"Can you be ready in a half hour?"

CHAPTER 12

Most people attend auctions because they are looking for something, whether it was to fill a purpose, seek a bargain, or make a buck. Michael, on the other hand, wasn't interested in any breed, grade, or age of horseflesh on the block. He would, however, shell out the price of this year's derby champion in order to make Sarah smile, and so far his scorecard was tallying up.

The transformation he saw in Sarah lifted his spirits. A smudge of pink gloss matched the soft tones of her blush, and long swept lashes fluttered over sparkling irises. The air was charged, it rippled her mood, and Michael couldn't remember when he'd had so much fun. While he drove, they sang variations of children's songs and he listened to Sarah's gentle voice read to her son.

Now, hand in hand, he walked along with Sarah. Like Ethan, he too, was filled with enthusiasm and anticipation. There was a question he wanted to ask her, so, as he threw caution to the wind, his thumb rubbed over the top of her hand.

Sarah jerked her hand free, a spark flared between them, and her eyes warned him. She grabbed Ethan's hand, and Ethan grinned back at him.

Michael didn't like auction houses, the inhumane treatment of the animals, or the sight of good sturdy horses sent for slaughter. A barter of sorts for injured racehorses, replaced and forgotten. Foals too young to be without a mother were sent to this place. There was a widespread use of mares bred for the purpose of raising future racers. Orphan foals, death, and sympathizers, like Sarah, attempted to turn fate. Part of him joined her in the effort as he thought of his clinic, Sarah's rescue, and the difference they could make together.

This was just like Sarah. She tugged Ethan along, gung-ho in her quest and drop-dead gorgeous. She adjusted the bag around her shoulder and kept a tight hold on her son. Along their way through the lot numbers of horses, she managed to take notes. By the end of the night, she'd fill his trailer as much as she filled his heart again.

The auctioneer started up at their arrival, and he wondered how long young boy could sit in the crowds of people without disturbance. He marveled at Sarah as she pulled out a box of juice and a bag of pretzels. This mother knew best, he decided.

Minutes after they settled, Michael said a quick prayer for Sarah, and one for himself. Selfish as it seemed, he needed patience and strength. He needed strength to restrain himself from touching her hand again, or brushing the twisted lock of hair away from her face. Strength.

"What are we looking for?"

"Foals." She drew Ethan closer to her side. "I'd like to raise a few to sell when they're older to help fund the rescue."

"Look!" Ethan pointed at a horse in the ring. The mare's dapple-grey coat was caked with mud.

"Better keep your hand down, Sport."

"Why?"

"They'll think you're bidding on that horse," Sarah darted Michael a quick glance. There were horses, and there were horses.

The scents of horseflesh, oiled leather, and Sarah's fragrance punctuated the air. From the first time he caught a whiff of her, Michael was sold.

Ethan's face lit up with the presentation of each new horse.

Sarah sat on the edge of her high-rise bench, and a euphoric lure of impatience stemmed from her like the thorns of a rose.

"Whoa there, girl. Patience."

She sniffed and nodded. The auctioneer caught her movement, but she relaxed at the twitch of the other man's hand. She sighed.

"Careful," he teased. "You don't want us taking anything home by accident."

"Excuse me?"

"Patience," he repeated, eyes locked on hers.

And patience paid off with the purchase of four horses, two of which were foals. Michael's purchase of the last two horses came as a relief to Sarah, both for the wellbeing of the horses and her pocketbook.

"That's all, folks." The auctioneer wrapped it up. "Nothing in the green pen tonight."

Ethan's head lay on her lap as he slept.

Michael stretched. "Looks like no seven-dollar deals tonight."

"What's that supposed to mean?"

"Dead horse walking, Sarah. There's no horses in the green pen tonight." He yawned.

"They sell the green pen last." Her words were slow. Deliberate.

"Yeah, why?" He stared at her as if she were daft.

Dead by morning …

"Nothing," her brows furrowed. "Bonnie was the last horse sold at the auction I got her from, and there was a horse in the green pen that night."

"They usually put them in there for a reason." Michael's lips moved, but she heard Josh's voice.

"He didn't want me to look in the pen." He probably thought she was crazy buying a horse in Bonnie's condition.

"Who?"

"Josh"

"It's not always a pretty sight. He probably wanted to protect you."

Like her father. Like her grandmother. Like the way she protected Ethan. And, for the first time in her life, she understood.

Around one in the morning, their rig pulled up at the motel. They arranged with the auction barn to keep the horses overnight. Sarah and Michael fed and watered each horse, and bedded the animals down for the night. Sarah would have preferred to load them up and drive through the night, but Michael refused.

There were horse thieves in every state and she didn't want her investments disappearing before morning. The two horses Michael purchased were bone thin, and she told herself she didn't want the animals to starve or suffer longer than necessary, but what she feared most was spending the night in the motel with Michael.

Yet, having a vet around had its advantages. Michael kept packets of milk replacer in his truck. For more than an hour, they mixed milk and coaxed to get the foals to drink. The stubborn little Percheron and Arabian mix dumped half the bucket on Sarah before taking a drink. Ethan slept through the whole process.

The owner of the auction barn placed their horses in a special section he used for his own purchases to keep them out of sight. Sarah speculated that many of the horses he purchased never walked through the ring, but tonight she would fret about her four. The owner assured her they would be there in the morning when they came to pick them up, yet Sarah couldn't help but worry.

Inside the motel room, two separate double beds greeted her. Sarah settled Ethan on a bed at the far end of the room, and the bright light of the bathroom flooded across his small form as she sponged the milk replacer off her arms. The sticky white substance also soaked her jeans, but she couldn't take them off with Michael around.

He stood by the doorway with his arms crossed, watching her.

She turned off the light. She yawned and stretched out beside

Ethan. It would be a few hours before they could hit the road again. She expected to feel unsettled with Michael standing there—instead his presence gave her comfort. This assurance escorted her into a peaceful sleep.

Michael watched Sarah spoon Ethan's small body and heard her sigh. Hours of driving put a dent in a man, but his mind refused to rest.

Could Sarah have been carrying his child when she left that summer? He wrestled with what to say to her about the boy, but couldn't manage to get the words out during the entire ride into Mayfield. That, and the boy had been between them.

He watched the way Sarah fussed over Ethan. He would to have to tread lightly in order to find out about the boy's father. He remembered the expression on Jenny's face when he tried to dig for information. Did Sarah trust him enough to tell him?

What did it matter who the boy's father was? It wasn't Josh, and the guy obviously wasn't in the picture, so he was free to pursue Sarah.

She would have told him if the child were his, wouldn't she?

Maybe if he had searched for her, she wouldn't have walked into another man's arms. The thought of Sarah with another man burned his throat.

He leaned back against the door. He knew he should leave, but his thoughts still lingered on Sarah. His eyes adjusted to the darkness of the room, where he continued to watch her sleep.

She appeared so vulnerable laying there beside her child. So trusting, yet she remained distant. If only he could reach out to her, but then Sarah's wall of defense would rise and they'd be right back where started these many weeks ago on the first day he'd found her asleep in the barn.

He was wrong to touch her all those years ago without being married, but he was young and ambitious. Yet, his excuse didn't ring true. If only he would have known his mother fired Sarah and sent her home. He would have … He didn't know. All these years, he assumed she'd left on her own. Left him.

It was in the past now, and he could only look at the future, even if it included another man's child.

Harold Kingsley adopted another man's child. Michael loved his stepfather, and how he made a family with his mother, Drew and him. He and Sarah could have the same thing. Ethan would know the love of a father as Michael's stepfather loved him.

Wow. A family with Sarah. He had settled down after the loss of his youth—his mother thought she'd never see it. She wouldn't have chosen someone of Sarah's background for him, but the blessings from God showered over him as strong as any perfume his mother wore.

Michael closed his eyes. He prayed silently, asked God to guide him, to open Sarah's heart, and to watch over them. He walked across the room and sat down on the edge of the bed beside her.

"Sarah," he whispered. For a minute, he assumed she slept, for she didn't answer. Then she rolled gently over on to her back.

"Umm?"

"The boy's father?" he asked.

"What about him?"

"Does he know?"

She groaned, rubbing her eyes. "Would it matter?"

"To me?"

"Yeah."

"I'd want to know," he hoped she'd remember their conversation in the morning.

Outside, a car traveled down the road. Its muffled sounds interrupted a town in slumber.

"Sarah?"

"Umm."

"G'night," he knew he wouldn't get an answer tonight. He pulled the blanket off the spare bed and covered her and Ethan. Tucking them both in, he brush back a damp tendril of her hair and kissed Sarah's forehead.

Outside the motel, he jiggled the doorknob to make sure it

remained locked before he headed across the street towards an all-night diner. If only coffee were a strong enough antidote for what ailed him, he'd be cured before sunrise.

One by one, the horses stepped into fresh new stalls. Michael checked each one of them, giving several medical attention. The saddle-bred sported a bad case of worms and rain rot. He issued vaccinations and treated scrapes, bites, and cuts. An older horse showed signs of soft hooves as it came up lame. Josh moseyed over in the commotion of getting the foals to separate. The smallest, a paint colt, captured Sarah's heart, and had been the heaviest on her cash-flow. But a set of papers came along with the extra expense.

Michael headed back to the clinic to unhook his trailer and check in with Jenny and Doc Miller. It was a little before lunch, so Jenny hurried up to the barn to see Josh and the new arrivals.

Doc Miller decided to head home and left Michael to his own devices. Exhausted from driving and a restless night in a motel, Michael headed up the back entrance to his house.

He checked messages on his answering machine—one from his mother, and a several inquiries about the status of the horse clinic. None of them needed taken care of right away.

As Michael pulled open the fridge to grab a can of soda, he heard a soft rap on the door. When he responded to the knock, he found himself engulfed by the voluminous brunette who greeted him on the other side of the door. "Michael!"

"Andrea." He embraced her in a hug.

"Are you surprised?" She stood on her toes to reach him.

"You could say that. What are you doing here?" He gently pried her arms away.

"Your mother told me you were here," she drawled. "Since I'm on my way to Shelbyville anyway …" She shrugged. "I couldn't help but stop by. It's been a long time." Andrea walked around the interior of his small second-story apartment, pacing like a caged lioness. "The jubilee and annual horse show are this week."

"I take it you're entering?" He leaned back against the counter.

"Me? With my riding skills? You flatter me." Andrea laughed.

"I don't recall your being that bad." It caused her to smile.

"I almost think you're trying to be nice now." Her pink glossy fingertip slid down his nose. "It's always good to see you." Andrea's eyes softened. "I've missed you, too." She ran her hand up his arm and gave him another squeeze.

"Andrea," he kept his voice light. "I've moved on."

"I'm glad." Andrea's lips attempted to reshape their former position. "She must be a very special lady."

He'd met Andrea at college.

"You're smitten?"

Michael looked down at her. "Is it that obvious?"

Andrea was a nice girl, and he knew long ago there would never be more than friendship between them. He might even consider her his best friend, and owed a big debt to her for helping him step over into a new light.

"So if you're not riding at the show, what are you doing?" He avoided any talk of Sarah.

"Sam's working here for the week. He's a Ferrier." He noted the uplifted change in her voice.

"Sam?"

"Yeah, we're getting married next month." She glowed. "I stopped by to invite you to the wedding." She reached back in her jeans and pulled out a small envelope.

"I wouldn't miss it," he told her.

Andrea jumped up on her tip-toes and grabbed him behind the head. She pulled him down to meet her unexpected kiss.

After lunch, Josh and Ethan walked fencerows. Jenny headed back over to work at Michael's clinic, and since Ethan tagged along after Josh, Sarah walked with Jenny.

"I'm going to tell him," Sarah said. She'd decided last evening.

She wasn't going to put it off any longer.

"It's about time." Jenny slung an arm around Sarah. "I've seen the way you two have been looking at each other. You can't tell me you haven't thought about being with Michael again."

Sarah fought the urge to turn back around. "He's probably already moved on with his life a long time ago."

Jenny gave her a short tug. "If he did, there'd be a woman around."

"I guess you're right."

The clinic came into view faster than Sarah expected.

"So when are you going to tell him?" Jenny frowned.

A silver car sat parked in the lot by the house. Only a few construction workers milled about. A blonde-haired man raised his hand in greeting and it didn't escape Sarah's attention, or the way Jenny flushed in response. Sarah didn't say a word. Jenny's love life was her own business.

"Now or never, right?"

"Right!" Jenny checked her watch and headed back to work.

Sarah walked around to the back of the house. Midway up the stairs, she paused. Michael may not even be home. *He has a right to the truth. Think about your son. Ethan deserves a relationship with his father*. Seeing a flash image of her own father's face gave her confidence to finish her journey to Michael's door.

Last night she became a girl again, wrapped up in her son's curiosity, and the anticipation of the sale. She felt the heat in her face rise. Why should she be embarrassed? It wasn't like she fell into his arms last night.

The door stood ajar. Sarah stepped through the doorway into Michael's apartment. Her hand flew to her mouth and she halted. Michael and a short, brown-haired, woman embraced. Michael's head snapped up. His eyes met Sarah's gaze. The woman reached up and pulled his face down for a kiss. Sarah gasped. Michael's gaze widened as he stared at her. Sensing his withdrawal the woman released him. "Sarah."

Memories unleashed from inside choked her. Dizzy swirls of locked-up emotions blurred her vision, and Sarah backed away.

"I'm sorry." She bolted out the door.

With each step down the porch stairs, hurt poured out from inside her like boiling water from a kettle that scorched her senses and burned her heart.

"Sarah, wait!" Michael untangled himself, stumbling for the door.

"That's her?" Andrea eyes rolled in Sarah's direction like a frightened horse. Michael grasped the door jam. Sarah's feet hit the ground off the last stair and she ran.

"What are you standing there for? Go after her!" Andrea shoved him out the door. Michael flew down the stairs.

"Michael." He heard his named called.

Sarah's fleeting form crossed the distance between their farms in a dead run.

"Michael!" He skidded to a halt in front of the clinic.

"Eberly's cow is having a hard time calving. He needs you to come out to his place right away." Jenny stood on the porch with her hands on her hips. Michael's eyes fixed on Sarah as she sprinted around the curve at the sign of Silver Wind Equine Rescue.

He'd have to catch up with Sarah later.

CHAPTER 13

As the dog days of summer followed, Sarah found it more difficult to face Michael. A piece of dust in her eye she could blink or wipe away. However, she could not bear the spasm, which was her heart, throbbing at the sight of Michael in another woman's arms.

She spent her mornings in the stables with Ethan, where they coddled and fussed over the new arrivals with presents of new halters and gentle rubdowns. She gave Ethan the privilege of giving all the new horses names, since a name was such an important thing.

The meaning of her son's name revealed his identity.

Michael turned out as a great asset to her mission, and a greater turmoil to her heart. *The Bible says you won't give me anything I can't handle, Lord, so why pile Michael on my plate*?

Now with the roof repaired, wagons of hay arrived to pay Sarah for her share of allowing Frank Dodson to farm part of her land. Josh, along with Frank's boys, worked throughout the day to unload wagons and help with the horses.

Sarah and Ethan slipped into the waiting room as Michael walked out of his exam room at the ring of the bell.

"Mike!" Ethan ran over and wrapped his arms around Michael's waist.

"Hey, Sport." He ruffled Ethan's hair.

"We're going to have lunch with Jenny."

"Sorry, Sport, you just missed her." Michael patted Ethan's back. "She asked for lunch early today, and went off with one of the construction workers."

"That would be Brad, her mystery man," Sarah held her hand out for Ethan. "Come on, Ethan. It looks like it's you and me."

"No!" Ethan grabbed onto Michael's jean-clad legs. "I wanna stay with Mike!"

Michael hunched down in front of the boy. "You should always listen to your mother."

Sarah inhaled deeply.

"I don't want to go. I want to stay with you." Ethan's lip stuck out.

"How about we all go?" Michael looked over Ethan's head at Sarah.

"Yeah."

She let out her breath slowly. "I have errands to run."

"You were going to have lunch with Jenny." He slipped off his white jacket.

"Come on, Mom." Ethan danced around her.

"Maybe another time." A picture of Michael and the brunette formed in her mind.

"Really want to disappoint him?"

There was no way she was going to get out of it. "Of course not."

"We could have gone to Mulberry." Michael checked on Ethan in the rear view mirror.

"My errand is in Shelbyville," Sarah said.

Large banners and streamers hung across the street in the downtown area.

Michael parked in front of a local sandwich shop. "Ethan and I will grab lunch and meet you in the park."

Sarah hesitated a moment. She pushed away fleeting thoughts of Michael stealing her baby boy, nodded, and headed down the street.

Fifteen minutes later, Sarah sat in the office of Peter Thompson, her family's attorney.

"I'm sorry, Sarah, but the terms of your grandmother's will are very clear."

Sarah fell back against the wingback chair. She'd known Peter Thompson her whole life. His hair was silver and his smile was like gold. She looked beyond him to the shelves of legal books and files lined in perfect order by a small stretch of window, than back at him.

"What am I supposed to do?"

When she'd first made up her mind to bring horses back to her father's stables, Sarah came to Mr. Thompson for help. Then, after he'd read the provisions of her grandmother's will, she'd felt her dream slipping away—like now.

"You could always sell off some of your land," Mr. Thompson suggested.

"Sell off my land? No, that's not an option. The land has been in my family for generations. Besides, if I have no land then how will I make room for more horses?"

"Your grandmother knew what she was doing when she sold off the horses. They were too much of a burden, then, as they are now."

Sarah sat up. "Horses are not a burden, Mr. Thompson, they're my life. I was forced to give it up before, and now I feel compelled to choose again."

"Now Sarah, I wouldn't go as far as that. We both know your grandmother had good intentions. Look at you, raising a boy all alone on that farm. What would you have done a few months ago if Grace wouldn't have put the revisions in the will?

You would have spent it on that rescue business of yours, and where do you think you and that boy of yours would be now?" He leaned back in his leather-upholstered chair and interlaced his fingers behind his head.

Sarah picked up her bag and stood. "Thank you, Mr. Thompson. I believe that will be all for today." She could see there was no point in further discussion with him. Especially now that she suspected he was the one who put Gran up to selling off the horses and withholding what little she had left of her inheritance.

Now that she thought of it, Gran was rather fond of Mr. Thompson and the man never went near anything with four legs.

Mr. Thompson placed his hands on top his cherry stained desk and rose. "Sarah, you've only a short time left, do you really need the money that bad? If it's something for you and the boy ..."

"That farm is *everything* to us. Good day, Mr. Thompson."

As she stepped out into the bright afternoon sunlight, she checked her watch. Ethan and Michael waited for her in the park. How long before Michael asked Ethan questions that her son couldn't answer?

A pang of regret swept through her.

She may not be free to handle her inheritance yet, but she was free to make her own decisions about her and Ethan's life. So why couldn't she bring herself to tell Michael the truth?

She crossed the street, waiting for the traffic to go by, and continued on her way.

Perhaps Gran had been right to sell the horses. Sarah didn't know what she would have done to care for them all, plus take care of Ethan. If it hadn't been for the advice of one Peter Thompson, would her Gran have sent her away in the first place?

At the hardware store, Sarah picked out a few supplies she needed, and crossed the street to order grain and pellets.

"You're all paid up," Mr. Kough informed her at the feed mill, as she'd been about to pull out her checkbook. She would talk with Josh about this. He was being too generous with his cash flow these days.

She wiped the beads of perspiration from her brow.

Crowds of people lined up at various vendors around town for lunch, and she hoped Michael and Ethan had beaten the rush.

She found them at the playground.

"There's a lunch for you on the bench." Michael pointed behind her. He gave Ethan another push on a swing. She sat down and reached for the bag. Inside the bag she found a roast beef sub, a bag of chips, and an orange soda.

"Okay?" Michael left Ethan on the swing to sit beside her.

"Fine." She tucked a napkin back in the bag. She took a bite of the sandwich. Having Michael sitting this close did funny things to her senses. One moment she wanted to scream at him, the next she wanted to cry, and today—today she wanted to enjoy his company.

"Liar," he said. "You're upset about Andrea, aren't you?"

"It's not my business." She picked up the orange soda.

"She was my lab partner in college. Time hasn't changed anything between us."

Sarah took a gulp of the sweet soda, hoping it would calm her nerves.

"You don't owe me an explanation, Michael, it's not like we are together or anything." Michael watched Ethan go down the sliding board and race around to climb the metal ladder again.

"I miss you, Sarah."

"We see each other almost every day." Or they did before she started to avoid him again.

"That's not what I meant, and you know it."

"I don't know what you expect me to say." She looked out to watch Ethan as Michael's gaze settled on her face. Her cheeks grew warm.

"You can start by being honest." His hand slid over hers. "Tell me you don't miss me? Miss what we once had together."

Sarah laughed. Inside her gut twisted. This time she couldn't run. This time she would have to tell him the truth. "We had a summer fling, Michael, nothing more." Her heart pounded. No matter how many times she tried to tell herself that, her heart always interjected with reasoning. "We hardly know each other anymore."

"Then we'll start over." He slid closer. Her empty soda can fell to the grass. "Let me take you out Saturday night. Mother is having her annual gala at the estate."

"I don't know, Michael; I have to think about Ethan." She

didn't want to go back there. She didn't want to see Michael's mother again, or relive that night which brought her a son.

"I've already checked with Jenny and she's fine with watching Ethan for the night."

"It's not that simple."

"Why not?" he asked.

"There are things you don't know."

"Like what?" he pressed, but Sarah shook her head. Some things were better off left in the past. Ethan hopped off the swing and trotted towards them. The words were stuck in her throat. It was now or never. She didn't have time to explain. *Not here—not like this.*

"I'll pick you up Friday afternoon. You can dress for the party when we get there."

She hadn't said yes. One glance at his face told her he wasn't about to take no for answer. She wasn't about to ruin their time together by arguing.

They walked hand in hand around the park, with Ethan between them. Michael treated them to ice cream from a vendor on the street, and they browsed the festival. A few women they passed would raise a hand and flash a flirtatious smile, but it went slack when they sighted Ethan and Sarah with the new veterinarian. Michael took no notice. Or if he did, he chose not to acknowledge it.

They arrived back at the clinic by midafternoon. Jenny sat at her desk and a small group of people sat in the waiting area.

"How was lunch?" Sarah asked.

Jenny grinned. "It was nice. We had a picnic."

"So did we," Ethan said. "In the park."

Jenny's eyebrows rose. "Really? With Michael?" She pulled out a folder from a stack on her desk. "I guess I don't feel so bad now."

"Are you sick?" Ethan fidgeted beside the desk.

"If that's what you call being in love." Jenny winked at Ethan.

He giggled. "Then I don't think I ever want to be in love."

"You will, someday." Sarah gazed down at her son.

Ethan scrunched up his nose and placed a hand on his belly. "I don't like to be sick. It hurts my belly and my head hurts."

"It's not that kind of sick," Jenny replied. "Love makes people do crazy things. Things that they normally wouldn't do."

Sarah crossed her arms. "Now what have you done?"

Jenny swiveled away in her chair. "Nothing." She pulled a sheet of paper off a printer at the far corner of her desk. "Yet." She turned back.

Ethan looked up at Sarah.

"Don't pay Aunt Jenny any mind, Brad must have put something in her soda," Sarah said.

Jenny gasped. Her eyes widened. "He did not!"

"We'll talk about it later. Now it's time for us to head home for a nap."

"Oh, Mom," Ethan huffed. "Naps are for babies."

"Even active boys need a nap once in a while, so they can keep growing strong," Sarah replied. Jenny ducked her head and Ethan stomped off in the direction of the front door.

Sarah lingered, while Jenny followed Ethan back to the house.

Later, scents of lavender and peppermint welcomed her as she walked into her bedroom—she wished the familiar fragrance would stay forever. She sat on the tattered brown carpet at the foot of the bed, lifted the lid of her mother's hope chest, and found her father's breeding charts and her mother's show ribbons.

She rubbed the soft satin awards against her cheek. *Only these three things remain, faith, hope, love.* Ethan was all that to her and more. She didn't want to be without him. Only now, where would Michael fit into her life? He and Ethan formed a bond. Like father and son.

She picked up the family Bible. Inside, every name of her bloodline was recorded in ink. Slowly, she flipped the pages. There, written in Gran's hand she found Ethan's name, but no marriage or father recorded.

When Ethan was born, Sarah made a promise to Gran, swearing on the life of her child, she would never tell Michael or his family about Ethan. All these years, she never broke her promise. She wouldn't make the same mistake twice. If she'd made a mistake at all.

She didn't think so.

How could she call Ethan a mistake when God created him inside her womb? God knew every single hair on her son's head and the purpose he would serve in life, and she refused to believe God made mistakes.

A long envelope fell onto her lap. The corners yellowed with age—the seal unopened. She recognized the elegant script on the front as her own penmanship. She'd forgotten all about the letter. Not since the day Mrs. Kingsley looked down her nose at Sarah—a fool's errand by a lovesick teenager. One that had cost her this letter, and bonded her to the promise she now struggled to keep.

She'd stood in the foyer. Behind her a uniformed maid shut the door, and blocked off any attempt for escape. Sounds of heels clicking across marble floors echoed through the mansion's main entrance.

Millicent Kingsley glided towards her.

Sarah's heart lunged. She drove over an hour in her little Ford, trying to talk herself into it. She'd had the last five months to plan.

Writing the letter had been the easy part.

She felt her child flutter from inside her womb—and pulled her coat more securely across her rounded abdomen. Her voice squeaked like a little barn mouse under the direct gaze of Mrs. Kingsley's stare. "Is Michael here?"

"Michael?" Mrs. Kingsley's smile fell short of her eyes.

"Yes, I'd like to see him. If he's not here, I can come back another time." She slipped her hand inside her pocket—resting on the letter, folded in half.

Her heart drummed.

"Michael's not here," Mrs. Kingsley said. "He's off at college."

If Mrs. Kingsley tried to smile any harder, her face would crack.

"He didn't come home between semesters?" She hoped with all her heart. She'd taken a risk by coming here. Gran forbade her to contact Michael, but in her heart, she knew it was wrong. Despite the promise she'd made, Sarah waited for months for this opportunity. With Jenny's help, she formulated a plan. Jenny swore she wouldn't tell anyone where Sarah went this night.

As far as Gran knew, Jenny and Sarah were at a movie. Since Jenny's parents were strict about whom she could date, Jenny jumped on the opportunity to go out with a boy her parents didn't approve.

Sarah's plan couldn't have worked better.

Except Michael wasn't here.

Of course he wouldn't be, she chided. It was like Gran said. Michael had no place for her in his life. He'd moved on and forgotten her. But, if he knew about the baby ...

"When he calls or comes home, will you let him know I stopped by?" Desperation flooded her. "Or could you give me his phone number or address?" She could mail him the letter. Anything, she prayed, that would enable her to get in touch with him.

Mrs. Kingsley's eyes were a mirror of pity as she folded her manicured tipped fingers together in front of her and sighed. "You're not the first, you know."

There were others? Sarah wrapped her arms around the baby she carried. How many others? No, she shook her head. She wouldn't believe it. Maybe—but that had been before, right?

Hadn't Michael told her so?

Tears release their hold from the pools of her eyes and trickle down her flushed cheeks. She reached up with her fist to nudge them away. At the same time, her jacket slid open revealing the small bump of her pregnancy.

Mrs. Kingsley's face grew pale. Her painted lips and dark eye shadow appeared on a hollow face as she went ghostly white. Her eyes grew large. "Oh, I see." She took a sharp intake of breath. "Well, I hope you didn't come here expecting to burden *this* on my son."

Sarah clutched her coat and pulled it back together.

"After all, we both know why you were dismissed during your employment here in the summer, now don't we?" Mrs. Kingsley's color seeped back into her cheeks.

Sarah's lip trembled. Anger spread through her chest and burned. Her throat clogged with words that rushed to her lips. In her mind, she heard the soft sweet voice of her mother whispering, "*Fools vent their anger, but the wise quietly hold it back*."

She was a fool. She fooled herself into believing Michael would find her, loved her and once he knew about the baby he'd want to marry her and become a family.

But the time for fools had passed. She bit back the words pressing at her lips and swallowed them. She looked Mrs. Kingsley in the eye, the same pale blue eyes as Michael, and her stomach tightened.

"If you would be so kind to let Michael know I stopped by …" Sarah sniffled back her tears and tugged at her jacket, a few sizes too small.

"Of course," Mrs. Kingsley pasted on a smile and motioned Sarah to the door. Frigid air from cold January winds hit her in the face and stole her breath away. Mrs. Kingsley stood holding the door wide open.

Without another word, Sarah slid her hands in her pockets, clutching the letter within, and braced herself to walk into the cold dark night.

Every day she'd carried this letter with her along with the hope that Michael would call or she'd find an address. Then Gran found the letter. All these years …

At the sound of footsteps coming down the hall, Sarah slid the letter back inside the Bible and slapped the cover shut.

Josh stood inside her doorway, his flashy white grin smudged with concern. She placed the Bible back in the chest and shut the lid. He walked across the room and reached out for her. She allowed him to tug her to her feet and wrap his comforting arms around her.

"What is it, Sarah? What's wrong?"

When she didn't respond, Josh said, "You can tell me anything."

Hadn't she always?

"I don't know anymore." She buried her face in his tee shirt. Her arms rested around his narrow waist.

"Is it Michael? What has he done now?"

Her throat constricted and she sobbed into his shoulder.

"I knew it. This was bad business from the start." He gathered her closer in his arms and rested his chin on her head. Sarah cried, unable to stop herself. Josh ran his hand down over the back of her hair.

"It's not Michael." Sarah sobbed. "It's me."

"What do you mean 'it's you'?"

She struggled to stop the waterworks of tears from flowing.

"What has Jenny gone and put you up to now?" He pulled her away from him. He hunched, putting himself at eye level with her.

Sarah shook her head. "I have to tell him, Josh." She sniffled. Her vision blurred with tears and concern.

Josh snorted. "Is this what all these tears are about?" He pulled a handkerchief out from his back pocket and handed it to her.

"I found the letter." She blew her nose.

Josh's face scrunched up. He shook his head when she offered him the handkerchief back. "It's a little too late for that don't you think?"

"I'm surprised Gran kept it hidden away. I thought she destroyed it." Sarah glanced back at her mother's hope chest.

"Maybe she wasn't all that bad. Just set in her ways," Josh

said.

"She wasn't the same after Mom and Dad died. It did something to her, you know?"

"She wasn't the only one. Look at you," he said, softly.

Sarah patted her cheeks dry. "My mother used to tell me that the best things in life were the hardest to achieve."

"I don't know about that, Sarah." Josh reached up, pushed a piece of her hair back, and tucked it behind her ear. "I don't know why you women insist on torturing yourselves."

Sarah smirked. "Is that what you call it?"

"I'd call it a waste of time. Why keep crying over the past, when you can change the future, you know what I'm saying?"

"You don't think I should tell him." Sarah turned away from him. She clasped her hands over her heart, Josh's handkerchief clutched in her hand.

"No I don't, but it's not my decision to make."

"If I don't tell him, Jenny will." Sarah sighed. "I'm surprised she hasn't said something to Michael before now." She glanced back at Josh. He leaned in the doorway.

"There's still time. You could always marry me before some gorgeous woman snaps me up." He dazzled her with one of his most brilliant smiles.

"Oh, Josh!" She swatted him. Her hand hit a rolled-up paper in his back pocket. She pulled it out. "What's this?"

"Nothing." He caught her hand in motion and gave her palm a tight squeeze. "Business."

She pulled back from him. "What kind of business?"

"Paperwork for the shoebox."

Sarah studied him. His face drew serious.

"You should ask Jenny to help you." Sarah let go of the paper.

"I've got it under control."

"I went in town to pay Mr. Kough." Sarah kept her eyes on him. "The bill had already been taken care of."

Josh smirked. "Sounds like a charitable donor."

"Sounds like a man with money to burn," Sarah said.

"Accept it for what it is, Sarah, not all gifts come in packages."

His eyes were sincere.

"You can't keep doing this, Josh."

"Who says I did?"

She walked over and hugged him.

"You don't seem to get it." He didn't hug her back. "I'm here for you, for Ethan, and for this rescue business of yours." He cupped his hand around the back of his sun-scorched neck.

Sarah stepped back. "It's not right for me to depend on you. I can't depend on anyone."

"Sooner or later you're going to trip, and when you fall, I'll be there to pick you up, just like I was when he dropped you the first time."

"He didn't drop me." Sarah turned her back on him.

"If you didn't get fired he would have, and he didn't come sniffing around afterward, did he?" Josh turned her around. "Did he?"

"You sound like Gran," she hissed. Her nose burned, and she sniffed back tears.

"I never liked that woman, but she had sense. Wish you had some right about now. When are you going to see what's been under your nose all this time?" He grabbed her arm, spinning her around to face him.

Silent rage crept over his tanned face, and dark freckles stood out like mud splattered across paper. His nostrils flared with audacity.

"You're hurting my arm," she said, soft and slow.

"Don't expect me to be around again to watch you fall." He released her.

"You're jealous."

"If he hadn't come …"

"You can't blame Michael. He doesn't know."

"And you think he would have come running to you if he did?"

"Maybe—maybe he would have married me. Or maybe he wouldn't have. But, it doesn't change how I feel about you." She brushed back the hair draped across his brow.

"And how's that?"

"I love you." She pressed her fingers to his lips to halt his attempted words. "You're the brother of my heart."

"Brother?" Josh grabbed her by the shoulder and kissed her. Sarah gasped. His lips pressed painfully to her mouth. Sarah blinked, and he pushed her away. "Still think I'm your brother now?"

She placed a hand over her mouth. She waited, waited for that euphoria feeling, but only numbness settled through her veins. Her eyes met his, and slowly she nodded.

Josh stared down at her for a moment, gave her a curt nod, and retreated down the hall.

Tears gushed forth, and she buried her face in her hands.

CHAPTER 14

Sarah and Ethan sat on a blanket beneath the shade of an old oak tree behind the house. Sarah waved a sandwich at Jenny.

Jenny snatched the sandwich from Sarah's hand and plopped down on the blanket.

"Josh called," Jenny said, between bites. Sarah reached out to tickle Ethan. He laughed as he dodged and tried to swipe Sarah's soda.

"You two have a fight?" Jenny reached for the unopened can of Pepsi near the tree.

Sarah reached for Ethan again. He took off from the blanket in a playful gait. "Why do you say that?" Sarah asked. She glanced over her shoulder at Ethan.

"He's going out of town for a few days. Didn't sound real sorry to be leaving." Jenny flicked open the tab of her soda can.

Sarah's lips tightened. "I think I broke his heart."

Jenny sighed. "I figured as much."

Ethan grinned at Sarah as he picked dandelions a few feet from Sarah's reach.

"I never meant to hurt him."

Jenny shifted on the blanket. "I know you didn't."

"Michael asked me to attend the gala with him on Saturday."

Jenny choked on her drink, and Sarah leaned forward to thrust Jenny's arm in the air. Choking fit gone, Jenny asked, "So, are you going? I told Michael I'd babysit, but I thought he was taking you out to dinner or something."

This wasn't any ordinary date. "I'd be gone overnight." Her brows furrowed. From the very first day she'd brought Ethan home, Sarah hadn't spent a night without him.

"You should go," Jenny waved her hand. "Maybe you'll finally tell him the truth and save us both a lot of trouble." A grin curved her lips.

Sarah shook her head, telling Michael was the least of her problems.

"It's one night, and this time *you'll* be Michael's date."

She hadn't thought about it that way, and it did appeal to her. But, she could also imagine herself walking alongside the road thumbing a ride home once Michael discovered the truth and ditched her.

"There's Ethan to consider ..."

"I've been helping take care of him since the day he was born. I think I can handle one night with him. Besides, he's potty-trained now, nothing to it."

"I suppose," Sarah said.

"Now, about what you're going to wear ..." Jenny drummed her fingers on her chin.

"I have something in mind." Sarah looked over at Ethan.

"Well, go and get a girl's hopes up, then spoil her shopping trip, why don't you?" Jenny finished her lunch.

"I guess you'll have to go to Wednesday night Bible study with me next week to make up for not going shopping," Jenny hinted. "We're starting a new book about forgiveness."

As far as Sarah was concerned, God forgave her a long time ago. Michael, however, she wasn't so sure.

"What about Brad? Isn't he going with you?"

Jenny's eyes sparkled at the sound of Brad's name. "He has other commitments on Wednesdays."

"I'll think about it," Sarah said.

"The invitation is always open. Claire Ashton has it at her place now. You know Claire and Jeff with their three boys?"

"Yeah." Sarah gathered up empty cans and plastic wrappers. "Jeff used to come around once in a while and give us a hand when something broke in the house."

"Maybe Jeff could help with the stables." Jenny suggested.

"The stables are coming along. Look at the improvements we've made, and the fence is almost finished."

"The barn needs a good coat of paint."

Sarah looked over at the old barn. The whitewashed boards faded of their color and the once rich green trim evaporated in the sun, peeling in places. Josh had almost finished repairing the outside corral, and the roof no longer leaked.

"You know Jeff's dad owns the hardware store. I'm sure if we asked, he'd donate the paint, and maybe Jeff would lend a hand with the project."

Sarah sat up on her knees. "We're not talking a couple gallons."

"Sarah, if we're going to restore this place, we have to accept what is given." Jenny got up, and helped Sarah fold the blanket. "We can't run a rescue off of love and determination alone." Jenny matched a corner of the blanket to Sarah's corner. "Make lists; if people don't know what you need, how are they supposed to know what to give?"

Saturday came quickly. Sarah packed her overnight bag, while Ethan sat playing with trucks on her bed. Mixed feelings swirled inside her. She watched Ethan crash two trucks together and flipped them over. She reached over and picked up a truck. Ethan made car noises and she drove her truck right in the path of a toy car. Ethan drove his car up over and settled it into the back of her truck. He would be safe with Jenny.

Ethan laughed and snatched the truck from her.

Michael would be there soon to pick her up. It gnawed at her stomach like an ulcer. He would have to accept the truth. Maybe it would bring them closer. Maybe, she'd trip at the gala and fall on her face. Or maybe, his mother wouldn't remember her. There was no such luck in her case.

She zipped her overnight bag closed. She needed to face the facts. Michael was no more in her reach now than he'd been six years ago. She couldn't deny her feelings anymore. It was useless to fight what always had been there. She was at the point of no turning back. She had made her decision.

Ethan scrambled to collect the pile of little metal cars and trucks scattered across her bed. Sarah pulled the strap of her bag over her shoulder as she tried to work up the resolve necessary to face her fears.

Michael met her at the front porch, dressed in a light pair of khakis with a blue-collared shirt. Sarah reviewed instructions with Jenny, while Michael stowed her bag in the trunk of his car.

"Don't worry," Jenny said. "I have Michael's cell phone number. Ethan and I will be fine."

Sarah looked down at Ethan. His face appeared like a wounded deer. Michael held open the car door, waiting for her.

She kissed Ethan's scowling face. "You be good. I'll see you after church tomorrow." His solemn blue eyes stared up at her. She couldn't think of a single good reason why she should get into Michael's car. Jenny smiled at her. She remembered all the times her parents left her with Gran, and the last time they traveled to the horse show without her.

A large ache swelled her chest. She ran her hand down Ethan's cheek. "I'll be back, I promise."

Ethan's voice quivered, "I don't want you to go away, Mom."

Sarah kneeled down. Her voice constricted. "I know." She pulled Ethan into her embrace and smoothing her hand over his hair. "Did I ever tell you about the times Gran and I would make cookies while my mom and dad went away overnight?"

She felt his body tremble in her arms, and he sighed. "Yes."

With tear-drenched lashes, she glanced up at Jenny. "There's flour in the tin, butter in the fridge, and chocolate chips in the cupboard."

"I don't like chocolate chip." Ethan sniffled, hugging Sarah tightly.

"There's peanut butter, too," Jenny said, hunching down beside him. "My favorite."

Ethan peered around Sarah's waist. "Can we make peanut butter chocolate chip?"

"Sounds delicious," Sarah said, "Save me one, okay?"

Ethan released Sarah and glanced over at Michael. "And Michael, too?"

"Of course," Sarah stepped down from the porch and left Ethan standing with Jenny.

Michael leaned against the car door with his arms folded in front of his chest. As she approached, he opened the door and held it for her.

"He'll be fine," Michael said. Sarah slid into the passenger seat and Michael closed the door. She stared out the window, hearing the car engine come to life, and waved to Ethan and Jenny on the porch. Her heart seized. *Please help me to keep my promise*, she prayed.

Her hand pressed against the glass pane of her window as she watched Jenny standing on the porch, waving, with Ethan at her side as they drove away.

"We can turn back."

Sarah's hand dropped to her lap. How easy it would be to turn around and go back? She gazed out the window watching the farm grow distant. "He'll be fine with Jenny."

Sarah didn't know if she could survive the next twenty-four hours.

Michael switched on the radio, and she rested her head back, listening to the soothing lyrics of the music. A solitary tear slid down her cheek. Michael studied her in glimpses, keeping his eyes on the road.

Green blotches of trees smeared the landscape as the car's momentum sped them down the highway.

"I've been waiting to get you all to myself." He admitted. "There are a few things I'd like to discuss with you."

Sarah's hand gripped the door's handle. "Like what?"

"Silver Wind."

She stiffened. He checked his review mirror. "Just hear me out," he said, as she turned her head towards him. "I know I've brought this up before, but you haven't ever really given me an answer."

"I haven't had a chance to talk to Jenny and Josh."

"I really wish you would consider it." He darted a glance at her. "I feel we have similar goals. Once the clinic is complete, I'll be able to help not only racehorses, but rescue horses too. We could join our properties and take advantage of the extra land on both sides to serve our mission."

Sarah's jaw went slack and her eyes widened. "*Our* mission? What makes you think you can step in and take over my rescue?"

"I'm not. I'm only offering my talents as a veterinarian and partnership of sorts."

Sarah considered his proposal. "What about Josh and Jenny? I didn't put together this operation on my own."

"For one minute, could we leave them out of this conversation?"

Sarah could hardly believe what she was hearing. "This is as much theirs as it is mine."

"No, Sarah. It isn't." Michael gritted his teeth. No matter what happened after this night, he would be a part of her life, one way, or the other.

Sarah looked away. She slumped in the seat next to him.

"The rescue is your dream, not theirs." He turned off the radio.

"That's not true."

"Jenny is divided between the clinic and the rescue, and Josh … he's not exactly helping the rescue by running off for days and leaving you to tend to the stables on your own."

"Josh needs an income like Jenny. I can't pay them," Sarah said wistfully.

"You could, if you got things running right."

"Maybe Thompson was right, I should sell the horses. Jenny

seems content working for you and Josh is set in his new venture. They don't seem to have time for the rescue anymore."

"Thompson, you mean the attorney?" Michael asked.

Sarah nodded. "I needed money to make repairs and pay overdue bills. I thought, maybe, he could find a loophole and I could have what little is left of my inheritance."

"And?"

"I think it was Thompson who convinced my grandmother to tie up my parents' estate in so many knots it would take a lifetime to straighten it out."

Michael reached over and touched her hand. "With or without Jenny and Josh, you can make the rescue work. Let me help you."

"By letting you control the rescue?" Sarah slipped her hand out from beneath his.

"All you need are a few good sponsors. You're running a nonprofit mission, Sarah. Sponsors would help keep the rescue running, and Jenny and Josh wouldn't have to be the only ones receiving an income."

There would be several important people at the gala tonight. Many with fat wallets willing to make charitable contributions to the right cause. But, how could she convince any of them to share her dream when she couldn't convince herself to tell Michael the truth about their son?

Two hours later, they stood at the doorstep of Kingsley Estate. A regal black-haired woman greeted them. From behind, a housekeeper shut the door.

"Mother." Michael smiled. Mrs. Kingsley held out her arms.

"Michael, darling, I'm so glad you could make it." She grasped him by the shoulders and kissed each cheek. Her bright red lips parted as she caught sight of Sarah. "You brought a guest." Mrs. Kingsley clasped her hands together as her sophisticated brow arched.

"Mother, this is Sarah Colvert." Michael slid his arm around her as he introduced them, “Sarah, this is my mother, Millicent.”

“Sarah.” Mrs. Kingsley laid a red-tipped finger to her lips as she stepped around Michael. “Have we met?”

“It’s possible,” Michael offered before Sarah could speak. “Sarah worked for father several summers ago.”

“I see.” Mrs. Kingsley pasted a brighter smile onto her cosmetic-plastered face. “That must be why your name sounds familiar.”

Sarah didn’t reply. Nothing inside the four-column mansion had changed since the last time she had been here. An eerie tingle ran up her spine, and anger seethed inside her. Mrs. Kingsley knew exactly who Sarah was.

“I’m afraid I’m not prepared for your guest.” Mrs. Kingsley fingered the pearls around her throat. “Had you let me know you were bringing someone ... we have so many guests attending this evening.”

Michael interrupted. “Sarah can have my room, I’ll bunk with Drew.”

Sarah stood between them.

“Drew brought a guest of his own, and they’ll be sharing his room.” Mrs. Kingsley’s eyes ran the length of Sarah’s form.

“I wouldn’t think you would find that appropriate, Mother.” Michael stepped closer to Sarah.

“Let’s not get into that here. Drew is a big boy.”

“As am I,” Michael reminded her. “Either way, Sarah will stay in my room.”

“Surely, darling, you can’t sleep outside—” Mrs. Kingsley’s lips parted slightly.

“I’m sure father won’t mind me stretching out on the couch in his den.” He placed his hand on the small of Sarah’s back and pressed her to walk past Mrs. Kingsley. Yet, Sarah’s legs remained rooted to the marble floor. Michael, with his carryall over his shoulder reached down and picked up Sarah’s overnight bag.

“Don’t worry Mother; we’ll manage on our own.” Michael gave Sarah a challenging look as he motioned for her to follow him. Looking back over her shoulder, Sarah smiled at Mrs. Kingsley—with the artificial sweetness of saccharin.

Michael pinched her in the hallway. "Ouch!"

"That wasn't very nice." He escorted her down the hallway to his room. "You shouldn't taunt her so." He opened the door and indicated for her to step inside.

This wasn't exactly how she'd pictured his room, with dark navy walls and deep burgundy curtains. The dark cherry trim coordinated with the matching furniture. A full-sized bed loomed in the center of the far wall, and the plush comforter atop it held a splash of navy, burgundy, and tan. Colors she recognized from his apartment.

"Make yourself at home. I need to find father and Drew before more guests arrive."

"Michael, wait," Sarah said, as he reached for the door.

"Relax. Take a bubble bath or whatever it is you women do to get ready. You have plenty of time."

Michael left her alone in the large room. "Plenty of time," she huffed. There wasn't enough time, as it was, to calm her nerves. She sat on his bed and prayed.

CHAPTER 15

It didn't take Michael long to catch up with the man he called "Dad" as he strolled across the front lawn. "I see you're avoiding Mother."

His father laughed. "You know your mother, parties always make things stressful." He stopped near an arc of pavement. Cars lined the driveway as guests arrived. Parking attendants in black ties stood awaiting the next vehicle.

"I don't suppose it will get any better through the evening."

Michael ran a hand through his hair. "I didn't help much."

Harold surveyed the lawn. "Can't imagine why."

Michael met his father's gaze. "Sarah Colvert is in my bedroom."

"Robert and Hannah's girl?" Harold's expression changed.

"She's my guest."

Harold scratched his chin. "Your mother wouldn't be very pleased."

"I would say that's an understatement."

Harold nodded. "And things at the clinic?"

Michael relaxed, "Progressing well. The barn should be finished before long, and the clinic turned out better than I'd initially visualized."

"Sounds like your place is really coming along." Harold smiled. "How did you come across the Colvert girl?"

"We're neighbors."

"Well, I'll be." Harold shook his head.

"She's renamed the place, *Silver Wind Equine Rescue,* and she's trying to save horses from auction houses and inhumane situations." Michael slid his hands into his front pockets. "I've been trying to convince her to agree to join forces—her rescue with my clinic."

"And how's that working out for you?"

"She's not fully convinced." Michael walked alongside his father.

"Sarah's a lot like her mother." Harold reminisced. "Hannah Colvert wasn't one to be easily persuaded."

"You knew them, then?" Michael looked at his father.

"That I did." Harold admitted. "Hadn't seen Sarah since she was a baby, until that summer when Grace called me about the accident." Harold's pained expression caused Michael to pause.

"Does mother know about Sarah?"

Harold stared, blankly. "I'm not sure what you mean."

"Mother fired Sarah that summer."

Harold took a deep breath. "I seem to remember something about that."

"Sarah says she was given twenty minutes to vacate the estate."

"I'm sure your mother had cause." His father frowned. "It was a sad summer for us all. The whole state mourned Robert and Hannah's death, but none more, I suppose, than Sarah."

"It's my fault mother fired her."

"How's that?"

"She was with me," he admitted.

Harold took a deep breath. "I suspected as much," he said, exhaling. "A father knows what his children are doing."

"We met in a stall that night, somebody locked her in. Josh was apparently letting her out when they got caught." Michael rocked back on his heels.

"I've only fired a few summer workers over the years, and very few have left on their own, but I don't recall any named Josh."

"Anderson. He has a twin, Jenny. Both redheads. Josh is the calm, and Jenny the storm."

"Ah yes—worked all summer, and the summer after too."

"Are you sure?" Michael's eyes narrowed.

"I might be getting old son, but I do remember most things."

"Why would Sarah be the only one to get fired?" Michael walked with his father.

"It's hard to say what your mother's reasoning was, but I'd be asking how the boy knew where to find her if she was sneaking off with you."

"Girl talk," Michael shrugged it off.

"Girls talk to other boys about meeting boys in the stables?" Creases formed on Harold's forehead. "Not that you should have been out there in the first place with a girl, but you're too old now for that kind of talk."

"Sarah has a son."

"Is he yours?"

Michael flushed. "I don't know. The age is right, but Sarah doesn't talk about the father. I honestly think she would have told me if he were mine," Michael hoped.

"A child is innocent of sin or shame in which they might have come into this world, Son. I'm glad you aren't keeping this as a reason not to pursue the girl."

"You always taught me to look at the good in people. You married mother when she already had a son. I guess I'm following your example."

"Your mother's situation wasn't much different." Harold appeared pensive. "I will always claim you as my child, Son. I'm glad to know part of what I tried to teach you sank in, even if it did take a while."

Sarah completed the last touches of her toiletry before Michael entered his bedroom. She wore the same dress those many years ago. Jenny urged her to buy a new gown, but this one still fit. Six years and a baby later, the exquisite black gown fit snug over her hips. She couldn't bring herself to pay the expense for another gown for one night. The cost alone would buy groceries for a month.

She closed the bathroom door, giving Michael the privacy to change. She heard him shuffle around the room, while she pulled out her rich plum-colored lipstick. Smacking her lips together, she smiled at the woman in the mirror.

There was a soft rap on the door. "Ready?"

As she ever would be. She pulled back her exposed shoulders and opened the door. Michael stepped back and whistled low under his breath. A warm blush swept over her face and down her neck.

She reached up and touched a thin strap looped around her neck meeting at the middle of the bodice. He offered his arm to her. "You look more beautiful in that gown then I remember."

"Thank you," she slipped her hand around his arm. "You don't look bad yourself."

His pale blue eyes sent shivers down her spine—she felt seventeen again.

Inside the dining room, a buffet laid spread out in front of them over several white linen-covered tables. Sarah graciously accepted the plate Michael offered her as she listened to conversations buzz from all directions in the room.

With the grace of a bird, she picked at an hors d'oeuvre from her plate. Michael hovered near, talking with old friends.

She wondered into the ballroom and caught a glimpse of Michael out of the corner of her eye. He was engaged in conversation with the younger Kingsley son. Andrew Kingsley had his father's dark brown hair and strong square chin. Only one similarity was evident between the brothers—their pale blue eyes, like mountain springs.

Men and women, known throughout the horse world, gathered at this event each year, and celebrated their victories of past races and speculated about those yet to come. Stud fees debated, alliances gained and broken over punchbowls, while jockeys rubbed noses in the hunt for new employers.

As the orchestra filled the room with music, a slender blonde woman came and pulled Drew away to the dance floor. Michael smiled and turned towards Sarah. Her heart raced, her legs became weak, and breath caught in her throat as he beckoned her to him.

Putting one foot in front of the other, she weaved her away around couples and found herself face to face with Harold Kingsley. Michael frowned as his father stepped between them a few feet from where Michael stood. Michael gave Sarah an apologetic look as Mr. Kingsley held his hand out for a dance.

Sarah accepted the invitation and stepped into his arms. After all these years, would it feel the same to dance with him again?

She looked over Mr. Kingsley's shoulder at Michael. "Save me a dance," he mouthed, backing away into the crowd.

Mr. Kingsley guided her around the ballroom floor. "These past few months must have been difficult for you."

"I'm not sure what you mean," she stammered.

"I am very sorry to hear about the passing of your grandmother."

So this was it. This was all the man had to say? "Thank you."

"Coming here must not have been very easy for you."

She nodded, feeling a lump in her throat.

"Michael tells me you purchased a few of our horses a while back." She searched the room seeking his tall frame and dark head in the crowd.

"It is possible. Robert always had good bloodlines." Mr. Kingsley led her into the next dance, and she momentary paused between dances, allowing her senses to evaporate any hope she felt building up inside her.

"There was a sorrel mare with a flaxen mane and tail. She would have been about four years old at the time. Irish Rose."

"You want to know if I have your horse." His eyes were kind, looking down at her with a fatherly aura.

"Do you?" Her voice squeaked from a hoarse whisper.

"No, I'm sorry." Mr. Kingsley turned her away from the crowd. "I purchased your father's stallions, and a couple of geldings throughout the years, but no mares."

As the next song started, Michael cut in, and Mr. Kingsley excused himself to find his wife. Sarah slid into Michael's arms. Shattered shards of hope fell like confetti from her heart. Her hand trembled as she placed it in Michael's and rested the other on his shoulder. He bent his head, whispering in her ear. "Is everything alright?"

"Your father didn't buy my horse." She nestled her head on his shoulder and allowed him to guide her through the waltz. They floated across the ballroom like a pair of swans on a lake.

"You miss Rosie, don't you?" He pulled her closer. Michael remembered her pet name for Irish Rose. Tears stung at the corners of her eyes. Would he remember what this night brought them, so long ago?

"I do, but ..." Her words muffled in the material of his jacket. "*Not nearly as much as I have missed you.*"

When the dance ended, Sarah held onto him. If only she could stop time to savor this first dance—she didn't want the feeling of being in his arms to ever end. Inside her, the seventeen-year-old girl dissolved, and the woman inside emerged.

Around them, couples danced, laughter erupted, and heads bent together in conversations. Wallflowers waited to blossom while crowds of men stood hovered together discussing politics and business. Michael tucked her hand in the curve of his arm and led her off the dance floor. "Sarah, there's someone I'd like you to meet."

They walked up to a small group of men. They all laughed and listened to Harold Kingsley entertain them with one of his horse stories. Michael wedged them into the circle. When Harold was finished, Michael tapped an older gentleman on the shoulder. "Mr. Wilkes, I'd like you to meet Sarah Colvert."

"How do you do, Mr. Wilkes." Suddenly, Sarah felt the stare of a dozen eyes turn in her direction. She glanced at Michael.

What did he think he was doing pulling her into the middle of all these people?

"Ah, yes, Robert and Hannah's girl. My—what's it been now—seven, eight years? A real tragedy."

"Six," Sarah said. She glanced around the crowd and took a step back. Michael's hand wrapped around her waist and held her from escape.

"Still ride like your mother?" Mr. Wilkes inquired.

"I haven't ridden in years." Sarah confessed. Not since Ethan was born.

"But I reckon she'll be getting back in the saddle again, real soon." Michael added.

"Seems a shame to waste all that talent," Mr. Kingsley said.

Mr. Wilkes took her by the arm and drew her aside. He reached into the pocket of his tuxedo and pulled out a handkerchief. "If you're interested in riding professionally again, I could use someone of your talents. Robert and Hannah only bred the best." He dabbed a dribble of sweat from his forehead.

"That's very kind of you. But I've recently founded the Silver Wind Equine Rescue."

"Rescue?" Mr. Wilkes' eyebrows shot up as he tucked his handkerchief back in his pocket. "What possibly could a horse need rescued from?"

Several members of the crowd gathered close. Sarah suppressed the urge to flee and smiled despite the seismic tremble in her arms. Michael wrapped his arm around her shoulders. She looked Mr. Wilkes straight in the eye. "What do they need rescued from?"

Sarah planted her fists on her hips. "How about abuse? Abandonment? Have you ever considered what happens to a prize racehorse when it's no longer bringing home blue ribbons? And, what happens to the foals whose mothers are too busy racing to raise them? You ask what kind of horses need rescued—those are a few of the types of horses that are saved, rehabilitated, and given a second chance at my stables."

Mr. Wilkes appeared taken back. He and all the rest of those who listened made mumbling sounds. Some turned away. "Isn't that what you are doing, Dr. Wolfe?"

Michael grinned. He pulled Sarah closer and responded, "Rehabilitate, yes. However, I'm afraid I'll leave the rescuing up to Sarah."

Several members of the crowd shuffled away. Harold and another gentleman lingered. "Now about that clinic of yours ..." Mr. Wilkes moved away from Sarah and dragged Michael along with him.

Michael held up his empty glass and Sarah pointed towards the balcony. *A waste of talent*. She shook her head as she walked outdoors. She welcomed the cool night air as it caressed her perspiring skin.

Sarah watched Mr. Wilkes and Michael cross the room to the far side where guests hovered around a refreshment bar. She turned, smiled, and looked out into the black velvet sky. Sarah leaned against a stone pillar, gazed upon the large crescent moon and remembered ...

Silence greeted her from within the stables. Several horses slept with their heads hung low, while others scavenged their stall floors for bits of hay left over from supper.

Sarah bit her lip until she was sure it would bleed. "I'm such a fool," she cried. She muffled her sobs as she leaned her forehead against the wall and hugged herself. She let go of the shoes that dangled them from her hand while she continued the pity party.

"Sarah," he whispered in her ear. Startled, Sarah's head jerked up. His strong arms embraced her. "You surprised me in the ballroom. I had no idea you would be there."

She rubbed her damp cheeks with the palms of her hands and swiped away the tears stuck to her lashes. She needed to get her act together or he would think of her as nothing more than a silly schoolgirl.

"After you said ... I thought you...," she sniffled.

Michael leaned closer. "I wish I had asked you, Sarah. You

look lovely tonight." She pivoted in his arms to face him. "You've been crying." He reached up tracing the tear stains down her cheeks.

"Go back to your date, Michael; I am sure she's looking for you."

"Ah," he whispered. "So that's why you're out here?"

"Leave me alone." She attempted to push him away. Her heart squeezed. She was foolish to believe he would want to be with her. Gran didn't even want her.

"I've hurt you." His eyes grew sincere. "My mother arranged weeks ago for me to accompany the daughter of a friend." Sarah's eyes cast down. "Oh, my sweet Sarah," he cupped his hand beneath her chin and drew her face to look into his eyes. Slowly, she lifted her gaze. "She's a friend of the family. She means nothing to me."

He captured her lips with his in a soft searing kiss. Her sandals slipped from her hand and she stepped into his arms.

The chill of a tall fluted glass against her bare arm brought her back to the balcony.

"Hey," Michael whispered from behind. Sarah turned away and wiped her mascara-stained cheeks. "Thanks," she took a sip of the sparkling cider.

"You seemed so far away, just now." His hand cupped her cheek. "Where did you go?"

She closed her eyes against the brush of his thumb, and a sob struggled down her throat. "It doesn't matter. What matters is here and now."

He set down his emptied glass on the stone railing. "Did something happen while I was gone?" He shouldn't have left her alone. The smiling woman he placed in this spot vanished. A more vulnerable Sarah stood before him.

Sarah opened her eyes. She closed her hand over his. "Michael." His name became a soft murmur from her lips.

He took her hand, pressed his lips to her knuckles and kissed each one. His thumbs massaged into the palm of her hand.

"I'm so afraid." She quaked in her laced-up heels. He reached for her glass, placed it beside his on the rail and gathered her into his arms. From inside the ballroom, music floated out through the night like a ship drifting across an endless sea. Sarah linked her arms around his neck. She laid her cheek on his shoulder. He rocked her back and forth. He cradled the back of her dark, swirling curls with one hand, and wrapped the other around her waist.

He breathed in the scent of her perfume, roses with a hint of jasmine—unlike her usual smells of grain and alfalfa. He felt her body relax in his hold, but his own heart raced.

He wanted to tell her he felt the same way, but the fear he saw in her eyes halted him. There was pain in her voice, and he wasn't sure what he felt anymore. What he felt these past few weeks was inconclusive for an early prognosis in his medical mind. He had to be sure, he had to have answers, and he had to have Sarah.

Her face turned up beneath his jaw. "You are the most beautiful woman here tonight." He hooked a finger under her chin.

"I never meant for things to end up like this." She pulled away from him, but Michael pulled her closer.

"I admire you, Sarah." He ran his fingers through her thick mass of soft dark locks. "It couldn't have been easy raising a son and trying to take care of your grandmother all alone."

"Michael, there is something you should know …" Her eyes were red with tears.

"You had no choice, Sarah. You can start over. *We* can start over."

"Michael please, I'm trying to tell you something."

"We'll find Irish Rose, Sarah. I promise." His thumb brushed softly across her lips, and Sarah gave way to the firm pressure of his lips as he kissed her. She'd have to wait for another time to tell him that he had a son.

CHAPTER 16

At midnight, she stood in the hallway outside Michael's bedroom. "Isn't this the part where you're supposed to invite me in?" he leaned back against the door. Tiny flutters erupted in her stomach. "I believe they are still serving coffee down in the dining room."

Michael chuckled. "I was hoping ..."

"We've already had our goodnight kiss," she prayed Michael wouldn't expect history to repeat itself. *Not tonight, Lord,* she pleaded. *Not tonight.*

She made a promise to herself and to God that not even Michael could make her break.

"No kisses, I'll keep my hands to myself, I promise." Arms up, he surrendered, then placed his hands behind his back like a gentleman. Down the hall, laughter floated past their room from the stairwell.

What did Michael want, coming into her room? *His* room. However, heady giddiness bubbled up inside her, and she fought to suppress it. She wasn't seventeen anymore, and this wasn't a horse stall.

Yet, as she gazed into his eyes, her hand twisted the knob and opened the door.

"Now that's my girl," he went into his room. On the corner of the bed he sat, kicked off his shoes, and loosened his bow tie.

She gulped. "What are you doing?"

"I would have thought that was obvious," Michael said. He pulled the bow tie from around his shirt collar and unbuttoned his shirt half way.

A cold chill swept over her and she felt the blood drain from her face. "Stop!"

Sarah held out her hand as Michael stood and discarded his jacket. "Stop, right now!" she panted for breath. Michael gave her an odd look and continued to take his jacket off. Sarah whirled around and faced the open door way, ready to flee.

"Relax." Michael chuckled.

A group of ladies gawked through the doorway as they passed. Mortified by their expressions, Sarah swiftly slammed the door.

"You didn't have to do that."

She heard rustling sounds from behind her, and glanced over her shoulder as the bathroom door shut.

Her eyes fell to the bed. At the corner, lay Michael's jacket. She glanced over at the bathroom door, heard the faucets running, and picked up the jacket. Rich spices and mint filled her senses as she pressed the jacket to her cheek.

What was Michael doing in there? Her hands trembled. Had she by some way led him on this evening? She made a mistake. She should never have let him inside the room. Now, he probably thought she wanted to tumble into bed with him, and he would be wrong. Definitely wrong.

Running water ceased from the other side of the door. Chatter softly floated in from outside the bedroom. She laid his jacket down and stepped back from the bed. Her heart, like her hands, quivered. Michael emerged from the bathroom, dressed in long cotton pants and a t-shirt. He appeared as handsome in pajamas as he did in a tuxedo.

Be still my heart. She silently crooned and closed her eyes briefly for another prayer. If God was listening, and she hoped

He was, Michael would walk straight out of this room and leave her alone for the night. One eye popped open, then the other. Michael grinned at her.

Oh, Lord, she thought, *I'm in a heap of trouble.* Her eyes darted to the bedroom door, then to Michael, and back to the door again.

"Find what you were looking for?" He gestured towards his jacket.

Sarah scratched her neck and attempted a weak smile. "I was just …" but how could she explain to him what she had done, when she didn't know herself? Her cheek tingled where it touched his jacket.

Michael tossed his tuxedo shirt and pants over a nearby chair. "Here," he said. "If you want, you can sleep in it."

Sarah shook her head. The offer tempted her. An awkward silence stretched between them as Michael zipped up his bag and took a blanket out from inside the closet.

He grabbed a pillow from beneath the blankets on the bed. "If you need anything, I'll be downstairs in the den."

Sarah's lungs loosened and she took a deep breath. He walked over, rested his hand on her cheek, and kissed her forehead. "Goodnight, Sarah."

Outside, the sounds of the hallway settled. A door shut down the hall, and Sarah yawned. She reached for the door and Michael caught her hand. "Thank you for coming with me tonight. I know how hard this has been for you."

She slumped, her body drained from what little mental and physical energy she had left. "About Ethan—" she started to say.

"You can use my cell phone before breakfast to call him, but I'm sure he and Jenny are fine."

"That's not it." She wanted to tell him.

Michael yawned. Releasing her hand, he opened the door. "I'll see you in the morning."

"Michael, wait." She reached for him, but he was too quick. "Ethan is your son," she said, as the door shut and she sat, alone, on the corner of the bed.

Dressed in a pair of tan slacks and white eyelet-trimmed blouse, Sarah willed herself to leave Michael's room. She spent the night in his childhood bed. After hours of not being able to rest, she picked up the small black leather Bible on his dresser. As the first streaks of morning cast shadows in his room, Sarah placed the Bible back atop the dresser and packed her bag waiting for Michael to come for her. Psalms 15:2, *He whose walk is blameless who does what is righteous, who speaks the truth from his heart*, repeated in her mind.

An hour later, her stomach growled in protest. Sarah descended the staircase, her hand glided down the smooth polished wood of the banister. Rich smells of coffee and croissants lured her.

Below, she heard voices and hoped one of them was Michael's.

She reached up to her neck and clutched her mother's simple gold chain, as if it were a lucky charm. As she walked into the formal dining room, Sarah observed the other overnight guests who drank coffee and sampled the breakfast buffet at the far end of the room.

Mr. Kingsley stood among the guests with Drew at his side. Sarah could see now the difference between Michael and his younger brother, like a moon that passed the sun.

Drew, was the younger version of his father. Like Ethan resembled Michael. Even though she'd never seen pictures of Michael when he was Ethan's age, she could envision the same crooked grin, black hair, and pale blue eyes.

She scanned the room for Michael.

A sinking feeling tugged inside her.

Mr. Kingsley's eyes met her gaze and he nodded. Sarah smiled and forced herself to walk across the room. Gold trimmed china lined the mahogany cabinet and burgundy damask draped the floor-to-ceiling windows like wine pouring out from the beige walls.

Several guests glanced her way, but no one spoke to her as she walked up and plucked a blueberry pastry from a woven basket. As quickly as she came, Sarah retreated.

Michael had to be around here somewhere. He wouldn't have left without her.

She felt a flutter of panic and pushed it away.

Michael didn't come back to his room this morning, but he wouldn't leave her. Would he?

She tore off a piece of the pastry and popped it in her mouth. She walked into the foyer and came face to face with Michael's mother.

"I see you found the breakfast bar," Mrs. Kingsley walked towards her in a vibrant yellow sundress with her white-heeled sandals clicked on the marble. Her hair was pulled back in a tight twist and she a diamond on each earlobe.

Sarah's spine stiffened. "Yes, I was actually looking for Michael." She caught her breath and held it. Her heart squeezed in response.

"Knowing my son, he's probably out at the stables or getting ready for church services this morning."

Sarah headed for the front door, but as Mrs. Kingsley stepped down off the staircase, she blocked Sarah's path.

"I'll go check in the stables," Sarah said. Her pulse pounded. She tried to step around Mrs. Kingsley.

"Why don't you and I go for a walk and have a little chat? I'm sure Michael will find you when he's ready to leave. That is why you're looking for him, isn't it?"

Sarah bit her lip. She wasn't that teenage girl anymore, so why was she quaking inside? She tore off another piece of pastry and stuffed it in her mouth. Mrs. Kingsley motioned for her to follow and Sarah found herself being led down the hall to a small sunroom filled with wicker furniture and bright morning sunlight. Sarah didn't feel nearly as cheery.

From the windows, Sarah could see the lush lawn filled with manicured trees, trimmed hedges, and a glimpse of the glossy black paved drive curving away from the estate.

Mrs. Kingsley sat in a chair and invited Sarah to do the same. "Would you like a drink? I could have some tea brought in."

Sarah settled in a chair across from Mrs. Kingsley. She took a deep breath and willed her nerves to calm. "I don't believe you brought me here for a tea party."

"You're a smart girl, Sarah. I can see why Michael was so infatuated with you all those years ago."

So Mrs. Kingsley did recognize her! Bitterness, like bile, rose in her throat.

Last evening, she read about forgiveness. Yet, even as she knew in her heart that she should forgive those who wronged her, it didn't change the fact that Millicent Kingsley held no love for Sarah. *So why then, Lord,* she asked, *should I find love for a woman I see as my enemy*?

"I suppose the little act you put on yesterday afternoon was all for Michael's benefit?"

Mrs. Kingsley laughed. "A mother does what she must to protect her son. Surely, you would understand that, now wouldn't you?"

An icy chill spread across her arms and prickled her skin. How did Mrs. Kingsley know she had a son? Not unless …

A slow smile crept across Mrs. Kingsley's powdered face.

Sarah's hands clenched and her pastry crumbled in her hands. Her pulse, like her thoughts, raced. She took another deep breath.

You're not a teenager anymore! Millicent Kingsley couldn't hurt her. Or could she?

She felt her hands tremble.

Mrs. Kingsley frowned as she folded her hands on her lap. "I take it you found your accommodations suitable for the night?"

"Michael and I didn't share a room together, if that is what you mean."

"Of course not," Mrs. Kingsley's hard-pressed smile relaxed along with the features of her face.

Sarah squirmed in her seat, as Mrs. Kingsley slanted her head and stared at Sarah.

"You remind me a lot of myself at your age—young, pretty, ambitious." Her smile broadened. "We both know where that got us."

"No, I don't," Sarah clutched the arms of her wicker chair for support.

"I think you'll find we have a lot more in common than you know." Mrs. Kingsley said, settling back in her chair. "I was young, like you, when I met Harold. My family, too, invested their life in horses. Only when I was seventeen, I fell in love with a young man who was not of my parents' liking. He ran off and joined the Army, and I stayed back waiting for his return."

Sarah relaxed. What did any of this have to do with her and Michael? She crossed her arms and listened.

"Not soon after Daniel left, my mother paired me up with a young man from a family whose wealth matched our own. It was a perfect set-up for my family. His name was Harold Kingsley."

Sarah started to get the picture. But why was Mrs. Kingsley telling her all this? Then, Sarah gasped with understanding. "You never married Michael's father."

"No, I did not," Mrs. Kingsley confessed. "By the time I realized I was pregnant, it was too late. I went to Harold, thinking he would call off our engagement, but instead he insisted on moving up the wedding."

Sarah was speechless.

"I named Michael after my father. A few months after he was born, I heard news Daniel had been killed overseas in a bar fight with another comrade over a woman. That's when I knew it was best I marry Harold. Daniel would have never been faithful. Michael's a lot like his biological father. Rather dashing isn't he, my son?"

Sarah was quick to her feet. "Michael isn't like that! Even if he was, he's a Christian now!"

Mrs. Kingsley arched a brow.

Bits and pieces of flaked bread trickled down Sarah's slacks and scattered across the stone-tiled floor.

"It's very clear you have feelings for my son." Mrs. Kingsley remained unaffected by Sarah's outburst.

Sarah stared at Mrs. Kingsley.

Mrs. Kingsley laughed, "One would have to be a fool not to notice the way you look at him, and the way he looks at you."

She motioned for Sarah to sit back down.

"Michael and I will work things out on our own," Sarah said.

"I have no doubt that you will. My son is a very ambitious man, wouldn't you agree?"

Sarah nodded.

"Why that clinic of his is going to take a lot of his time, with tending to all those injured horses and gaining clientele. I understand you are attempting to manage your family's stables again."

"You could say that." Sarah studied Mrs. Kingsley's profile. "Michael believes we have similar goals, rescuing and rehabilitating horses."

"Do you?" Mrs. Kingsley asked, her voice soft.

Sarah shrugged. "I'd like to think so."

Mrs. Kingsley reached back and pushed a tendril of hair behind her ear. "Then let me ask you this. When two people come from opposite sides of the road, which one must cross the road in order to meet the other?"

Sarah frowned. Mrs. Kingsley's words slithered into her heart and sunk. What place did she have in Michael's life?

"Do you really think you and your child have any place in Michael's life or will you have him cross the road and leave his ambitions behind to trap him in yours? Sometimes, we are better off allowing someone else to step into our lives and move on."

CHAPTER 17

Blue skies stretched above him as far as the eye could see, and fat clouds drifted overhead. A faint yellow globe peeked out through the haze, but Michael knew rain was imminent. He smelled it in the air and felt it in the brisk winds that swept across the fields.

Clyde felt it too. His horse stopped and looked around, ears twitched in opposite directions like an old television antenna. Clyde's head swung this way and that, his thick mane mussed in the wind. Michael seated himself deeper in the saddle and felt Clyde tense beneath him.

Something was coming alright. He'd felt it even before the storm, since the day he and Sarah returned from his parents' estate. The tension had been thick and dark like storm clouds.

The powerful horse shot out from underneath him like a bullet.

Michael grabbed a tuft of Clyde's mane. Together they galloped across the field.

He yanked back on the reins. "Whoa Boy, whoa!"

As Clyde refused to let up his breakneck speed, Michael tugged on one rein pulling Clyde's head to the side—forcing the animal to run in circles.

Eventually, Clyde slowed to a walk.

Michael looked up at the clouds as he leaned up and patted Clyde on the neck. There was no doubt about it—a storm was rolling in fast upon them.

A high-pitched scream pierced the air.

Clyde went still.

Blood roared in Michael's ears. As if Clyde sensed Michael's intention, the horse took off in the direction of the scream. Blades of grass and heather blurred together as they darted through the field.

Clyde's chest heaved as Michael pulled him back into a slow walk. His ears perked and Michael scanned the field, listening for the sound again.

He was sure it came from somewhere near. *Be still and know that I am God.* Michael closed his eyes, taking deep breaths, and willed himself to listen. The horse craned its neck and stood alert while Michael held tight to Clyde's reins.

Agitated, the horse snorted, then jerked his head up and turned—pulling at the reins.

Sounds of faint sobbing echoed in Michael's ears and he opened his eyes.

He nudged Clyde in the direction of the sobs. Around a grove of trees, tangled in the fence row, he spotted Sarah.

She'd fallen to her knees—a piece of barbed wire clutched inside her fist. Michael jumped down from Clyde, threw the reins over Clyde's head so they dangled to the ground, and ran to Sarah.

He couldn't find enough breath to fill his lungs and gasped at the sight of a steady stream of blood running down her arm. Wide-eyes glazed with pain pleaded with him to help. Her sobs dissolved into hiccups as she gritted her teeth to keep from crying out. He pushed back a tendril of hair and noticed her ghostly white complexion.

He knelt down beside her. "Can you let go?"

Sarah sniffled. "It hurts too much."

"Sometimes it's harder to let go than it is to hold on," he said.

Michael unbuttoned his shirt and took it off. He heard Sarah's sharp intake of breath. With his shirt wadded up in one hand, he gently glided his hand up Sarah's arm to her injured hand.

"What happened?"

Sarah's terrified eyes never left his face. "I was trying to tighten this strand of wire, but when I pulled, it snapped and I put my hand up to shield my face. I caught it in my hand." She moaned as Michael's thumb pried up one of her fingers.

The wire's barbs embedded themselves into the palm of her hand. It came as no surprise to him the wire had snapped. Glancing down the fencerow, rotted posts appeared to have fallen years ago.

"You shouldn't have been out here alone," he scolded.

"Josh and Ethan went into town to grab a few new posts."

Michael sighed. "I wish you would have asked me to help."

Sarah took a deep breath and appeared as though she'd be ill. "I don't need your help, Michael."

"I'm not going to leave you Sarah, not like this."

Her lips trembled. After the night at his parents' estate, he was sure things would change between them. Like now, she'd been so vulnerable in his arms. What had happened between that night and the car ride home?

He leaned over, pushed back her hair, and kissed her forehead. "This is going to hurt."

Sarah's eyes grew wider and little spots of pink stained her cheeks. She ducked her head away and bit her lip.

"On the count of three: one ... two ... three ..." Michael flipped up her fingers and yanked the wire out of her hand.

Sarah screamed. Michael stuffed his shirt into her tender palm and closed her fingers around it.

Sarah wept uncontrollably. He gathered her into his arms and held her as she buried her face into his bare shoulder. Her face felt clammy against his naked flesh but her tears came hot and steady.

"It's alright, Sarah." Michael consoled her. "I've got you."

Michael rested his chin on Sarah's head and rubbed her back

as she cried. He prayed until a few minutes later Sarah pulled away from him. She reached up with her good hand and wiped her eyes.

"I guess I should go put a bandage on this."

"I'll give you a ride." He got up and pulled her to her feet. Sarah wavered and Michael held on to her. Her hand went up to the side of her head.

"Dizzy?"

"A little," she admitted.

"It's probably shock. When's the last time you had a tetanus shot?" He led her towards the horse.

Clyde jerked his head and watched them approach. Michael released her long enough to grab Clyde's reins and flip them back over the horse's head.

"Last year, I was chasing Ethan around the barn and stepped on a loose board with old nails."

Before Sarah could protest, Michael lifted her up in the saddle and handed her the reins. Clyde danced as Michael put his foot in the stirrup and swung himself up behind her. He pulled her onto his lap and wrapped his arms around her taking hold of the reins.

Sarah leaned back against him cradling her bad hand against her heart. "It's been a long time since I've been on a horse."

"Ever ride double?" he asked.

"Not since I was a kid. My dad would lift me up in front of him and we'd ride around the fence rows."

Michael heard the wistfulness in her voice. "Maybe someday, once you get the right horse, you and Ethan can do the same thing."

He nudged Clyde forward in a slow walk. Sarah melted into his hold. Her back against his chest, he liked the way she fit in his arms. He was careful to keep Clyde walking as to not jolt Sarah and cause her pain.

The last thing he ever wanted to do was hurt her.

Michael lost sight of the sun. The sky darkened, and the winds rushed by them.

"You're going the wrong way." Sarah said.

"My place is closer."

As they reached roadside, Clyde tripped. Michael tightened his hold around Sarah and Clyde's hooves clicked across the blacktop.

In front of the clinic, Michael tied Clyde to a porch rail and lifted Sarah down into his arms. He carried her up the stairs.

"You can put me down now."

"As soon as I get you to the clinic," he replied.

Sarah winced. "You can't treat me like one of your patients."

He grabbed the door handle and gave it a jerk, holding open the door with his foot as he turned sideways and walked inside the clinic's waiting room. Jenny looked up from her laptop and gasped. "What happened?"

"Barbed wire," Michael explained, as he carried Sarah into one of his exam rooms down the hall. Jenny followed close behind. Doc Miller walked out of the room next door and chuckled. "Now that's something you don't see every day."

"I'm fine." Sarah looked over Michael's shoulder towards Jenny.

"Barbed wire!" Jenny exclaimed. "Where is Josh? Wasn't he supposed to be fixing the fence?"

"I sent him and Ethan into town to grab posts."

"Why didn't you wait?" Jenny asked.

"Only thing that's waiting around here is my next patient," declared Doc Miller from the doorway. "Now, if you don't mind, I got a schedule to keep. If I were you, young lady, I'd be getting myself a real doctor." Doc Miller winked at Sarah.

"We should probably take you to the hospital, you might need stitches," Jenny said. Michael sat Sarah on an examining table in the middle of the room.

Sarah shivered.

"Are you cold?" Michael asked, pulling open drawers and pointing to the first-aid kit on the wall. Jenny grabbed it and handed him the case.

Sarah shivered again.

"Is it shock? Sarah?"

"I'm fine," Sarah said, as a smile attempted to spread across her pale complexion.

"Girl you look like you're going to pass out," Jenny replied. "I'll go call an ambulance."

Sarah's shook her head. "I'm fine, besides Michael's a doctor, he'll take care of me, right?"

"That barbed wire must have wrapped around your brain, too. Earth to Sarah." Jenny waved her hands. "VMD means four-legged patients."

"I left Clyde tied to the porch." Michael turned to Jenny. "If you could return him to the barn before the storm hits, I'd appreciate it."

Jenny's eyebrows rose as she shot a look at Sarah.

Sarah lifted one shoulder in response.

"Right after I send in Doc's next patient. But when I get back I'm taking you to the hospital!" Jenny pointed at Sarah.

Michael watched as Jenny turned and departed.

"Thank you," Sarah said, when his gaze returned to her.

"I'm not sure you want to be thanking me yet. I am, after all, the man who's about to put you through a great deal of pain."

"No one knows pain greater than I do," Sarah whispered.

He walked up to her and unfolded her arm from her chest. She diverted her gaze.

"It's a flesh wound, the bleeding should have stopped by now." He opened her cold fingers from her clinched fist and massaged them.

Sarah gasped and flinched. He took his shirt from her hand and tossed it on a counter behind him. Sarah sucked in her breath.

"Perhaps we should take you to the hospital." Michael grimaced. Her palm was pierced in several places from the barbs. Dark red welts formed in the deepest spots of the wounds. Michael stretched his neck up to look out the window. Rain pounded against the window in streams. "I hope Jenny is alright."

"She'll probably complain about getting wet."

"Not squeamish are you?" He lifted his gaze. Her hair tumbled forward around her face. "I thought Jenny would pass out on me last week stitching up a pup's foot."

Sarah laughed, soft and weak. "You should have seen her when Ethan was born."

Michael pulled out a bottle of antiseptic and bandages. Inside he felt his gut twist. "So, Jenny was there when Ethan was born?"

As she spoke, Michael cleansed the wound. "Jenny was my birthing coach. She stayed up with me all night when I was in labor, and never left my side at the hospital. Gran was there too …" She frowned.

"And Josh, where was he during all this?" Michael stared at her hand while he worked.

Sarah sucked in her breath before she replied, "Pacing outside the delivery room doors like an expectant father, I suppose."

Michael grabbed a wad of gauze and pressed it into her palm. She winced.

"Not nearly as painful." Michael brushed his fingers down her arm. Their gazes locked. He reached back and grabbed more gauze, quickly slipping out the old and sliding in the new. Sarah's lip trembled as he wrapped more gauze around her hand and taped it.

"That should do it." He placed the last piece of tape around her knuckles. "You're lucky. The barbs pierced the flesh of your palm, but it doesn't appear you'll need stitches. Keep the wounds clean and put some salve on them. Once they scab over you should be able to remove the bandage. Try not to open and close your hand too much for a time. You could cause the gashes to reopen."

Sarah slid down from the table with Michael holding her injured hand. He bent over and kissed her palm.

Sarah took a sharp intake of breath. "What was that for?"

"To make it all better, of course." He grinned.

Sarah's cheeks turned scarlet. He heard the jingle of the door and footsteps down the hall. He reached around her and scooped his shirt from off the table.

When Josh stepped through the doorway with rain-drenched clothes, Sarah stepped back. Michael released her hand. Josh's gaze narrowed as Michael felt Sarah pull away.

"I heard you got hurt," Josh said, his eyes on Michael.

"I'm fine, it just a scratch." Sarah tried to shrug the incident off. "Where's Ethan?"

"In the barn with Jenny. They're wiping down Dr. Wolfe's horse." Josh tore his gaze away from Michael and looked at Sarah. His expression softened.

Michael slipped on his shirt, not bothering to button it.

"Oh, Michael, your shirt." Sarah exclaimed.

Michael looked down at the bloodstains on his white shirt and shrugged. "Don't worry about it, it's *just* a shirt."

"Come on, I'll take you home." Josh put his arm around Sarah and led her out of the room. "Hey, thanks man, for patching her up."

Sarah looked back over her shoulder and attempted to smile as Josh led her away.

When they left, Michael stepped up to the window and watched Josh hold open the door of his truck for Sarah as she slipped in out of the rain.

He leaned his forehead against the cool glass window and watched the truck back up and drive away.

Sarah flicked on the light switch in the stable's office and searched the drawers until she found the envelope. She sighed and fell back into the chair. She'd spent so much time reading Gran's Bible she'd been afraid to keep it anywhere else. There in her hand, laid the truth.

She took one look at her wounded hand and winced. Her heart pounded then too, when Michael carried her into his clinic. She attempted to wiggle her swollen and bruised fingers.

Pain jetted past her wrist and up her arm. She hissed, expelling a sharp intake of breath.

Like her heart, these wounds would heal.

This time, however, it would be different. Michael came to her. It was as if God heard her silent pleas for help during her time of bondage with the barbwire fence.

If she hadn't prayed, would Michael have come and untangled her from the mess she'd created?

She rocked back on her chair.

Yet, part of her refused to believe God had anything to do with Michael finding her in the field. If he could find her now, he could have found her years ago. Her lip trembled. She could no longer deny Michael a place in her life.

Then, why was it so hard to give Michael this letter?

It would unravel the web she'd woven around her heart. Hadn't she already felt the strings pluck one by one? Even now, she felt the electric tingles over her flesh when she thought about him.

Outside, she heard the gentle roar of a motor and vehicle tires crunching in the gravel by the stable.

Ethan was at the clinic with Jenny.

She placed the letter back inside the back portion of the drawer. Briefly, she picked up a stack of bills and glanced through them. There was no bill for the construction crew that showed up and fixed the barn roof. She would have to ask Josh about it later, she decided, and slid a stack of bills atop the letter before pushing the drawer shut.

She got up and walked out into the stable's walkway. All but one of the horses were out in the fields. Thanks to Josh, the fence was finished and the horses could graze.

She walked outside and looked around.

She could have sworn she'd heard a vehicle. She shook her head and turned back inside the shade of the stables. Halfway down the walkway, she heard his voice.

Michael.

She found him in a stall with the little Morgan mare they'd purchased in Mayfield. She leaned against the stall and peered in at him. He hummed "Amazing Grace" as he worked. He ran his hands down each of the horse's legs and cleaned out the bottom of each hoof. The mare stood perfect like a statue.

Tempted, Sarah reached for the stall door latch and grinned.

"Now who is locking whom in?" Michael asked, undistracted from picking the horse's hoof.

"How did you know I was here?"

Michael set down the horse's hoof and patted the Morgan on the neck. "The only thing that smells rosy in this stable is you." He flashed a white-toothed grin.

She flushed and ducked her head. She peeked at him through the strands of her hair covering her face.

"I didn't expect you to come over until later this evening."

Michael straightened and cleaned the hoof pick off on his leg. He slipped it in the back pocket of his work pants. "I had a client drop me off. Jenny mentioned this one was limping." He nudged the horse's head away from his shirt front. The horse grunted and swung its head around to finish picking at its grain.

"I would have called you if I thought I needed you."

"Going to let me out?" He gave the stall door a light tug.

Sarah tossed her hair back. "That depends, Doctor. What's the prognosis?"

"Stone bruise. I'd keep her in her stall for a few days. Then I'd see about getting this pretty filly a good pair of shoes." He pulled open the stall door and Sarah stepped back. The little Morgan shook her head up and down as if she agreed.

Sarah thought about the stack of bills in the drawer of her desk, the unbilled roof repair, and now a farrier fee and grimaced. Since the day Josh discovered the leaky roof, Jenny insisted on donating a portion of her paycheck to the rescue, but it wasn't enough to cover all the cost.

She glanced at Michael; his proposal to help out with the rescue tempted her. Doubts pushed aside any hope that rose inside her. What would happen if she let Michael become a part of the rescue? Would he change his mind when he found out the truth inside her letter?

She had to think of Ethan.

She jerked her chin up when she heard Michael slide the stall door shut.

If only Michael hadn't shut the door on her at the gala....

Suddenly, she felt a sharp pain in her hand, and realized she clinched it in a fist. She released her fingers and took a deep breath. Michael stared at her intently.

She licked her lips and looked around. They were alone. She cradled her wounded hand in front of her.

This was the perfect time to give Michael the letter.

CHAPTER 18

"How's the hand?" Michael's gaze lowered to her hand cradled close to her heart.

She held it up for his inspection. "I took the bandage off. The doctor says it will be sore for a little while, but no scarring."

"So you did go see a doctor, then?" He reached over and took her hand.

Sarah shrugged, "Josh insisted."

Softly, he ran his index finger over her palm. Her skin felt smooth except for the three small areas where her flesh was dark red and bruised across the middle crease of her palm. How many other scars did Sarah have? He prayed they, too, would be healed.

"They came and fixed the barn roof."

"Who?" Michael suppressed a smile.

"Some outfit Josh hired, I suppose." Sarah answered.

Josh? He bit back his response. He cleared his throat and felt as if he'd swallowed a fly. "I suppose now you'll be prepared for the hay when it arrives."

"Dodson called a few days ago, he is going to start delivering hay again this week. He would have brought it sooner, but I asked him to hold off with all the forecasted rain. Things are finally starting to work out for us around here."

Sarah walked down the walkway and left small puffs of dust at her feet. Michael fell into step beside her.

"Josh seems to take care of things quite well around here, doesn't he?"

"I suppose he does. Josh is a good foreman and he's a good friend." Her voice lowered.

Michael bent his head and their lips met. She melted into his arms as he drew her closer. It was like spring rain, each kiss more refreshing than the last. He looked into her eyes. "I didn't come here to be your friend, Sarah."

His chest pounded from the drum of his heart.

Sarah pulled away from him. "I know what you're trying to do Michael, and it's not going to work." She frowned, causing creases in her delicate forehead.

He took a deep breath as she walked towards the stable's office. She lingered at the office doorway.

"What am I trying to do?" Michael wished they could still be kissing, not talking.

She took in a deep breath, like she was exasperated with him. "You, me, and this clinic rescue business you've got in your head."

"Ah," he said. "So, you have given it more thought."

She lengthened her strides. "Given what thought?"

"Us." He urged his heart to slow and his lungs to breathe steadily. He'd prepared himself at the beginning of summer, determined to have a relationship with Sarah. Only then, his emotions hadn't been as strong as they'd grown now.

She glanced at him, sharply, "It would never work."

"Can we talk about this? What are you running from, Sarah?"

Her gaze fell inside her office. She sighed and spun on her heel to face him.

He held up his hand as her mouth opened. "I've been trying to give you all the time you need. But listen Sarah, the clinic is behind schedule and I have several clients putting on the pressure. If I don't take their horses soon they'll find a different clinic."

Sarah turned away. Her gaze fell to the office again. Slowly, she swung back around to face him. "You want to bring them to the rescue? That's why you came over here?"

"Until the clinic is ready," He explained, "I'd pay you board, like I do for Clyde."

Michael's pulse raced. Maybe now Sarah would see how much they needed each other. How much *he* needed her.

Sarah bit her bottom lip as they walked out of the shaded interior of the barn and into the bright sunlight. He blinked and Sarah kept walking. They headed down the farm lane. As they walked, Sarah brushed a piece of hair back from her shoulder. "How many horses?"

"Two, maybe three." Michael couldn't be sure. Like Sarah, he didn't want to ever have to turn any horse away from his care.

"I don't know ..." She kicked a stone from the farm lane into the grass.

"It's only until the clinic is finished and we can board the horses—a few months."

Sarah slowed her pace. "A few months? No, I don't think so."

"Two months max." Michael felt a heavy weight upon his chest. "Come on Sarah, these horses need as much care as any horse you bring into your stables. It's not like you don't have room."

They're shoulders brushed. Michael leaned into her.

Sarah scowled at him and picked up the pace again. "What if I take these horses in and then don't have room for a horse that needs to be at the rescue because your horses have taken over their space?"

"Be reasonable Sarah, you have plenty of space. Do you really think you'll take on that many horses in a couple of months?" He felt his ire rise. Beautiful stubborn, Sarah. He wanted to shake her and at the same time kiss her again. He fought the urge to drag her back inside the barn and lock her in a stall, only this time it would be different. This time he had God walking alongside him.

He stuffed his hands in his pockets.

"What if your clients don't want their horses intermixed with rescue horses?"

His jaw tightened.

He rolled back his shoulders. "Exactly what are you getting at?"

"All I'm saying is your clients might not like their fancy-bred horses being stabled next to my horses. Mine are, after all, of lesser value." Sarcasm dripped from her mouth.

"You haven't told Bonnie have you?"

Sarah's eyes narrowed. She glanced over at him. "What about Bonnie?"

"Only that you don't feel she's worth as much to you as Clyde."

Sarah's jaw dropped. "I didn't say that!"

"Didn't you?" He was unable to resist grinning as he stepped onto the main road.

Sarah stood at the end of the farm lane. Her lips pressed together in a flat line and her features turned dark.

She was so cute when she was mad.

As Michael walked away, he said. "The horses arrive a week after Thursday. I knew you wouldn't turn them away."

He waited until his back was turned to let out a chuckle. From the corner of his eye he spotted Sarah at the edge of the road, as if she couldn't decide which side she wanted to be on.

Back inside his clinic, Michael strolled up to Jenny's desk and rapped his knuckles on the hard wood. Jenny's fiery head lifted. Beside her, Ethan looked up from his Legos.

"Mark my calendar, would you? We've got horses arriving on Thursday."

Jenny's brows drew together. "Horses? Where are you going to put them?"

Michael grinned. Jenny's eyes grew large and her mouth formed an "O."

Ethan got to his feet. "Look, I made a horse, like Clyde. Except it's not black." He frowned, holding up the block horse.

"I take it you and Sarah worked things out." Jenny's face appeared hopeful.

"That's great, Sport. Reminds me of a horse I had once." Michael left Jenny to wait.

"You had a blue horse?" Ethan exclaimed.

"Sure I did, except he wasn't really blue." Michael admitted.

"Can I put my horse in the stable with Clyde?"

"I don't see why not. Who knows, maybe someday you'll wake up and find a real horse of your own in its place."

Jenny rolled her eyes, "If he starts asking, I'm blaming this one on you."

Michael chuckled. "Wouldn't be the first thing I've been at fault for."

Jenny turned back to her computer screen. He heard the clicking of her nails on the keyboard as he inspected Ethan's block horse.

"Done." Jenny beamed. "Now you have a farm visit and you'll be done for the day."

"Can I go?" Ethan asked, his body trembling with anticipation.

Michael shrugged. "Sure, but I suppose we'll have to ask your mom."

Ethan frowned; Michael felt the same expression taking over his features. If there was anything he'd learned from Sarah since they got reacquainted, it was her protectiveness over her son.

"Don't worry, Sport. I'll sweet-talk her if she says no."

Jenny snorted. "Go, it's not like you're going to take Ethan and run."

Michael and Ethan looked at each other. Ethan's slim shoulders lifted and dropped. Michael mirrored the action. They both stared at Jenny. She shooed them away as the telephone rang.

Michael put his arm around the boy's shoulders and turned to walk out.

"What's sweet-talking mean?"

Michael chuckled. "Stick with me, Kid. There's a lot you got to learn yet." He winked back at Jenny, who pointed to her watch and made a face.

"Like that?" Ethan asked, attempting to wink as they strolled out the door.

Sarah rose early, as was her habit. Dawn scattered gray with dusty pink. August in Kentucky was a transitional time for the weather. It strutted in hot and muggy, but skipped out cool and comfortable for the approach of autumn.

She crept quietly into Ethan's room and found him asleep in his bed. She didn't bother with her monitor this morning. Jenny's room was directly across the hall from Ethan and if he made a peep, Jenny would hear him. She always did.

Sarah walked down the stable's walkway and tended to each of the horses. Bonnie's soft neighs welcomed her in the dim light of the florescent bulbs that hung overhead. The little Morgan Michael purchased for the rescue stomped a hoof, impatient to be fed, and the bay thoroughbred's muzzle dropped low, still dozing. Many of the other horses acknowledged her in their own way. Ears perked, a soft whoosh of morning sighs, bared teeth with the wideness of a yawn, all watched for Sarah—yet still reserved due to their previous abuse and neglect. Each horse waited for its morning oats with little regard as to who fed them, just as long as she kept her distance. She knew only time, patience, and trust would change their temperaments.

Clyde, as usual, was missing from his stall. Michael rode every morning to exercise both beast and man. She missed that feeling of the wind in her face as she raced down through the thick grassy fields. But she also missed the comfort of a dear friend, the exhilaration of a good ride, and the pride she saw in her father's eyes. She wished she could be sixteen all over again.

Bonnie nickered when she passed the mare's stall to finish the morning feeding. She back tracked her steps and opened the stall gate to hug the outstretched neck of the horse. Of all the horses, Bonnie welcomed Sarah's attentions without reserve. The mare was underweight, but her skeletal frame no longer visibly protruded against the horse's flesh. Bonnie developed a healthy appetite in the past months of recovery since being rescued, and Sarah didn't think she'd be able to part with her once she was ready to adopt. Technically, Bonnie belonged to Sarah.

She reached for a lead rope and halter. The mare lowered her head as Sarah slipped on the halter and clipped the lead rope to the metal ring under the horse's chin. She led the horse out of her stall. They headed outside into the cool air of the morning.

Sarah found the gate open to the field, led Bonnie inside, and they walked the fencerow. She stopped occasionally to allow Bonnie snips of grass along the way.

Sarah closed the gate and felt as if she entered another time. The horse was gone and she could hear her father's voice. A beautiful sorrel thoroughbred trotted in a circle. It obeyed his commands. The horse's coat gleamed in the sun like a new copper penny, as its long legs broke into a canter. Muscular shoulders propelled the animal forward. Its smooth muzzle tucked and proud neck arched.

She saw the silhouette of her father. He turned towards her and smiled. He commanded the horse to slow and halted out of her reach. "She's yours," he told her. Sarah stepped forward to pat the horse affectionately on the neck, but the horse shied away from her touch. She looked at her father, whose eyes filled with sorrow. Droplets of tears ran down the sun-tanned creases on his face. An invisible lasso wrapped around the middle of her chest and pulled tight. She reached out again for the horse, this time more slowly, and murmured soft praises for the horse's ears to adjust. She took a step forward, her hand a mere breath from the warm velvet muzzle.

As she reached closer, the image of the horse faded away.

Her father was gone. She stood there with Bonnie's lead in her hand.

The tall empty grass rustled around her. Her arm dropped to her side, and she looked around. There was no one. No other horses.

It all had been a mirage.

Her mind had turned her into a sentimental fool, always

dwelling on the past. Always wanting what she could no longer have. Always feeling she would forever be alone.

She was six years old when her father placed her on a horse for the first time. It would have happened even sooner if her mother had allowed. There wasn't a horse on the farm she couldn't ride by the time she turned nine. At ten, she accompanied her parents to various horse shows throughout the state. Once she witnessed the races at Churchill Downs. At fourteen, her parents gave her Irish Rose. She and her mother rode together every day, and trained under her father's supervision. Many times, he joined them to ride around the borders of the farm. They were always together, the perfect family unit.

On her sixteenth birthday, her parents bought her a new saddle. She could still smell the strong scent of leather and oil. If she could never ride again, she still would have held on to her saddle forever.

But shortly before her seventeenth birthday, despite her desperate plea to go with them, her parents left her behind. Sarah would never forget the last time she said goodbye, or the smiles on their faces, or the sounds of their voices.

She could replace the saddle. Yet, it wouldn't be the same. Nothing would ever be the same again.

Sarah brushed her hand down the blaze of the horse's long face. Bonnie rubbed the flat of her forehead against her arm her footsteps stumbled in a drunkard's stance.

Bonnie's head rose with the approach of horse and rider as Sarah shielded her eyes from the rising sun. Michael pulled Clyde to halt inches from where she stood, and Clyde snorted. The gelding shook his mane, arched his neck and chomped at the bit. Sarah stepped back and bumped into the mare. Like his rider, Clyde was a magnificent creation—tall, dark, and impressively made.

"Good morning," Michael called, his hair tousled by the ride.

Sarah smiled wearily at Michael. Her stomach tumbled with summersaults. "Good morning."

Michael dismounted in a single fluid motion, taking the

horse's reins into one hand, while Clyde stomped his feet with impatience. Sarah tugged on the mare's lead, continued to walk, and Michael fell into step beside her. Both horses trailed behind them. Clyde whinnied at Bonnie and the mare nipped at him. Bonnie pushed the domineering gelding to the side. Clyde sidestepped away and tossed his head in defiance. The two stable mates fussed like an old married couple.

"I suppose now you'll head back to the clinic now," she said. She'd spent the night thinking about what Mrs. Kingsley said, about her and Michael. Then, she'd prayed. She seemed to be doing this a lot lately, turning to God.

"I am," he admitted. "I've got a few things to put in order before the horses arrive, but I hoped we could get together for lunch."

Bonnie stuck her head in Sarah's back and gave her a shove. "I can't. The truth is ..." Fear gripped her and at her slight hesitation, Michael interrupted.

"What about tonight? You can bring Ethan if you like."

She sighed. There was no easy way to do this. Whether she fit into Michael's life or not, she'd held the truth from him long enough.

"I have to tell you," he grinned. "That boy is really beginning to grow on me like a vine around a trellis."

Sarah grew queasy and she feared she'd be ill before she reached the house. At the mention of her son, Michael's face lit up like last Fourth of July's fireworks. A little voice in her head prompted her. *Tell him. Tell him.*

"I can't. I have plans with Jenny and Josh," Sarah said.

"Then Ethan can stay with me."

Sarah stopped and looked at him, skeptical. "Have you ever watched a five-year-old before?"

"Only the day we were in the park," he admitted. "I'll come over tonight and sit with Ethan while you go out. What else were you going to do with him?"

"Mrs. Dodson keeps him for me on occasion." Since Jenny and Josh moved on the farm Mrs. Dodson was on the bottom of her call list these days, but tonight was special. Mrs. Dodson, with three teenage boys and a girl in college, out-qualified Michael's one day in the park.

However, Ethan would rather stay with Michael. The two of them became closer as each day passed. What would the harm be? Ethan would be able to sleep in his own bed, and Michael would get to spend more time with their son. Perhaps it was best, under the current situation, for her to grant him babysitter's privileges.

"All right, but no matter how much he begs, bedtime is eight o'clock."

Michael glanced at her, "You're no fun."

She laughed. At the gate, Clyde stood while Michael uncinched the saddle and slid it from the horse's back. Sarah watched as Michael swiftly traded Clyde's bridle for a halter that hung from a post near the gate. She unsnapped the lead and gave Bonnie her freedom. Together, she and Michael watched the two horses run across the field in full gallop. Michael hitched the saddle over his shoulder and took Sarah's hand.

As the sun rose higher into the clear morning sky, the crisp air seemed to sizzle around them despite the cool temperature. She plucked the tip off a tall weed growing up a fencepost. She inhaled the subtle scent of milkweed and gazed out over the land. Each post connected to the others by strands of wire created a boundary. For a long time, those boundaries had been broken. How would she mend them when they became broken again? She glanced down at her hand.

"So now that tonight's settled, when do you plan to ride any of the horses?"

Sarah's brows furrowed together. She felt her stomach become queasy. "Not for a while. I don't have a saddle." The old stone house loomed closer.

"If any of the horses are ready, it would be the bay I got." Michael eased his saddle to the ground. "The one Ethan calls Goliath."

Sarah glimpsed in the direction of the house. "We may introduce a saddle in a week or so, but I'll have to get one first."

She bit her lip. Shame burnt her cheeks at the admission. What would happen when she confessed her secret to Michael? She looked away before his eyes met her gaze.

That nagging uncertainty pulled heavily on her chest.

She heard Michael sigh, felt his thumb rub across her hand, and she instinctively withdrew her fingers from his grasp.

"What happened Sarah?" Michael asked, as if he read her destitute thoughts.

She glanced over at him then, his eyes filled with unspoken questions.

"Life happened, Michael." Sarah stepped away from him.

Michael waited, a few feet behind her. She looked back over her shoulder. "You wouldn't understand."

"Maybe not, but I do know we all have to get back into the saddle again."

"When I'm ready, I'll let you know," she said. She headed for the house.

"What time should I arrive?" he called out after her.

"Six."

CHAPTER 19

Michael watched Sarah disappear into the house. She'd seemed so lost as she stood there in the field when he approached. As if she'd been in her own little world.

He picked up his saddle from the ground and strolled to the barn. He decided not to give Clyde a good rubdown; the horse barely broke a sweat when he spotted Sarah with the mare in the pasture, and then the rambunctious gelding ran off with the mare across the field.

He hung his saddle and bridle in the tack room then went back to his clinic. He could hear Sarah's soft wistful voice in his head. She sounded regretful at the way her life turned out. Saws squalled, men shouted and things got hammered. As every morning, the construction crew showed up early and worked late to build the facility for Michael's equine clinic. He wondered how Sarah would react, if she knew the truth he'd made anonymous donations towards the rescue. Would it shed the barrier between them once and for all, or would it only create an impenetrable wall?

There were moments, Michael assessed, as he stepped up onto the clinic's porch, that the barrier faded and Sarah allowed him to get close. If not for her parents' deaths, or her abandonment by her grandmother, what could cause her such grief? Why couldn't she let go of the past? It was the boy, no doubt.

Would Sarah love him now, if she knew he would love her son as his own?

Oh Lord, he prayed, *what must I do to show this woman that my love, like yours, will never fail*?

Michael opened the door to the clinic.

At least tonight, he would be given another opportunity to demonstrate to Sarah his unfailing love.

Sarah wiped her feet on a rug and headed down the hall. She entered the kitchen and turned on a kettle of tea. From inside the battered old fridge, she searched for some cream while she waited for the kettle to boil.

Across the top freezer portion of the fridge, stuck with magnets, a picture colored by Ethan drew her attention. Her hand paused on the refrigerator's door handle. She touched the drawing and admired the large scrolled letters of his name at the bottom.

"Mrs. Dodson says he's a great kid, one of the best behaved in the whole Sunday school class." Sarah leaned in the doorway and glanced over her shoulder at Jenny. Jenny's red blouse hung loose over a pair of snug jeans. Her face lacked the artificial color of cosmetics, yet her fingertips gleamed like cherries.

"He enjoys going," Sarah said.

"Claire gave me an extra book for Wednesday." Jenny tossed the paperback on the table with a soft thud, and Sarah stared at it for a moment. She opened the refrigerator door, ducking her head.

"I offered to bring brownies for afterwards."

"Did you? How thoughtful," Sarah reached for the creamer in the door.

"You know I always burn them, so I thought maybe you could give me a hand. Help me bake up a dozen or two."

Sarah shut the door. "I can do that." She set the creamer on the table and picked up the book. She thumbed through the pages.

"Does this mean you'll go?"

Sarah leaned back against the fridge. She spotted a glimpse of hope in Jenny's eyes, the same gleam she saw each time Jenny asked her to come back and be part of their church family again.

"If you're going to say 'maybe' again ..." Jenny started to sputter, "I'm not taking 'no' for an answer." Sarah liked that about her.

"Of *course* I'll have to go." Sarah's lips twitched. "I can't let those ladies go on thinking you can bake; think of the disaster at the next bake sale."

Jenny grinned. "This Wednesday at six-thirty. Ethan can come too—Claire's got a boy his age."

Sarah nodded.

"I got to get going. I don't want Michael catching me coming in late," Jenny said.

"Then you'd better run, because he was heading back to the clinic when I came in." Sarah grabbed the kettle before it whistled and set it on a cool burner.

"See you tonight," Jenny called, as she headed out the door.

Jenny greeted him from her desk with a red flush to her checks and her shaggy red hair clinging damp at her neck. "Getting an early start this morning?"

"Miller's out sick today, so I'll be filling in." Michael reached for his white lab coat.

Jenny hit a few keys on her keyboard to view appointments. "It should be a light day. Henderson called and cancelled. His dog passed away last night. You should be done by three o'clock, if nothing comes up."

Michael nodded as he watched the small sedan pull into the parking lot.

"I was hoping to get out early today," she kept her eyes on the screen. It seemed like she skipped out early a lot these days or hugged the clock minutes before closing.

"Ah, that's right; you've got a date with Josh and Sarah."

"In a matter of speaking." She cocked her head towards him. "We're taking Sarah out for her birthday." Jenny eyed Michael. "Maybe you'd like to join us?"

He watched a young girl and her mother carrying an armful of puppies through the doorway, and could smell Jenny's pungent plan before she'd proposed it.

"Can't. I already told Sarah I'd watch Ethan." After the way he'd pressed her for the privilege, he wasn't going to back out.

He strolled over to the door and held it open with his foot and scooped up a few of the puppies in his arms as the young girl entered the clinic.

Promptly at six, Michael knocked on the front door—with a squirming bundle of fur tucked under one arm. He heard the patter of feet racing down the hall and skid into the door. A few rattled turns later and a spaghetti-smeared face poked out grinning from ear to ear.

"A puppy!" Ethan's bright eyes confirmed—this was a good move.

"Hello to you, too," Michael laughed. Ethan bounced up and down. "Mind if I come in?" Ethan nodded and then ran to the kitchen. Michael stepped through the doorway and closed the door. In his arms, the puppy squirmed and barked.

"Mom! Mom! He's got a puppy!" Ethan shouted down the hall. Michael found Sarah in the kitchen. She wrestled Ethan as she attempted to clean his sauced face. "See it Mom!"

Sarah's gaze followed the direction of Ethan's finger. A tiny pup wiggled in Michael's arms. Then her eyes switched back to catch Ethan's expression. He flashed a grin in her direction. As the puppy barked and attempted to escape Michael's hold, Ethan broke free of Sarah's grasp.

Carefully, Michael placed the anxious pup down on the kitchen floor.

"If that thing does its business on my floor, you're cleaning it up," Sarah glared at Michael. Ethan giggled as the little pup licked his face and he struggled to hold it in his arms. Giggles erupted into laughter, and Sarah's stern gaze fell on Michael.

"Mrs. Peterson's beagle had pups. She didn't know what to do with them all." Michael shrugged. He tried to hide the hidden amusement that played on his juvenile grin.

"I bet," Sarah said. "You're taking it home with you."

Ethan's mouth opened to interject.

"Now is that any way to treat a man's birthday present?" A brow arched in answer.

"Mine!" Ethan stood, hands on hips, staring up at his mother.

"Now look what you've done." Her hands flared out from her sides, and Michael chuckled.

"Can we keep him, *please*?" Ethan dipped down on his knees with the pup as it jumped to reach his face.

"It would be rude to return a man's gift." Michael crossed his arms, smug, challenging her decision. Sarah's lips thinned. Her gaze fell to the puppy as it licked her son's face. Ethan's eyes filled with delight and his laughter sounded with pure joy.

"How can I possibly say no?"

"Yes!" Ethan jumped up. He spun in a circle and caused the pup to bark. He took off down the hall with the puppy not far behind him.

"There's spaghetti in the fridge. Jenny wrote down Brad's cell phone number and it's taped on the wall by the phone. Bedtime is eight; he likes to be read to, and he'll find every excuse why he can stay up later. Last night, he told me he was too heavy for his bed."

Michael chuckled. "He'll be fine."

Sarah looked wearily at him. "It's not *him* I'm worried about."

A little while later, Sarah emerged down the stairs dressed in a simple white blouse and long peach skirt. A pair of white, low-heeled sandals strapped around her slender ankles, and her hair hung in loose curls down her back. A smear of pink gloss kissed her lips.

From the bottom of the stairwell, male voices floated down the hall. Sarah was tempted to follow them, to kiss her son one more time, and reassured herself Ethan would was fine with Michael. As a mother, she wanted to check one final time before she left. But because she cherished her relationship with Michael, she wouldn't interrupt them. Quietly, she escaped out the front door.

Twenty-three years old—the days of her youth, gone. Her life would never turn back. In her youth she'd learned to grow up too fast. Rather than go out with friends, she'd prefer to spend the evening with Michael and Ethan. Her time with them at the park or the pizza parlor, trumped tonight's plans with Jenny and the guys. In those brief excursions with Michael and Ethan, she felt like part of a family again.

"Hey you." Jenny made one last attempt to secure the flare of her gelled hair. "I've got something for you." She thrust a long rectangle box wrapped in shiny silver paper into Sarah's view. Sarah's heart beat faster.

"What's this?"

"I don't know ... you'd better open it and find out." Jenny's face beamed as Sarah took the present from her hands. "Go on." She shooed Sarah to open it.

"You shouldn't have," Sarah slipped her index finger beneath the seam of wrapping paper. It was pulled together in neat squares of clear tape. Jenny's eyes rolled upward with the shake of her head.

"What?"

"It's alright if you rip into it."

"And spoil the paper?" Sarah peeled away the flashy foil wrapping in one smooth motion. She tucked the paper under the box and shuffled the lid free. Her jaw went slack.

Jenny laughed.

Mesmerized by the gift in her hand, Sarah allowed Jenny to pull away the remaining tissue. Leather straps dangled in her grip as she plucked the gift from its wrapping. Thick braided reins and a broken bit hovered in the air, and Sarah's eyes prickled with tears.

"Oh, Jenny, you really shouldn't have!" She clutched the bridle close to her chest.

"Josh pitched in. We wanted to get you a saddle ..." Jenny flushed.

"No ... no, this is great. I-it's perfect." A lump stuck in her throat. Perhaps turning twenty-three wasn't so bad after all.

"You like it?" Jenny fussed over the discarded wrappings. "It's okay to say if you don't."

"I love it. Really." Sarah gave Jenny a quick hug. At the sound of an engine, they both turned, watching the red jeep pull up to the house.

"That would be Brad." Jenny reached for Sarah's arm, drawing the face of the watch clamped on her wrist in view. "Right on time."

Sarah clutched the bridle and scanned the distance from the porch to the cottage house where Josh stayed. Jenny touched Sarah's arm. "I'm sure Josh will be here any minute."

A tall, fair, broad-shouldered man slid from the driver's seat of the jeep. Jenny released Sarah to give him an open-hand wave.

"Why don't you go on?"

"And leave without you on your birthday?" Jenny shook her head.

"There's no sense in you and Brad waiting with me." Sarah looked back at the front door. Brad approached, his silver-tipped boots gathering mud from the driveway.

"We'll wait until Josh gets here." Jenny stepped down from the porch, careful of her red stilettos on the stairs. Brad reached out and took her by the hand to help her down. Jenny's face flushed.

"We can meet there—you go on with Brad." Sarah pressed. Down the farm lane, she searched for any signs of Josh's truck. It wasn't like him to be late.

Jenny frowned, caught between her best friend and her boyfriend.

"Josh is probably on his way right now," Sarah said.

Jenny, however, didn't look at all convinced.

Brad pushed up his Stetson." You can ride with us."

"Knowing Josh, he probably hauled some livestock into the auction barn tonight and is running late. You two go on, I'll wait here for him."

"Are you sure?" Jenny asked.

"Go. We have reservations, remember?"

Jenny made a face. She slipped her hand around Brad's arm. "I don't like leaving you like this."

From inside the house, she heard the muffled sounds of a dog bark. Brad's eyebrows lifted and he stuck one hand into his jean pocket.

"I'll be fine," Sarah said. She imagined Michael and Ethan rolling around and playing with the puppy on the living room floor. By nightfall, the puppy would have a makeshift bed in Ethan's room if her son got his way.

"Josh will be here soon," Sarah said. Josh never kept a lady waiting. Even now, with their relationship strained, she doubted Josh would let her down on such an important occasion as her birthday.

"Come on, Jenny, we'll hold the reservation until they get there." Brad took Jenny by the hand.

Her face crinkled and her mouth turned down. "I don't know ..."

"Go!" Sarah nearly shouted, about to physically push Jenny into the jeep.

"Okay, but we won't order until you get there." Jenny walked to the jeep. As Brad opened the door, Jenny glanced back at Sarah.

She motioned for Jenny to go and Jenny slipped inside the Jeep. Brad tipped his head in Sarah's direction as he walked across to the driver's side. All she needed to do now was endure the wait.

She watched the jeep bounce down the farm lane.

According to her watch, five minutes passed. Perhaps if she'd been a leggy blonde or a cheeky brunette, Josh would be here this second. Suspicion seeped into her bones like a sponge to water. Because he said so, she believed Josh would come.

That was before she'd crushed his heart and dissolved any illusions he could be her love interest.

Clutching the bridle, she stepped down from the porch. Tempted to sit down, she didn't want to snag the polyester skirt on the rough boards. From inside the house, she heard the sounds of Ethan's laughter and Michael's voice. She yearned to join them.

Michael would think she was checking up on them, and she didn't want him to think she was having second thoughts.

Josh would come any minute now.

She imagined Ethan, Michael and her as they strolled down the farm lane on a Sunday afternoon. Their voices and laughter would carry across the fields. The image she sketched in her mind ran away and left a blank canvas of reservation behind. That was exactly what it would be like when Michael found out. Maybe it didn't have to be this way.

She sighed.

Where was Josh? He hardly spoke two words to her since the day Michael patched her hand. He skipped suppers in the evening and left a few bills on the table for take-out on the nights he was responsible for supper. Sarah tucked the bills in the cookie jar and prepared dinner for three—or sometimes four, if Michael wasn't on call at the clinic. And, more often than not, the three of them, when Jenny slipped off with Brad after work.

They became more like a family as days passed. Her stomach twisted, and her head throbbed.

Another five minutes went by, and she turned as the lace curtains swayed back in place behind her. She continued to listen to the muffled sounds of television and voices. Maybe she would go inside with them and tell Michael the truth she'd been keeping from him.

She tugged at the hem of her blouse.

Sarah checked her watch again. No sight of Josh, nor any signs of an old green pickup coming down the road. She strained to hear the whistle of rubber rolling down the blacktop from afar, but only soft sounds floated from within the house.

Two minutes, three minutes, four minutes ... Sarah counted as time passed. Ten minutes passed and Josh failed to appear.

If Josh didn't show up in the next minute she was going to—going to—she didn't know what she would do. This wasn't like Josh at all.

From inside, she heard the telephone shrill. Maybe it was Josh on the phone? Most likely it was Jenny since she hadn't showed up yet.

She Glanced at the window and then walked away from the porch. The late afternoon sun was positioned high, unprepared yet to sink down below the horizon.

She waited long enough.

She walked across the yard into the shade of the stables. Hungry muzzles sorted and rusted hay. The pungent fragrance of alfalfa floated through the breezeway. Clumsy knees and unshod hooves bumped walls or pawed sawdust covered mats.

How she longed to have it all back.

Her father would be proud of her. She pictured his smile, Gran's frown, and her mother's soft eyes looking down. She accomplished everything she'd set out to do.

The barn was no longer empty, and neither was her heart.

Yet, one thing remained between her and Michael—Ethan.

How could she ever have let it go on this long? Hadn't it become clear that Michael loved her son, as much as Ethan loved him?

A trickle of excitement ran in her veins. She brought this place to life again, and soon, very soon, Ethan would make memories with Michael as she had with her own father. She was surrounded by the people and the things she loved.

She stole into the tack room, and placed her bridle on the hook beside the door. She refused to think about the saddle absent from the rack on the wall. Instead, the black smooth seat of

Michael's hunt saddle hung in the corner. One day, she'd have another saddle to hang there, and she'd ride again. Maybe not the Olympics, but someday she'd go national. *Just once. Just so I can tell my grandchildren I went there.* She left the stable occupants to munch on their supper.

Outside the stable, she walked a familiar path. Blades of soft grasses tickled her ankles and quickened her strides. She ran through these fields as a young girl, racing after her father to fetch a horse, or frolic—like she had seen Ethan play on many occasions.

Several horses raised their heads from the field and snorted into the air. Sarah stood in front of the gate. A few horses stayed out in the evenings to graze and wander the boundaries of the pasture. Sarah stepped up on the sturdy bottom board of the gate and crossed her arms as she gazed across the pasture.

Bonnie, catching sight of Sarah, swished her tail and bobbed her head while she grazed.

Months ago, nobody thought a horse like Bonnie would make it past morning. Now, the mare grazed alongside several other horses rescued from the same fate. None of them in nearly as bad of shape as Bonnie, but if Michael hadn't appeared back in her life at that moment ... Sarah cringed.

Long blades of grass swayed in a gentle breeze, much welcomed in the heat. Trees reached their limbs out from unusual places providing a shelter of shade during the day. One tree particularly called out her name, but Sarah rested her chin on her arms. She watched the horses as they accepted her presence and resumed their grazing.

Where was her future in all of this?

She felt alone, a single mother looking at the world from outside the arena. She wanted more, but did that make her selfish?

Where was a shoulder when she needed one? She always needed, always yearned. The longing inside burned her very core. For what?

Lord, I need You. Sarah slid carefully down off the gate and tried not to snag her skirt. She unlocked the gate and entered the field. Two heads popped up and watched her stroll across the distance to the large dominate tree. Here she sat under the guarded protection of her large four-legged bodyguards.

The horses gazed at her with curious stares. They watched her, waiting for her to make a move. When she didn't, they shook off flies and ignored her. Each of these horses had suffered in some way or another, but the one thing they had in common was her. She rescued them when they were abandoned by their owners. But who—who was there to rescue her?

"*I will never leave you nor forsake you.*" She heard the voice deep from within her heart. *Everyone has left me.* A tide of sorrow built inside her throat. The pools of her eyes flooded down her cheeks. *Now, I'll lose Michael too, and possibly Ethan. Oh Lord, I don't want to lose anyone else.*

She leaned her head against the tree trunk and gazed at the leaves above. Sarah closed her eyes—tears pour over her lashes. She traced the tears down her cheeks as the wetness dripped down the exposed flesh of her slender neck.

He leads me to green pastures. He restores my soul.

She brushed the tears from her cheeks and smoothed her hair back.

"I'm scared and confused. What do I do?" The answer was there inside her before the words came. *Trust me* …

She did.

Inside, the shell around her heart broke, like a walnut crunched in the vise of steel bands. It splintered.

A single golden leaf fell from the tree above her and floated onto her lap. She plucked the leaf from her skirt and twirled it in her fingers. *Trust me* …

She leaned back into the bark of the tree and closed her eyes once more as the orange streaks of sunset drizzled across the sky. She listened to the sounds of horse teeth ripping grass, and the rustle of the branches above swaying in the breeze.

She would have to return to the house, return to her son, and face the truth. It was time she stopped running and started trusting someone other than herself.

She looked out over the field again, then stretched and eased herself up. Her equine companions ignored her slow, graceful movements away from them. None of the horses, except Bonnie, acknowledged her. They would not be grieved by her exit.

There was an unspoken rapport between her and those big animals. Horses were her life's ambition. Ethan was her hope. Only now, Michael added complication to her life. But if she let him in, allowed him to be a part of their family, maybe, just maybe everything would work out for them.

A second chance, like Jenny hinted when Michael first appeared back in her life. A chance with Michael was worth the price of all the sorrows she had in the world. She owed it to herself, Michael, and her son to confess the secret she'd kept all this time. The promise she made to her grandmother would be broken, and the bound around her heart would be free.

By the end of this night, Michael Wolfe would know the truth. God would take care of the rest, even if it meant Michael walked away from her—even if it meant facing life alone.

CHAPTER 20

Gran parked the car and slammed the door. Startled, Sarah jumped. Her eyes dried from tears, she stared out beyond the windshield to the house that was now her home. She watched Gran hobble onto the porch.

Gran yanked open the screen door and it banged shut behind her.

On the ride home, Gran didn't speak a word. When Sarah turned towards her, Gran held up her hand. She'd kept her eyes to the road.

Sarah turned and stared out the car window at the landscape, memories of the morning blurred—her mind numbed.

Josh, bless his soul, offered to drive her home. That made her smile. Even when the situation looked bad for them both, Josh held his own—unlike Sarah, cowering in the corner of Harold Kingsley's office with his wife Mrs. Kingsley coolly dismissing her.

Sarah never got a chance to explain, not even to Gran.

Nor did she get to say goodbye to her roommate, Jenny. She'd been given enough time to pack and leave Jenny a note with her address and telephone number. She hoped their friendship wouldn't end, like her employment.

She slumped in her seat. Eventually, she would have to go inside the house and face the old woman. What would Michael think when she didn't show up for their morning ride? Deep within her heart, she felt Michael would seek her out—it was only a matter of time.

Gran couldn't stop her from seeing him.

She was seventeen. One more year and she'd be free to move back into the cottage house, where she and her parents once resided, and take over her father's stables. It would be like they'd dreamed about on those lazy afternoons as they lay under the giant oak tree in the west pasture.

Together, they'd run a stable and Michael would have his own clinic. She'd become a champion equestrian rider like her mother.

Someday.

Sarah got out of the car. She heard the door shut softly behind her. A sense of absence settled over her.

The farm was too quiet.

Even the smells didn't seem familiar anymore. She craned her neck. Odd. Where was Rosie? She glanced at the stables. All the barn doors were shut. A cold sweat broke out over her skin.

Slowly, she walked. Gran wouldn't have ... Her pulse pounded and her heartbeat thudded in her ears. Sarah broke out into a run. She flung open the barn doors. A jolt struck her spine. Inside, the stables were dark. Silent.

Sweat beaded on her forehead, and a chill swept over her.

Sarah sprinted down the walkway.

Every stall was vacant. Her blood grew cold. She sprinted to the fields. Panting for breath, she slowed at the sight of an open gate.

Her father's horses were gone.

"Rosie!" She shouted and cried. She clutched the stitch in her side as she ran.

She scanned the fenced landscape for any sign of a horse. She raced to the next field and the next one after that, until she reached the far end of the farm.

Her lungs burned and heart squeezed. After several hours of

walking aimlessly through barren fields, she returned to the barn near dusk.

Back inside the stables, she fell to her knees and sobbed.

Approaching the porch, Sarah watched the sky dissolve into the darken shades of night. She walked up the stairs, leaned against the porch post, and searched the blank universe above. To her left beyond the barn, she waited, she watched, as the first star for the night came to bless the sky.

Every night for years, she wished upon one of those stars, but not tonight. Wishes were like miracles, they only happened in the most unforeseen times. This wasn't one of those times. A star wouldn't give her the courage to face the truth. *Trust me* …

Courage and strength forged inside her from those simple words. "I do," she whispered, "I do."

"Sounds like the answer to an unasked question." Sarah jumped at Michael's voice. How long had he been standing there?

"Where's Ethan?" She scrubbed her tear-stained cheeks with her hands.

"Asleep with the pup," Michael eased down on the swing. "I don't know how you do it. I was exhausted before the second book was done."

"You learn to cope."

"Jenny called shortly after seven. She wanted to know if Josh picked you up yet."

Her cheeks flushed.

Michael patted the swing beside him. "I get the feeling your boy never showed."

"Something must have come up." Her voice trembled despite the confidence she built up on her walk back for this very moment.

"It wasn't a very noble thing of a friend to do."

Sarah shrugged. "It's not like him." She continued to stare at the dotted sky as a new rash of stars appeared. White connect-the-dots against the blackness.

She twirled the golden leaf stem between her fingers. The creak of the swing broke the stretch of silence between them, and she glanced over at him taking the few necessary steps to reach her.

"You've been crying." He caressed her cheek. "He let you down."

"This isn't the first time someone has left me stranded or alone."

"Sarah, look at me."

She didn't want to, but somehow she managed to lift her gaze to his face.

"I'm not going anywhere. I promise." Michael reached up and smoothed the tangled locks of her hair.

A knot formed in her throat. Gently, he tucked her head to his shoulder and cradled her close. Her hands faltered at his waist and she slid her arms around him. She no longer held control. Her body trembled.

Tender, soft-spoken words washed over her and soothed the storm that raged within her. She found the solid shoulder she sought. She fought to bring her unbridled emotions under control. The golden leaf fluttered from her grasp and floated to the ground.

Her face slanted towards him. He inhaled, sharply. His fingertip softly traced across her cheek as he bent closer. His breath warm at her temples. He kissed her forehead. He kissed each tear that shimmered on her eyelashes—each one that slid down her cheeks.

"I love you, Sarah," he whispered. Her lungs held her last breath. Speechless, her lips parted in effort to respond. When she was unable to produce words, he simply kissed her again.

Air rushed out of her lungs and she breathed in the scent of him. Her ears rang with the sounds of his gentle voice. Maybe she heard him wrong. Even she couldn't remember why she thought he couldn't possibly love her. All that mattered was that he cared—that he said she'd never be alone again. Instantaneous fireworks of joy exploded inside her.

Trust me ... Sarah winced and the fireworks faded. Her entire adult life, she'd yearned to hear "I love you," but it wasn't enough. It wouldn't be all right until Michael knew the truth. Then would he still love her?

"Michael." She didn't trust her own voice. "Th-there's something I need to tell you." She pulled back and gazed straight in his eyes, their usual pristine crystal hue.

"I know."

Sarah blinked "You do?"

"Every time we're together." Michael hooked his finger beneath her chin. "Did you really think you could hide the truth from me?"

Oh Lord, thank you, thank you.

He didn't appear upset like she feared. They could be together now, a family, and Ethan would know he had a father. She felt a great heaviness lifted from her heart.

"You don't have to hide, Sarah. I know you love me." Michael's voice grew husky.

"I-I do." She stammered. That wasn't what she'd wanted to tell him.

She loved him, loved him with her whole heart, but there was more. She wanted to cry out, say she was sorry, but what good would it do now? The weight—temporarily lifted—slammed against her.

She needed to trust God, and, in trusting Him, she would do what was right. She braced herself. *Hold me, Lord, I'm about to fall.*

"Michael." She licked her dry lips.

"It would be nice to hear you say it."

It wasn't the words that frightened her. It was his reaction to the words she left unspoken, the opportunities she shied away from, the moments when she didn't have the strength or courage to confess what mattered most.

"I love you," she whispered.

He gathered her in his arms.

"W-what are you doing?" The night was broken by a serenade of nearby crickets. Sarah's heart raced in her chest.

He chuckled. "You act as though you've never been kissed." He bent his head, the curve of his lips formed into a smile. "Hold still. This won't hurt a bit." Softly, he kissed her mouth. He coaxed her and waited for her to return the favor. She kissed him back.

A strangled sob caught in her throat.

"Good night sweet Sarah," he reached down and drew her hand up to his lips. "Happy Birthday." He stepped down off the porch into the cascading darkness. She heard him whistle a tune in the distance as he walked to his truck. Two headlights flashed in the direction away from the house, and as he drove away, she remembered she hadn't told him anything at all.

Sarah's cantankerous little Ford let out a sputter of fumes parked in front of the clinic. "ol' dependable" developed a rattle under the hood on her way back from town.

She looked over at the scrapbook she'd laid on the passenger seat. She waited so long to hear Michael say he loved her. Now she feared she would never hear him say it again. *Oh Lord, please let him still love me.*

Drawing a deep breath to settle the quake in her stomach, she reached for the large scrapbook. Her fingers caressed the trim edge of the pages. Each and every page recounted her son's life. Now she'd share these precious pages, and the life they created.

The old metal door latch clunked shut and she pressed the heel of her foot against the door. She tucked the awkward weight of the book in the crook of her elbow. Any second thoughts she may have had vanished when she pushed open the door to enter the clinic.

Jenny's head peeked over the pile of folders on her desk at the sound of the bell ringing. Sarah weaved around a barking Saint Bernard. To reach safe footing at Jenny's side, she skirted around the stretched-out collie, and dodged the grunts of Mr.

Myers' nine-year-old pot-bellied pig he affectionately referred to as "Missus."

"Busy morning," Sarah remarked.

On a bench nearby, a woman picked up her caged ferrets and sat them on her lap.

"We're overbooked." Jenny flailed her arms across the folders.

The ferret owner motioned for Sarah to take a seat. Sarah shook her head and waved the woman off. "You don't say."

"It's not usually so packed." Jenny flipped open a folder.

"Epidemic?" Sarah teased.

"Miller's day," Jenny clicked her pen and scribbled in the open file.

"I thought he was supposed to retire." Sarah glanced around at the menagerie.

"The pasture must not be green enough for him." Jenny hooked a thumb at the exam room door.

"Any idea where I can find Michael?" Sarah tried to remain casual.

"Over yonder in the barn," Jenny shuffled papers into a folder as she turned to place them in the drawer behind her.

"So it's finished." She remarked more of a statement then a question.

"One down," Jenny attempted a smile, "Only a dozen more to go." Her voice was wistful.

"I'd better let you get to it." Sarah stepped back to avoid the scurry of a panicked cat.

"It keeps stacking up." A smile flourished on her glossy-pink lips.

"Any word from Josh?"

"I haven't heard from him in days."

"I'm sure he'll come back around." Sarah hoped.

"He stood you up." Jenny pointed her pen in Sarah's direction. "Mark my words, that boy is going to be in trouble."

"Maybe that's the problem, Josh isn't a boy."

"So you noticed." Jenny cocked an eyebrow as she opened another folder.

“Friends.”

Jenny brushed back short spikes of orange hair. “So where did you go last night?”

“Nowhere.” Sarah grinned. She couldn’t bring herself to become angry with Josh. If Josh had shown up and she went out on the date, she may not have finally found peace with God that finally filled that lonely void.

“Care to share, Miss Silly Grin?” Jenny pointed towards the scrapbook beneath her arm; then rolled her eyes as she reached for the shrill of the phone. “Wolfe Clinic,” Jenny answered brightly, and Sarah waited for Jenny to handle the call.

A stout woman came out of the exam room with her sleek Doberman and walked the dog outside—locking her pet securely in her vehicle before she returned to take care of her bill.

Miller slapped the folder on the pile while Sarah stepped out of the way. Jenny hung up the phone and scribbled down the appointment in the book by her hidden keyboard.

Sensing Jenny’s haste Sarah said, “I’ll catch you later.”

“He’ll be leaving soon, you best catch him now.” Jenny flipped open the new folder.

“Well, maybe I’ll wait for a time he’s not so rushed.” Sarah tapped the scrapbook, as she looked out the window. She had waited this long, after all.

“Oh, go on with you.” Miller exclaimed. “Draggin’ your feet.” He shook his balding head, and Jenny shooed her away while the owner of the collie reached down to pull the animal to its feet in order to follow Miller into the exam room. Sarah wove through the room.

“Hey,” Jenny called out from the hall. “Remind Michael that we’ve got another horse showing up this afternoon for the clinic.”

“So much for keeping things separate,” Sarah muttered.

CHAPTER 21

Gravel crunched beneath the worn soles of her tennis shoes. Sarah spotted Michael's truck parked near the front entrance. The aluminum trailer parked around the corner of the house gleamed in the sunlight. She walked towards the barn with the large scrapbook in front of her chest like a shield.

Michael's new equine clinic was a two-story barn situated diagonally behind the old converted plantation house. The back dome-shaped extension was a testimony that the doctor went all out on this project.

Lights strung overhead illuminated her path as four long rows of stalls greeted her. Steel-bar sliding gates, black corner feeders, and piney sawdust spread throughout reminded Sarah of the stables at Kingsley Estate. The aroma of fresh-cut lumber mixed with antiseptics made her nose twitch.

At the end of the last stall, the barn split in three directions. To her left was the dome structure closed by large stainless steel double doors. The right led to another set of closed doors, but straight ahead was an exercise ring. Michael stood in the middle.

He spotted Sarah down the walkway and strolled towards her. "Hey there."

"Hi, yourself."

He swept her into his arms, cradled her close to his chest, and Sarah wrapped her arms more tightly around the book.

She brought her face up for him to kiss her. When he continued to hold her without a kiss, she wiggled out of his embrace. She couldn't allow him to hold her, not until she faced the demon she'd come to conquer.

Here I am, Lord. Please bring peace and understanding between us.

She willed her nerves to ease that she might be able to speak in a calmer tone, but the light brush of his hand against her cheek distracted her. She leaned against him and combed her fingers through the thick strands of her hair. When his lips brushed a gentle kiss on the side of her face, she sighed. This was not going to be easy.

Of all the times in her life she'd felt God's presence, this moment she needed it more than ever. She could not accept the entirety of Michael's feelings for her without him first accepting her son. *Their* son, she corrected. She pulled away and put a few steps of distance between them.

"Want a tour?" he offered.

"Sure." She adjusted the book under her arm. A tour would give her an opportunity to relax and find the words she needed to tell him about their son.

"Have you given it any more thought?" he led her to the left set of double doors.

She frowned. "What?"

"You and I." Michael opened the door for Sarah. He ushered her inside the bright, sterile room.

"A lot, actually." She stood inside the threshold. The room was stainless steel, including the large platform which rose electronically to floor level and tilted by remote control. She had never seen a veterinarian operating room such as this one.

"I didn't want to press." Michael led her out of the room. "But, I figured you needed some time to think it over."

"We should have talked about it a long time ago." Sarah stepped outside the room.

"I did drop it on you suddenly."

"Time has always been our enemy, hasn't it?" When they reached the set of doors on the other side, he stopped.

"You've changed your mind?"

"No, I've wanted to do this for quite some time now." Her palm beneath the scrapbook grew damp with sweat.

"Really?"

"Absolutely." She tried to sound certain.

"This is going to work out for both of us." He stood in front of her, reaching up to brush a lock of hair from her shoulder. Sarah tensed. "You don't think so?"

She shook her head "No—I mean yes."

"Which is it?" he asked, confusion furrowed his brow.

"Yes, definitely yes."

"I'll be bringing Clyde and the others over in a few days." He slid open the doors, this time to the domed entrance, and she hesitated.

"Jenny said to tell you there's another one arriving this afternoon."

"Excellent, we'll send him over here instead of your place since this part of the clinic is finished."

Sarah adjusted her hold on the scrapbook. "I'll hate to see them go—especially Clyde."

Although, the board money had been nice while it lasted, she wouldn't charge him more to stay.

Michael snorted. "I thought you didn't like Clyde?"

"Bonnie is going to miss him. They've grown so close these past few months."

"Actually, if it is alright with you I'd like to bring Bonnie over for a while. There's a paddock on the other side of the barn where they can run with plenty of grass."

"I'll think about it." She, too, had grown quite attached to Bonnie.

Michael swung upon a set of doors and motioned for her to step inside. Sarah gasped at the sight of an indoor pool. It sparkled beneath the skylights.

He slid his arm around her waist. "Want to go for a swim?"

"Somehow, I don't think this was meant for us." She spied the four-foot-wide ramp leading down into the pool. Cables, harnesses, and bars dangled above the water.

"Where's the boy?" He asked.

"School." She almost didn't want to let him go, but knew he'd be fine without her. She'd placed the life of her son, as well as her own, in God's hands. This morning she put on a brave face and forced a smile for Ethan as she dropped him off for his first day of kindergarten.

"I've got some time," he suggested playfully.

"The clinic is packed and Jenny says you've got to go soon," she said, both amused and thrilled at the thought of diving in the pool with him.

"Miller's problem. I don't do dogs and cats anymore. That's his department."

"Why not?"

"This, my love, is my true ambition." He spread his arms wide and turned about inside the room, and then stopped and took hold of her shoulders. "Think of it, Sarah, a horse off the track not even suitable for riding, coming through here and leaving as a dressage horse or a trail poke. Your horses, Sarah, scooped out of auction houses badly neglected, given another chance, a new owner—rehabilitated and receiving urgent care. There are countless possibilities here."

Dawning rushed through her veins like a splash of cold water. She stared at him, unblinking. "Is *that* what this has been all about?"

"What?" His arms dropped and he looked at her, befuddled.

"This," her arm flew out and gestured around her. "This clinic."

"We talked about this." He lowered the tone of his voice.

"What was I thinking?" Sarah crossed her arms over the book held snug at her chest.

"This is the perfect situation for us."

"No, Michael, it's not! It's perfect for *you*." Sarah's stomach wrenched and she rubbed a hand over her forehead.

"Sarah ..."

"I came here because there was something I wanted to tell you." She waved him off as he reached for her, and pivoted away.

"I love you," he said.

Thousands of little pins prickled her flesh at the sound of his words. Last night, those words sounded so beautiful, uplifting—so refreshing. This morning, however, they fell stale to her ears. "I've wanted to hear those words since I was sixteen."

Confusion etched in his eyes, and his eyebrows drew together. Sarah wanted to scream. Why couldn't she do this? She stomped her foot and stared at him. *Say something. Say anything*!

His silence unnerved her. His eyes sought hers, unspoken questions darting like arrows between them. All he had to do was ask and she would answer. Yet silence dwelled between them until Sarah could take it no longer. "I have to go."

"I thought you had something you wanted to tell me."

She turned on her heel. "Not now."

"Running again, Sarah?"

She spun around and almost dropped the scrapbook along with her composure.

"What's this?" He pulled the book from her hands.

"Give it back!" She grabbed it from him.

"Sarah ..."

"I had something I wanted to tell you. I wanted to show you this, but can't. Not right now." She stomped off—grief and confusion suffocating her. She took quick breaths in an effort to catch her breath. This had gone bad, very bad. *I'm sorry, Lord,* she sniffled. *I'm not strong enough to let go. Help me, please.*

"Sarah." He followed behind her.

"I'm sorry." Her quick strides turned into a flat-out run. In the parking lot, she jerked open the driver's side door and jumped in.

She tossed the book on the seat across from her and banged her head against the back of her seat. *Way to go Sarah*. She closed her eyes for a second. When she looked up again, Michael was only a few steps away.

She slid her key in the ignition. "Come on, Come on."

At the first sound of the engine whine and the familiar "clank," she popped the car into gear, flew out of the parking lot, and left Michael to choke in her dust.

From inside her office, Sarah heard the truck park near the stables. She looked up at the clock on the wall. It was too early yet for the horse to arrive for Michael's clinic. At this time, he should be out on his morning visits, or at least she could hope.

She wasn't quite ready to face him after their last encounter. Maybe it was better if she didn't show him her scrapbook of Ethan. Would any father want to find out he had a son by having a bunch of pictures thrust onto his lap?

She sighed.—the morning wasn't halfway over yet and already she'd managed two strikes against her where Michael was concerned. Nothing worked out the way she thought, everything was a mess, and she didn't have a clue how to fix it. She would have to trust God to get her through this, and trust Him not take away any more loved ones.

Sounds of an idle engine and the slam of a door snapped her out of her slump. "Hello?" Sarah turned the corner from the stable office and came up short. The steel edge of a stock trailer pointed into the stable entrance a hair's breath away.

"Got room for two?" Josh walked out from around the trailer.

"Always." Sarah perched up on her tiptoes attempting to peer inside.

"Shut the doors in the back, and pull the gate across," Josh directed. "This one is a little wild."

"Where did you get him?" Sarah didn't wait for his response. She jogged back the length of the barn, pulled the gate closed, and ran down the other two stable wings to shut those doors too. The barn was empty except for the Morgan, which had bad feet.

"Stand clear," Josh yelled, as he opened the trailer door. The buckskin reared back from the sudden motion as the door swung.

Its eyes rounded with fear—nostrils flaring at the strange new barn scents. Sarah noticed the horse's patchy mane, and deep gashes welted the animal's neck and flanks.

Standing at the edge of the trailer, the horse trembled, and its skin became sleek with sweat.

"We'll have to herd him inside a stall," she called.

"Watch yourself!" Josh yelled, when the terrified beast ripped out of the trailer in a scramble of hooves. It dashed directly towards her.

"A little late!" Sarah glared at Josh. She watched for the horse's next move. The buckskin came to a halt in the center of the walkway. Burrs nestled in the short length of his tail. Sarah couldn't be sure, but suspected he was a stallion. Rippled flesh crawled up the sides of the horse's ribcage. The buckskin tossed his head back and forth while he pawed the dirt.

Sarah stood like a statue.

Josh took a step forward, and the horse's ears flew back. Sarah raised her hand slowly and motioned for Josh to halt.

The buckskin snorted, lowered his head to the ground, and back towards Josh. From inside a stall, the Morgan whined. The buckskin stallion took off, and then skidded to a stop in front of the Morgan's door. A barrage of hooves from the Morgan banged the stall door, and the buckskin attempted to attack through the barrier of wood and bars.

Sarah inched back away from the action, and slid open a stall door at the very end of the barn. The buckskin's head turned in her direction, and she held her breath. Digging in hooves, the horse darted towards her.

"Move!"

Sarah swung into the next stall and slid the door closed. The buckskin sneered at her, and by a split second she avoided its teeth.

Josh stood rigid at the opposite end of the barn. The buckskin sniffed and snorted. It lowered its head to the opening of the doorway beside where Sarah closed herself inside. The buckskin jerked its head and flashed teeth in Sarah's direction. She stepped back from the door.

With cautious steps, the buckskin entered the stall next to her. It snorted and pawed in the doorway, and Sarah jumped back as the horse rammed its shoulder into the partition between the stalls.

Josh ran towards her. Shards of wood and high-pitched squeals erupted and Sarah leapt back. Startled, she cried out as the wall between her and the buckskin bowed towards her. Josh slammed the stall door shut. The buckskin spun around and kicked in every direction. Splinters flew from the walls inside the horse's stall.

Josh leaned over. He clamped his hands on bent knees. "I wouldn't mess with this guy on your own."

Sarah eased her stall door open and stepped out beside him. Inside the stall, the buckskin continued to spin and lash out at the walls in a wild frenzy.

"Where did you get him?" She stepped farther away from the stalls.

"Don't ask." He walked back to the open trailer door, and jumped up inside to release the middle gate. "I brought you another one."

Sarah gasped. Her hands flew up and covered her mouth. Inside laid another horse. She felt light headed. Its front leg was broken, the bone protruded against flesh, and the horse's body was little more than a skeleton with skin. A trickle of blood dripped from the horse's nose.

"We'll have to get Michael," Sarah glanced at her watch. There wasn't enough time.

Josh left the horse lie inside the trailer. "It's probably too late, but if I know you, you'll try anyway."

She already mourned the inevitable loss of this horse. She pushed away the grief—she had to keep her head clear to act fast. This pitiful horse still had a chance if they could find Michael in time. She was torn in three different directions at once—the horse, Michael, and Ethan.

"We have to try." Her gaze remained on the fallen horse—its

breathing shallow. "We can't let it lie here and die!" This was by far the worst condition she'd witnessed any horse.

"It's a horse, Sarah."

"Any life is worth saving."

"You're not always going to be there."

"Speaking from experience?" she shot back at him. Of course, she couldn't save them all, but she could try, couldn't she? She needed to find Michael.

"I deserved that." He readjusted his billed cap and cupped a hand around the back of his neck.

"You could have called," she said, even after she'd told herself she wouldn't be angry.

He slammed the trailer door shut. "I thought you'd understand."

"Is this where you were?" Sarah crossed her arms.

"I brought the horses, didn't I?" He latched the door, then turned and lean against it. "Besides I'm sure Wolfe didn't have any trouble filling my spot." Sarcasm dripped from his voice.

"That's none of your business."

"Listen I'm not arguing with you. I made a choice; obviously you feel I made the wrong one." He shrugged.

Sarah looked again at the trailer, down the walkway towards the last stall, and back at Josh. Another hoof pounded on a petition not far from them. She sighed. "I would have done the same thing."

She shouldn't be this upset, anyway. Maybe if Michael hadn't stirred her up this morning she wouldn't feel the slightest bit hurt. Maybe she should stick with horses instead of men and let God worry about the rest. Yeah, she definitely liked the idea.

"Forgiven?" He ducked his head. He looked at her with apologetic eyes.

"Rain check?" Her mood lightened a bit.

"Sold!" Josh swung his arm like an auctioneer.

Together they laughed.

Sarah checked her watch. "Listen, Josh, I have to pick up Ethan, but the horse—."

"First day?" Josh asked.

"It's been rough." She thought how sappy she'd become as Ethan walked through the front doors of the school. While other parents waved and watched their child walk inside, Sarah had snapped pictures with her camera and called out, "I love you" to her son until the bell rang.

"I'll stop by the clinic."

CHAPTER 22

Michael's cell phone vibrated at his hip. He was up to his elbow in an internal examination. He peeled off his shoulder-length glove and pulled his phone from his pocket. He recognized the clinic's number. However, the text flashed Sarah's number across the screen along with the word, "emergency."

Michael congratulated the ranch owner on the conception of three more foals—due to come this spring and packed up his equipment. He pulled down his dark overalls, worn for farm visits, and kicked off his rubber boots.

His truck rumbled to life with a turn of the key, and he shifted the diesel-dually into gear, leaving the rancher behind. It was possible for Jenny to text him at Sarah's request, but the text message said emergency. One of the horses? Why else would Sarah have Jenny contact him?

He reached over and tapped the folded laptop beside him. He really muddled things up this morning. While she talked one way, he'd assumed another, and they hadn't resolved anything. No matter, he'd straighten it all up when he saw her.

He relaxed his grip on the steering wheel.

Whatever it was Sarah wanted to show him, or was trying to tell him, was important enough for her to seek him out. He'd been so wrapped up in the excitement of sharing the clinic with her, he hadn't noticed the book under her arm until she fumbled and nearly dropped it.

His mind drifted back to the farm, to the mares he'd examined. Each one was bred only a few months. They would come due this spring.

He remembered Jenny's question from the first day she came to work for him. He heard the grind of the truck, felt the shimmy of the front end, and reached for the gearshift. He switched it into third.

There hadn't been anyone else in Sarah's life, except Jenny and Josh. He kept his hand on the gearshift. All this time, he'd assumed the boy belonged to someone else. Yet, the evidence couldn't have been any closer—staring right at him.

The boy was his.

The ebony locks of mussed hair. Blue eyes mirrored his own. Sarah's straight nose. He wasn't blind, but how many times did Sarah come to tell him? How many times did he prevented her doing so?

His chest burned inside. How could he have missed it all this time? It wasn't as if the clues hadn't been there all along. He groaned.

His truck seemed to drive itself into Silver Wind's lane. He'd been so distracted he'd lost track of time and place, and he parked beside the smaller version of his stock trailer. Painted red, with thin strips of white across the sides, the trailer budged little to give a man room to walk inside the doorway of the barn.

Josh spotted Michael and tilted his pitchfork against the door of an empty stall. He tipped the brim of his faded cap back on his head. "I guess you got the message?"

Michael rolled back his shoulders. He should have known Sarah was nowhere about. "What can I do for you?"

Josh ambled towards him and pointed at the trailer door.

Michael flipped up the gate latch and left the door swing open.

"Have a look for yourself." Josh stepped up in the trailer, beside a sprawled-out horse.

"How long has she been like this?" Michael moved closer for a better look.

"Don't rightly know," Josh said.

"There's not much I can do." Michael ran his hands over the horse's caving chest. "She's too far gone."

The horse breathed in short shallow breaths and the fine hairs beneath his hand were stiff like a wire brush. This horse was beyond his help, and there was nothing he could do. *Lord, be merciful.*

"I could put her down." He looked up at Josh. "Might be dead by the time I return with a syringe though." His lips pressed firmly in a flat line. He didn't like taking lives of animals, even if it brought relief from an uncomfortable death, for it was God's place to give life and take it away. Those of the four-legged kind, included.

"Can't save 'em all," Josh shrugged. "Do whatever you think is best." He leaned against the inside of the trailer and crossed his arms.

"This is a real shame." Michael patted the horse's neck and stood. The humane thing to do would be to put this horse down. He watched the mare stretch its muzzle up a notch higher and knew it was too late.

"Sarah will think so." Josh's hand pressed against the rotted plywood lining the inside of his trailer.

"She would," Michael agreed. Sarah wouldn't take kindly to the news that one of her horses wasn't rescuable. Probably the same way he felt right now. When she found out about this, how was it going to impact her decision about his proposal to link the clinic and rescue? She might never want to join forces with him!

"What shall we do with her?" Josh asked.

"Ordinarily glue or some other byproduct they're making these days."

Josh's expression changed in amusement. "Sarah?"

Michael chuckled. "Now there's a tempting thought."

"She's got a habit of sticking to things," Josh said.

"Sometimes it's harder to let go than it is to hold on." Michael wiped his hands down the sides of his pants.

Josh frowned. "Can't hold on to something you never had."

Michael assessed Josh's appearance. Manure splattered his shirt and the hem was torn at the bottom. His jeans were worn and stained. He pushed the cap back on his head, revealing a smear of dirt on his forehead. "You've known Sarah a long time, haven't you?"

"Same as you, only I stuck around."

"Fond of her, are you?" Michael felt the muscles of his jaw work. Was he actually jealous of Josh? No, Sarah saw Josh as a friend, and he admired their friendship. He trusted her.

"You could say that." Josh straightened, widening his stance.

"I would have thought she'd have gotten married by now."

Josh glowered. "You think I haven't offered?"

Michael shrugged. "Seems to me she turned you down."

"She had someone else in mind."

"Ethan's father?" Michael arched a brow.

"What you getting at?"

"Does Sarah know you're in love with her?" Michael crossed his arms, leaning a shoulder against the trailer.

"Yeah—maybe. Well, someday she would have taken me seriously, but then you came along."

"Then it's a good thing I'm not going anywhere." Michael looked back at the horse. He expected it would perish in a few breaths.

Neither man heard Sarah or Ethan walk up beside the trailer.

Josh cleared his throat, "So what do you propose we do about this?"

"Bring your trailer down behind the clinic. We can drag the carcass off down there. I've got a truck stopping by in a few days." Michael stepped back.

Josh pushed the trailer door shut when he was clear.

Ethan darted from around the opening. "Uncle Josh!" He wound his arms around Josh's leg.

"Hey there, Partner, want to ride shotgun?" Josh brushed his hand through Ethan's hair, looking between Michael and Sarah.

"Can I, Mom?" Ethan's eyes, round like a basset hound's, stared up at Sarah.

"You'll have to take Elephant with you." Sarah glanced briefly in Michael's direction.

"Elephant?" Josh's lips twitched.

"Yep," Ethan giggled, pointing at the staggering pup sniffing at the wheel of the trailer.

"Nice name," Josh said, following Ethan over to the trailer wheel for a formal introduction.

"Mike gave him to me."

Josh's eyebrow rose. Ethan picked up the puppy. He held his chin up in an effort to avoid any more attacks from the puppy's sloppy pink tongue.

"You know she's a girl, right?" Michael walked over to scratch the pup on the head, his gaze squarely settled on Sarah.

"We agreed 'Ellie' for short," Sarah said.

"Come on, Squirt, we've got a delivery to make." Josh picked up Ethan with pup in arms and carried them to the cab of the truck.

"Seat belts!" Sarah shouted, and Josh waved his hand.

"Where are they going?" Sarah moved down the walkway, inspecting cleaned stalls.

"You could have asked." Michael stepped over beside her.

"I did. I asked you." So, that was the way it was going to be with her. Always two steps forward and three back when it came to Sarah.

"They're headed to the clinic. I should go. Josh will probably need a hand." Michael didn't move. He wanted to stay near her.

"Trying to steal one of my horses, Dr. Wolfe?" Sarah teased.

He felt the furrow lines of his brow draw together. "Not the way you're thinking."

"So now you know what I'm thinking?" She flashed a flirtatious smile.

He stopped, turned, and grasped her shoulders. "I didn't get here in time, Sarah."

He watched her deep intake of breath. Her eyes filled with lost hope and deep sadness. For a moment, she appeared as though she would cry. "And there was nothing you could do?"

He pulled her into his arms. "It was too late."

She laid her head against his chest and she chewed at the tip of her fingernail. "If only Josh would have brought the horse in sooner, then maybe ..."

"It would have been too late." Michael sighed. He stepped back from her and held her at arm length. "The horse was beyond help when Josh picked it up."

"How do you know? Did he tell you that?"

"He didn't have to."

Her expression hardened. With dark penetrating eyes, she stared up at him. "What did you do?"

For the second time in his life, he felt as if he'd failed her.

"There was nothing I *could* do." Michael gritted his teeth.

She shook her head in disbelief. "I thought you wanted to save horses. Isn't that why you wanted us to join forces?"

"I do, Sarah." He relaxed his hold.

"You're mad about this morning, so now my horses don't matter anymore."

"That's not it, and you know it!" He pushed her away. "There was nothing I could do. The horse was beyond my help when I got here."

Sarah bit her lip and shook her head again.

"I meant it when I said I wanted us to be together. Don't you see, Sarah, that together, we are one?" His voice churned rich with emotion. "We belong together, Sarah; it's all part of the plan."

"What plan? To save the horses?" She laughed, bitterly. "You talk about plans, but you don't want to help save the horses, you want what's best for *your* clinic. When you said you loved me, whose plan was that?"

Michael reached for her and ran his hands down the length of her arms. Her pulse jumped beneath his touch. He interlaced their fingers together. "It's never been about *my* plan Sarah; it's always been about seeking God's plan for our lives."

He lifted her hand, brushed his lips across the knuckles, and then the other in a tender caress.

Sarah's eyes grew watery as she stared at him. She took quick uneven breaths as he spoke. "If I could have done anything to bring the horse back to life, I would have. You know it and I know it. It's all been leading up to this, Sarah. Why else would God choose this place for me to move in and build my clinic? Why else would He bring us back together after all these years?"

Sarah's lip trembled and her chin quivered. A strand of hair caught in the corner of her mouth. Even as he yearned to tuck it back behind her ear, he held on.

"This morning you were trying to tell me something. I should have been listening then, but I'm listening now."

She shook her head—puddles of her tears collected at the edge of her dark lashes. "Why do you always do this to me?"

"I don't know. What am I doing?"

Tears spilled across her cheeks. "You always seem to make me cry, and no matter how hard I try, I can't ever seem to let you go."

He raised one hand to her cheek and rubbed the tears with his thumb. She placed her hand atop his as he leaned in and kissed her, a gentle lingering of their lips, and he felt her tremble in his arms. Hesitantly, he lifted his head. He wanted to memorize this feeling before it ended. Gently he rocked their bodies in a soothing motion as she laid her head against his heart.

Still curious about what she had been trying to tell him, Michael resisted the urge to press her further. He didn't want to shatter this moment.

"How did it go?" Jenny entered the kitchen. Sarah rummaged through the refrigerator, scanning options for supper.

"What?"

Jenny washed her hands to help Sarah. "That great, huh? I assumed this morning, the way you were toting that scrapbook, you were finally going to tell him."

Sarah pulled out a casserole dish. "I planned on it," she sighed.

"But?" Jenny leaned into Sarah.

"Every time I try, something goes and messes it all up."

"What happened?" Jenny turned the oven on to preheat.

"He loves me, Jenny." Sarah hesitated. *Excuses … excuses …* This had gone too far.

"Did he say that?" Jenny's expression went aghast. "You have to tell me everything!"

Together they compiled the makings of a decent meal, while Sarah told Jenny about the night Josh stood her up.

Jenny sighed. "Isn't it amazing how God works wonders in our lives?" Jenny went all dreamy-eyed.

Michael seemed to think God planned for them to be together, but had God put this obstacle between them? Sarah shook her head. Did God know she loved Michael, even after all these years?

Of course, God would know. God knew everything, and she heard those familiar words again. *Trust me …*

"I went to see Michael this morning, to tell him the truth, and it got all blundered." Sarah's shoulders slumped. With a casserole dish on the stove, she laid out thick wide noodles across the bottom of the pan.

"Keep talking," Jenny pulled out a head of lettuce, tomato, and a cucumber for a salad from the refrigerator.

Sarah listened down the hall; she heard Ethan and Josh's voices, and then turned back to Jenny.

"Things got confused between us, and I got mad. I thought he was talking about us, and instead he was talking about that clinic of his." Sarah reached for a bowl and poured its contents over the noodles in her dish. "Do you know Michael asked me if I'd let him join forces with us and combine the clinic with the rescue?"

Jenny's eyes grew wide. "Really? What did you say?"

"At first, I told him I'd have to talk to you and Josh. Then it slipped my mind." She busied herself with setting the dining room table.

Jenny gave her that look, the one that said she didn't believe her. "Slipped your mind, huh?"

"All right, I admit." Sarah confessed. "I kept pushing it back. How was I supposed to know Michael loved me after all this time?"

"The clinic would be a really great asset to the horses." Jenny grabbed a knife from the block and chopped tomatoes while she spoke. "Besides, it would mean all of us working together, in which case you've got my vote." Jenny wrinkled her brows.

"Mine, too," Josh's voice interrupted. Both women simply stared at him.

"I thought you were in the other room." Jenny grumbled.

"The way I see it, Michael's not going anywhere, so better to join up with him rather than try to avoid him, know what I'm saying?" Josh scooped up a piece of lettuce and took a bite. Both Sarah and Jenny continued to stare at him speechless.

Josh shrugged. "Walls can be thin with two women yakking."

"Whose side are you on?" Sarah placed the last dish on the table and sitting down.

"We're on nobody's side, Sarah. We want what is right for you and Ethan. Isn't that right, Josh?" Jenny gave her brother the eye.

"Sure."

"You have to tell him about Ethan, you can't let it go any longer than it already has." Jenny pressed, "He loves you."

"I'm trying." Sarah said. If anything, she owed it to her son, as much as Michael, to tell him the truth. After this morning though, it was a wonder Michael hadn't already figured out her secret on his own. But if he had, why didn't he say anything in the barn this morning?

"Seems a little cold to leave a man hanging," Josh glanced into the living room.

"You're one to talk," Jenny gave him a gentle shove. "Where were you on Sarah's birthday?"

"I had to go out of town." Josh scoffed.

"Ever hear of a phone?" Jenny pressed.

"Lost signal."

"It's done and over," Sarah interrupted. "But, I'll expect something elaborate next year." Her eyes crinkled with sparks of mirth, as their bantering brought her back to the issue at present.

"Back to our Dr. Wolfe." Jenny said.

"It's complicated," Sarah admitted.

Josh snorted. "How complicated can it be? You love him, he loves you."

Jenny rolled her eyes at him.

Sarah pulled at her hair. "I wish it were that simple."

"We can pray about it together if you want," Jenny placed her hand over Sarah's.

"You two do whatever you need to do." Josh rubbed a hand over his jaw. "Holler when the food is ready." He walked off towards the living room.

During supper, the conversation took a turn towards rescue business. Somehow, Sarah would have to find people who could pay the adoption fees for the horses.

Ethan paid little attention to their adult conversation. He ate, and politely excused himself. No matter how determined Sarah was not to speak any further about her relationship with Michael, Jenny dragged it back up. They debated, and Sarah was still not convinced any one option was best where Michael was concerned.

Josh kept silent. He stuffed his mouth with noodles when either woman looked directly towards him.

He retreated to the carriage house soon after the dishes were dried. Jenny withdrew to her bedroom, and Sarah was left to her thoughts. She was still awake when Ethan complained of a tummy ache. She curled her son close and held him through the night.

She prayed, and rocked, and sang, "Jesus loves me" to her son.

CHAPTER 23

The stiff ivory page of stationary crumpled in his fist.

Michael sat in the deep cushions of the loveseat, barely able to draw breath, and his eyes fixated on the smashed letter in his hand.

Words of a desperate teenage mother, marred by blots of dried tears, haunted him. Those were the words of Sarah.

Words he'd always longed to hear, and now he never would.

She'd spoiled them with ink.

He breathed deeply through his nose and exhaled a hissing noise between his teeth. Like a right hand jab to the ribs, her words packed quite a punch. A hot iron on a horse's flanks would have felt better than he did right now. And, so it should, he thought with the irony of it all.

Why hadn't she told him the boy was his?

Instead, he'd found the envelope on the seat of his truck, his name scrolled across in bold black letters. The yellow tinged envelope proclaimed the note's age.

Yet, the letter he read inside the envelope shot a bolt of lightning straight down his spine. How could Sarah have kept this from him?

Michael squeezed his fist tighter, clenched his teeth a little harder, and braced himself to hold back the rush of emotions threatening to break forth from inside. He ground his teeth, feeling his nose burn.

He looked down at the brittle paper.

Ethan, Sarah's son, belonged to him.

Hadn't he already known the boy was his?

He refused to listen to the soft whisper of his heart. The truth as he knew it was clasped tightly in his hand.

A letter.

If only she knew, he thought. If only she'd trusted him enough to seek him in person. However, by the penmanship and sloppy words, he could almost imagine the state she would have been in when writing this to him.

It was over now.

He clenched his jaw so tight, a pain shot down his neck. He threw up his fist and screamed—one long agonized cry that came from deep within his throat.

He didn't feel any better. Only worse.

He thought of his father, his mother, and the announcement of his own birth. His mother never did tell his biological father he existed. It was too late now. Daniel Wolfe died serving his country, and the letter Michael's mother sent came back unopened. At least that is what his mother once told him.

What did it feel like when a man found out his wife carried their first child?

What did it matter now? It didn't apply to him.

He and Sarah weren't married, and he wasn't off in another country fighting a war. He'd been right here, all these months, and she hadn't said a word.

Lord, how did things come to this? He stared at the wad of paper in his hand.

All this time—it was right in front of him the whole time.

The boy's age—his name—Sarah distancing herself from him.

It all made sense, now.

There was other hints too, from Jenny. He was too thickheaded to pick them up. He'd have to give Jenny credit for trying.

That's more than he could say for Sarah.

Yet, he'd simply ignored the clues. He'd been so infatuated with Sarah he hadn't bothered to press hard enough for the answer. *Who was Ethan's father*?

Only days ago, he'd foreseen this coming.

But not like this.

Not the impersonal smudges of ink scrolled across faded lines of a piece of notepaper. Michael supposed he could forgive her because he loved her. And, he could love her because, through God, such love was possible. She'd always been in his heart, that wouldn't ever change.

However, trust was an entirely different issue.

Where there is no trust, there is no love, and that was most painful of all.

Sarah didn't love him enough to trust him with the knowledge of their child.

He buried his face in his hands and wept.

A little while later, when the tremors left his body and he'd no more tears to shed, he looked up.

Sarah stood in the doorway. A pair of faded Levis hugged her hips. Her moss-green blouse split open to reveal the white cotton tank top beneath, and her long twisted strands of hair were pulled back by a piece of ribbon.

He spied the old scrapbook, the same one from days before, tucked under her arm. She shifted her weight.

How long had she been standing there?

"I k-knocked ..." Her lip trembled as her voice trailed off. Her gaze fell to the paper in his hand. A startled look stole over her face as she pulled the book in front of her chest like a shield.

"Please—Michael, you have to understand."

For an instant, he almost felt more sorry for her than himself. Her remorse was probably only because he'd found out. Didn't matter.

"Where's the boy?" He croaked.

Sarah bit her bottom lip until it turned white and took a shaky breath. "School."

The scrapbook slid down her arms and cradled in her hands.

He tensed and waited for an explanation. Of course, he knew that. How easily he'd forgotten that the boy started school.

"When he comes home..."

Her eyes riveted on the crumpled letter in his hand. "I—I was p-planning on p-picking him up." Her eyes pleaded with him, their glazed expression echoed his pain, and he tore his gaze from her.

"Don't, I'll be going that way this afternoon."

Sarah's face blanched. Michael's impatience mounted and twisted his shoulders into knots.

He didn't trust himself not to hurt her, with the heat of his anger pumping into his veins like full octane gasoline. He wanted to burn through and settle the fumes of his emotions later.

And he would have, if Sarah hadn't shown up.

Tears pooled in her eyes as she blinked rapidly. "Michael, please ..."

Her words tortured his soul as much as his head throbbed at the base of his neck. He could no longer contain the storm that built from within. Like a shot of lightening, he flung the crumpled letter across the room. "A letter?"

Frustration surged. He became even more irked that he'd fallen in love with her again, only to find himself stuck in this position. She wasn't any better than his mother, who also claimed she loved him.

"Why? All this time—and you never told me!" He refused to restrain the disapproval in his voice. Each word came out a decibel louder than the first.

Quaking hands fumbled to hold on to the scrapbook dangling at her side. Sarah's lips rolled inward, and tears trickled down her cheeks. She blinked rapidly. "I tried—I tried to tell you." She swallowed. Her voice strangled by the sob, and she cried in a soft voice. "If you'd just let me explain."

Anger welled up inside him and spilled over like an active volcano. He needed to be alone. He wanted nothing whatsoever to do with her at this moment. Never again.

"Get out." He commanded her through clinched teeth.

Sarah jumped, startled like a wild rabbit. Her eyes, huge and filled with tears, stared at him. Her lips parted but no words escaped.

Not only had she lied to him, she'd made him believe there was hope for them as a couple. He stared at her.

She'd caused all this!

He wanted to yell at her and shake her at the same time. How could she have allowed their relationship to get so close—and now this?

His chest ached and his head pounded. Incensed, he released the pent-up anger boiling inside him. "Get out!"

He jerked his gaze away and ground his teeth. Hazel eyes bulged from her paled face. They begged, pleaded with him. One more look into those eyes, he feared his resolve would cave.

Her pained expression mirrored the gut-wrenching feeling inside him. He couldn't bear to look at her again. He'd become lost somewhere in the red fog roiling in his mind.

He clinched his eyes shut to block her out. The truth was, her presence lingered even when he tried to ignore her.

He prepared himself to be the boy's father like Harold was his father. He hadn't expected *this*.

A letter! He drew his own conclusions, and now proof. He was actually the boy's father. *Father*. The word turned bittersweet on his tongue. He felt the urge to laugh. Or vomit.

He was a father.

All these years, he surmised, he had been a father.

What would he have done back then? Any possible action back then was blotted out in his mind by the here and now. The realization stung.

"Please," Sarah begged.

Michael still refused to look at her. "You could have come to me."

"It w-was Gran's idea," Sarah cried. "She—she made me p-promise!"

He shook his head. "Promise?"

Sarah hiccupped. Tears flooded her cheeks.

His head pounded harder. He lowered it slightly to ease the knot winding up at the back of his neck.

"She said you wouldn't c-care about the b-baby."

His eyes startled open. "Wouldn't care?"

Sarah took a step forward, and as she went to speak, he held up his hand. "I t-tried to t-tell you ..."

"Just get out." He said, as he pointed towards the door. An image of his father, Harold Kingsley, lifting him up on a horse for the first time floated across his memory. He saw his mother, her laughter pierced his mind like a siren, and he winced. Why couldn't she have told him?

"We—we can work this out, I know we can."

"I said get out." Michael shot her a lethal look. "I can't bear to look at you." He rose and turned his back to her, no longer able to view her inconsolable face.

"He's my son!" Sarah shouted and sobbed.

Michael whirled around. "He's mine! *My* son! And, he should have my name!"

Her face grew pale, white almost, and she backed away. She dropped the scrapbook on a nearby table and dashed out of the room.

He waited. His chest heaved as he listened for the door to slam, and walked over to where she'd dropped the scrapbook. Not bothering to look inside, he picked it up and threw it.

It hit the wall with a dull thud. Several photographs fluttered to the floor.

Tears stung her eyes, and Sarah swiped at them. Her brisk pace fueled by the flames of rage licking inside her. She wasn't being rational. She needed to find a place to cool down. There was only one place she wanted to go.

So, she ran.

Coward. She should have stood her ground, and made Michael listen, but the fury she saw in his face frightened her. What difference would it have made if she pleaded her case?

Michael held the truth in his hands.

It was her writing, her letter, and by all rights her responsibility to tell him.

Only, where had he gotten the letter?

Out of breath, Sarah came to a halt back at her own place. Her chest expanded to take in large gulps of air as her lungs raced to catch up with her. She placed her hands on her hips and leaned slightly forward and puffed for air.

Lord, why would you let this happen? I was going to tell him!

A flock of geese flew overhead in a V-shaped formation. The trees turned from lush greens to warm golden hues of color in preparation for the seasons to change. A smell of fresh hay drifted across the farm.

She inhaled it all; the fresh scents of what should have been a beautiful autumn morning.

Then, she spotted Josh as he led the little Morgan gelding inside the barn. Sarah's eyelids drooped. Slowly, she straightened. Her pulse sped.

There was only one person who would do this to her. One person who would be so irresponsible and so careless. If anyone would hold a grudge against her, it was Josh. And she didn't have to go far to find him.

Josh looked up from tying the horse to a ring on the wall inside the stable's walkway. He picked a comb out of his back pocket and pulled the steel teeth through the horse's ratty mane. A warm breeze rustled the leaves on the ground outside. The placid Morgan shook a neck full of briars towards him.

"Something caught in your hair need picking?" Josh tossed prickly thorns from the horse's mane into the dirt at his feet.

"How could you?" She walked towards him. She clenched her fists at her sides. He combed the horse's hair.

"He wanted out, Sarah. You can't keep him cooped up all day."

"I was going to tell him. Why did you have to interfere?"

Josh frowned. "I don't know what you are mad about."

He put the comb in a tuft of mane and pulled.

"Michael is picking up Ethan from school." She felt heart palpitations in her chest. Chills prickled her upper arms as her bottom lip quivered.

"You let them hang out any other time." Josh plucked more briars.

"This is different. He knows!" She stood on the other side of the horse, and swore she wouldn't cry anymore.

"It's about time," Josh said.

"About time?"

"And now you've got your panties in a bunch over it." Josh replied, with his eyes focused on his task.

It took every ounce of her strength not to shake him. "Don't you understand? He's taking my son!"

Josh glanced over at her. "The way you've got yourself all wound up, I'd say he's done more than that. He's got you tied in knots."

Josh gritted his teeth as he struggled with a few knots of his own. He pulled on the comb, little by little, as he worked to untangle the briars.

"You don't think this is a knot? You don't think Michael taking my son is something to worry about?"

Josh looked over the horse at Sarah and rested his arms across the animal's back. "Looks to me as if it's out of your hands now."

"Out of my hands?"

"You wanted to tell him, Sarah. Got yourself all googly-eyed over him and now you're running to me over it."

Sarah made an estranged noise in the back of her throat. The Morgan jerked its head away.

"I tried to warn you he would hurt you again. Didn't I?" Josh picked at another briar. "If you think you can run to me every time—well, I'm done."

"Done?"

"Done, as in finished! As in, I've run the race and I'm tired of always coming in second!"

"You caused this!" Sarah accused.

"I'm not the one who got myself in trouble in the first place." Josh attacked the horse's mane with a new vengeance.

Sarah sniffed and nodded.

This was coming back to fall on her. Gran would flip in her grave to see Sarah now. All she ever wanted was to bring this farm back to life, to give Ethan a part of her childhood, and make a future for her son.

Only, she'd been weak.

Gran refused to allow her to send Michael the letter, and she'd obeyed. She didn't want Sarah to be humiliated, and telling Michael wouldn't solve her dilemma, or so Gran said.

Gran was right—it had made it worse.

She could deal with the consequences of her actions alone. Except, she wasn't alone. She saw it now, the blessing of the Anderson twins in her life, and God watching over her.

If it wasn't for getting locked in the stall that night, or if Josh had not found her ... How did Josh find her? Unless he was the one who'd locked her in! Only then would he have known exactly where to find her.

It was Josh who caused her misery!

"It was you! You gave Michael the letter. You locked me in the stall that night all those years ago, knowing I'd get fired. Why would you do this to me?" She rambled.

"Because I didn't." He ground his teeth.

"Then why didn't you get fired like I did?"

"My mother and Mrs. Kingsley are in the same ladies group." Josh's neck turned red.

"You gave Michael the letter. You saw it in my room. You could have found it in the office." She said, calmly. It all made sense to her now.

"I did no such thing." He tossed strands of hair and briars down at his feet. "No matter what you think of me, I wouldn't do that to you."

Sarah glowered. "I don't believe you."

"Believe what you want. I'm tired of covering every one's behind around here." He tossed the comb in a bucket.

"I don't need you to cover anything for me!" Sarah crossed her arms.

"Good!" Josh yanked on the horse's lead.

"Fine!" Sarah turned on her heel. She marched down the walkway and into the office. She kicked the door shut with the bottom of her foot. Alone, she scanned the room for something she could throw, but it was useless.

She gave the door another swift kick, turned, and slumped to the floor in a puddle of despair.

CHAPTER 24

"Push, Sarah, push!"

Sarah screamed as pressure swept across her hips and pain clamped around her midsection. It jolted through her trembling thighs, and sweat tumbled down her forehead. Dr. Alexander sat at the end of the bed, and Jenny stood by her side, holding her hand.

Gran lingered on the opposite side of the bed close enough to watch but not within arm's length, should Sarah have the inclination to reach for her.

She kept her eyes on Jenny. Her friend attempted to smile while the worry in her eyes reflected back to Sarah. Hot streams of sweat rolled down Sarah's face and dripped from her nose. She groaned as she pushed.

"That's a girl," Dr. Alexander said.

A few moments later, Sarah felt the contractions release. She fell back against sterile white sheets. Her thighs quivered as her legs remained in stirrups—like riding a horse bareback while lying down.

A nurse offered Jenny a cool cloth, but Gran yanked it away and dabbed Sarah's flushed face.

"Deep, slow breaths, like we practiced," Jenny encouraged.

"You're doing great."

"I can't do this." Sarah wept, no longer aware of how much time passed since Jenny drove her to the hospital. The pains started gradually, first in her lower back—now intensified. Pressure built again in her pelvic area.

"It's a little too late to quit, Girl." Gran admonished.

Jenny looked up at the monitor beside Sarah's head. "Brace yourself—here comes another one."

Sarah took a deep breath as she bore down and squeezed Jenny's hand.

A moan escaped as her belly tightened and threatened to squeeze the life out of her. A tidal wave of hot searing pain washed across her hips and midsection. She cried out as Gran took hold of her other hand. Together Jenny and Gran helped pull Sarah forward.

A nurse grabbed her wobbly knees, providing extra support.

"There's the head!" The doctor announced.

Sarah sobbed, pushing through the pain. Then suddenly she felt it. Slowly, her body relaxed and she felt the release of the baby she'd kept protected in her womb all those months.

"There he is! I see him!" Jenny exclaimed.

Gran released her grip, and Sarah slumped back until she felt the pillow at her head. She turned her face from the bright lights overhead. Sweat soaked her face and dampened her neck. Dr. Alexander rolled the exam chair back and held the baby up.

She wrestled to prop herself up on her elbows. "It's a boy."

Fresh tears welled in her eyes as she gazed at her son. A sob caught in her throat. Jenny squeezed her shoulder. "He's beautiful, Sarah, just beautiful."

Through the blurriness of her tears, Sarah saw Jenny's eyes were moist too.

A high-pitched wail echoed through the hospital's delivery room.

"That's a good sign. He's a hearty one, that's for sure!" Gran said.

"Would anyone like to cut the cord?" Dr. Alexander cradled

the baby in one arm. A nurse handed him a pair of scissors as he clamped the cord, looking up expectantly at Jenny, then Gran.

"Modern nonsense," huffed Gran.

"If you want, we can let the father come in now." The nurse suggested.

Sarah looked over at Jenny whose face paled and her large green eyes appeared like emeralds in white sand. Sarah squeezed Jenny's hand. "Do you want to go tell Josh?"

Jenny nodded. Hesitant to leave, she clung to Sarah's hand. Sarah put on her brightest smile and slipped her hand from Jenny's. Jenny glanced at Gran, the nurse, then back at Sarah. "I'll be right back."

As Jenny dashed out of the room, Sarah turned her attention to Dr. Alexander. "The baby's father isn't here."

Gran held onto the side rail of Sarah's bed. "Let's get on with it so I can hold that great-grandson of mine."

Sarah nodded and Dr. Alexander cut the cord. He handed Sarah's son to a nurse, holding out a receiving blanket. Once her newborn son was swaddled, Sarah watched as a team of nurses swarmed around her baby. Gran shuffled over to the other side of the room in order to watch.

Dr. Alexander patted her knee. "You're a strong young woman Sarah. You're going to be a great mom."

"Thank you," she whispered. Hearing him say that bruised her heart. Hannah Colvert had been a great mother, too. The best. If only her parents were here to meet their grandson.

She kept her eyes on her baby. A new stream of tears ran down her face. In the midst of her great joy, her thoughts trailed to Michael. He should have been here. It should have been Michael, not Josh pacing outside her door. It should have been Michael to cut their baby's cord, instead of the doctor.

"Got a name picked out for the little guy?"

Again, Sarah glanced over where Gran held her hands out for the baby. The nurse refused, shaking her head. "This little guy goes to his momma first."

Gran's nose wrinkled and her lips tightened.

Sarah held her arms out. The nurse stepped past the doctor and laid Sarah's son into her arms. Chubby cheeks, a square little nose, and lots of thick black hair reminded her of Michael. As the baby opened his eyes and stared up at her, Sarah's breath caught in her throat. They were pale blue. "Like Michael's."

"Michael what?" Gran demanded.

"He has blue eyes." Sarah ran the tip of her finger lightly across the side of her son's face. She kissed his head and breathed in the scents of a new baby, like the air after a summer storm, despite the lingering stench of antiseptics floating through the room.

"All babies have blue eyes." Grace walked over towards Sarah.

Jenny came through the door with Josh.

"Michael is a fine name," Dr. Alexander replied, as if he hadn't paid any attention at all to Sarah, but to his duties.

"That boy is a Colvert," Gran reached to take the baby.

"Michael Ethan Colvert." Sarah held her son close and gazed down upon him. She shifted her hold, pulling the baby out of Gran's reach.

"Well, I suppose you should hand that boy over now, so I can have a look at him."

Jenny and Josh walked over to the opposite side of Sarah's bed from where Gran stood. Sarah looked up at both their beaming faces. At the sound of Gran's impatience, Sarah glanced over, "I want to hold him, Gran, and I'm never going to let go."

"You're all bright-eyed and bushy-tailed this morning." Jenny poured a cup of coffee, holding it out for Michael as he shuffled down the hall. The steaming mug ignored, she gawked at him. He didn't have to look in the mirror to know the tip of his nose was red, and there were dark rims around his bloodshot eyes.

"You alright, Boss?" Jenny followed behind, cradling the hot mug in her hands. "You look awful ... um ... tired. You look tired."

Michael pivoted on his heel into an exam room. He took his

white coat off the hook and slid it on.

"It's regular," she held out the cup again. He held up his hand and shook his head. "You're not coming down with what Miller's got, are you?"

"Don't you have work to do?" he asked.

"I think I can find something to do." Jenny cocked her head. "You might want to tuck in your shirt and comb your hair before you go looking at patients like that." Jenny pointed to the tail of his shirt sticking out.

"Let's just get this over with," Michael said. He pushed his shirt hem down in his black jeans and pulled up on the waist.

"I've been told I'm a good listener. That is, if you want to talk about it."

"Sister, I'd bend your ear half come noon." Michael rolled his shoulders to adjust his lab coat.

"You know where I am if you change your mind." Jenny sat the mug of coffee down on the table.

She waited, watching him with her keen eyes. "The offer is always open," she said, as she left the exam room.

"Minx." Michael grabbed the cup and took a drink. "You probably say that to all the boys." He attempted to grin, but the soreness made him groan.

He really did feel the need to talk to someone, and his father came to mind. He stuck his head out the doorway and looked down the hall as the first appointment strolled in the door. There was always enough time for a phone call, he decided.

"Kingsley Estate."

"Mother?" Michael gripped his cell phone. "What are you doing answering the phone?"

"Michael, darling, how good it is to hear your voice. What do you mean, 'why am I answering the phone?' I live here."

"Where is Jeffery or Marie?" He leaned against the wall inside the exam room.

"I sent Marie to the market, and Jeffery drove her. Sometimes I wonder if anything could get done around here without me."

"Is Dad around?" Michael hoped the hitch in his voice wasn't evident.

"No, darling, he's at the Jockey Club today for a meeting."

Michael paused. He needed to ask his father a question. His gut gnawed at him. His mother would have to do, for now. He looked up at the ceiling, praying God would give him insight.

"I need to ask you a question." He could visualize her unclipping an earring to rest the phone more securely against her ear.

"Of course darling, what is it?"

He took a deep breath, releasing it slow through his nose. "You once told me that right before I was born you wrote a letter to my father, my biological father. Do you know if he ever got to read that letter?" There was a crackle of static in the line.

"Oh, Michael, that was so long ago. Why bring it up now?"

"It's important. Please. I'd like to know." His gaze moved around the room as he waited for her answer. He felt the coffee he drank earlier slosh in his stomach.

"No, darling, I don't suppose he ever did."

Time held in place with the crackle of the phone.

"Is it that girl who has you asking questions? What has she done now?"

"I have a son, Mother, *Sarah and I* have a son." Michael pinched the bridge of his nose. The phone crackled and cut off in the middle of his mother's proclamation of a response. He was relieved not to hear it all.

"After all I did to keep that dreadful girl away from you! When is the baby due? There are ways ..."

"He's five, and what do you mean by keeping Sarah away from me?"

"I have eyes and ears all over this place, darling, I know what my children are up to, and in your case, under." She laughed.

"You didn't seem to think so badly of Drew's date at the gala." Michael reminded her.

"Andrew's date is the daughter of the Mayor's cousin."

His lips formed a thin straight line. "What did you do to Sarah?"

"I simply fired the girl and sent her away. You were young,

you could have gotten in a lot of trouble, and you hadn't finished college yet."

"You set her up so father wouldn't ask questions." Michael felt ashes reignite in blazing anger. His own mother betrayed him.

"I only had your best interest at heart." He heard his mother sigh. "Sometimes, it's best, darling, for a child to be raised with a different father: Look at you and Harold. Daniel would have never been the father Harold was to you."

"I never got a chance to know. I've missed all these years with my own son," he rasped.

"Trust me, darling, it was a blessing the day Daniel Wolfe didn't come back from the war." She paused. He heard the static in the phone increase and he barely made out the words, "For both of us."

He lost her then, when her words became jumbled in the mix of crackle and dead air. Michael snapped the phone closed and stuffed it back into his pocket.

His mother tried to protect him, first from a father he never knew, and second from a career he'd surely have given up if he'd known. Everyone, including Sarah, had good intentions for him, but when did he have a say in all this?

He closed his eyes in prayer. Holding out his hands, he offered everything he had to the Lord—his son, Sarah, this clinic—if God would direct him to the path he needed to take.

Jenny tapped on the doorway. Michael's praying hands drooped as he opened his eyes. "Don't blame Sarah, this isn't her fault."

"Eavesdropping?" he looked over his shoulder at her.

"I think everyone in the clinic heard you. But don't worry—they won't tell. Dogs only bark and Mrs. Beck is hard of hearing."

A knowing settled deep inside him. He looked at Jenny. "You've known all along."

"Forgive us for our trespasses as we forgive those who have trespassed against us," she said.

So be it, he thought, for Jenny to quote scripture to him. But for some reason, this time those words held no effect on him.

"It's not about forgiveness, it's about trust."

He cupped the back of his neck with his hands. Why would he even bother to stand here and talk to one of Sarah's friends? *Because she was willing to listen.*

Yet the question remained in his heart—how would he ever be able to have a relationship with Sarah, if he couldn't trust her?

For the sake of his son, he had no other choice.

"Sarah trusted you. She gave you something precious, and you broke her heart. Are you saying you can't forgive her when she's forgiven you?"

A mental image of Sarah pregnant as a teenager and struggling to raise Ethan became more vivid of a picture to him than before. He saw now the blessing Jenny and Josh had become in Sarah's life where he'd been absent. "I didn't say that."

Jenny sighed, as if she were about say something out of strict confidence. She looked around the room and made sure they were alone.

"She pined for you, even after Ethan was born. She held on to this crazy hope you'd come looking for her—but you didn't, and Sarah accepted it."

"She did?" Michael asked, stupefied.

"She went so far as to go behind Grace's back one night in order to stand on your door step, but you weren't there."

"So she wrote a letter." Michael realized how much he'd misjudged Sarah's attempts to tell him the truth.

Jenny reached out and touched his arm. "Forgive and you will be forgiven. Isn't that what you want? To be with Sarah?"

"What I want doesn't matter." His throat felt tight. He couldn't deny his disappointed in the manner in which he'd discovered he had a son. Any other way, he thought, things might have turned out different.

A sense of grief came over him.

"That's what Sarah said. She had to give up everything she had in order to keep hold of Ethan." Jenny walked out of the room, tossing a folder at him on her way out.

Sarah stood outside Michael's door, looking in through the pane glass window. Soft light spilled out and splashed across the small backpack she clutched to her bosom.

From inside she heard Ethan's laughter. Her heart cast downward. Her eyes fell to the backpack containing everything Ethan would need to spend the night with Michael.

For a moment, she shied away from the light.

Trust me …

That inner voice whispered in her ear all afternoon.

Open his eyes Lord. Help him understand.

She raised her hand to knock, hesitant she was doing the right thing. God would not have put it in her heart otherwise. She sighed.

The clinic closed hours ago, and Jenny offered to make her favorite, lasagna, for supper. However, Sarah lost her appetite. The only thing she was hungry for was to see her son. She walked through the quiet house all afternoon in anticipation of hearing his voice and praying once Ethan knew the truth that he, too, would forgive her.

Finally, she mustered up enough courage and knocked.

"Hey, Mom!" Ethan flung the door open.

"Sarah," Michael walked up behind Ethan and placed his hand on her son's shoulder.

She swallowed past the sudden lump in her throat. "I—it was getting late."

"I would have brought him home after supper."

Ethan exchanged glances between them.

Her motherly instincts screamed for her to grab Ethan and run. However, God's hands on her shoulders held her in place. She had nowhere to run. She hitched her shoulders back and her spine stiffened.

Ethan was the first to break the stretched silence. "Come on, Mom." He grabbed her hand. "We made fried chicken."

He tugged her through the doorway.

"I—I don't think that would be wise." She stammered. The ice-glazed chill she received from Michael's eyes made her shiver. "I didn't mean to interrupt."

"Didn't you?" he asked. He stood, feet apart, with his arms crossed. Ethan looked up at Michael, with narrow eyes.

Sarah had not come to pick a fight with him. She'd hoped in the hours they'd been apart that he'd simmered as she had. He apparently needed more time.

She wrung her hands around the straps of Ethan's backpack.

Let go …

"I brought your bag." She held up the pack as she fought to maintain a calm composure. "I thought you would need fresh clothes for the morning. Your toothbrush is in there, and your blanket."

She was near her breaking point. She refused to cry. There was no sense in crying over spilled beans, as Gran would have said. She would have to pick them up one at a time until the jar was full again.

"Does this mean I'm staying the night?" Ethan looked up at Michael, then at Sarah. His little face beamed with anticipation.

Sarah lifted her eyes to Michael. Their icy glare melted.

"I'll pick you up in the morning and take you to school," Sarah said. Ethan's eager face crushed her resolve. She bent over and kissed him on the forehead, then turned to leave.

"Why don't you stay for supper?" Michael blurted.

Sarah turned back and looked at him.

"Yeah, Mom. Come on, let's eat."

"We have plenty."

Although she wasn't hungry, Sarah nodded. "Alright."

As they sat down and ate in the dining room, plain beige walls mocked her.

Ethan chewed his chicken, chattering a mile a minute about school. "Bobby in my class, his dad picks him up after school. His parents don't live together."

"Not all parents do."

"Oh, I know. Maya—she don't have a dad." Ethan frowned,

"Kind of like me, huh Mom?"

Sarah paused in mid-bite of the mashed potatoes Michael pushed in front of her—she had to force herself to swallow.

All eyes were on her. "You have a father, Ethan."

"Yeah, Mrs. Miller at Sunday School says we all got a father in heaven. Isn't that right, Mom?" Ethan was trying so very hard to impress Michael. Sarah's heart swelled with pride. Her son cared a lot about this man, who was his father. This was harder than she expected.

Michael turned the conversation away from the subject of fathers, which relieved Sarah. It wasn't the right time to pop the fact that Michael was Ethan's father. Ethan would need time to adjust. They *all* needed time.

"Thank you," Michael told her when she saw Ethan snuggled securely in Michael's bed for the night. He would probably fix up the guest room now for when Ethan came to stay. It was funny how after the storm of rage blew over, the shower of wisdom rained down. However, little comfort came to her as she walked back home alone, knowing Ethan was across the road in someone else's home.

"Keep him safe, and warm, and happy," she prayed, as she walked down the lane to the old stone house. She chided herself. Ethan was only spending the night. Michael wouldn't take off with him—she warded off the fear. She would have to learn to share her son with someone else. Hadn't God shared His only son? Then she could share Ethan with Michael.

Above her, the stars in the sky brought loneliness to walk as her companion. "So this is the path I have chosen."

CHAPTER 25

Sarah walked across the bridge with Ellie running circles at her feet. Indian summer brought beauty to the farm. The leaves changed to golden yellow, chocolate browns, apple reds, and burnt orange.

Autumn was Sarah's favorite season. There was so much color to drown out the everlasting greens of spring and summer, and the bright new colors of the season signaled change.

Jenny grinned when Sarah entered the clinic. Ellie raced around the waiting area. There was only one man with his large Dalmatian sitting on a nearby bench. The Dalmatian tried to ignore the yipping little puppy at its heels, but soon became interested in the bitty beast. The owner pulled up a tight leash.

"Michael and Ethan got back a little while ago. They're upstairs grabbing lunch," Jenny said.

Sarah snapped her fingers at the obnoxious pup, but the command went ignored.

"You can go on up if you want, I'm sure he won't mind." Jenny waved her hand towards the hallway which led to the rear entrance of Michael's home.

"I'll wait." She stomped a foot at the pup, and the young Beagle barked at her. Sooner or later someone was going to have to teach that dog some obedience. It wasn't going to be her. It wasn't her idea to have a dog in the first place.

Then she felt a slow grin spread across her lips. Michael would have to deal with it. The last thing she needed right now was a pesky pup that wasn't even house-trained.

"He shouldn't be too long, his first appointment is scheduled in about ten minutes, and you can see the patient's already here." Jenny tapped her pen towards the man with the dog. "Sarah."

"Don't," Sarah held up her hand. "What's done is done." Since Michael found out about Ethan, she felt his withdrawal from her. For the past week, he picked up Ethan after school and brought him home after supper.

Each night she tucked Ethan into his bed. On Friday, Ethan stayed over with Michael and this morning Ethan accompanied Michael on his morning rounds. However, Ethan didn't question the change in routine.

She supposed the next step would be to tell Ethan the truth.

She was baffled Michael hadn't told Ethan by now.

She imagined there would be questions. She could see Ethan upset, perhaps even angry with her when he found out Michael was his father.

Would he still love her? Did a five-year-old boy even know about hate? Now that he started school, she was sure he did.

It didn't make her heart ache any less or bring her any peace of mind where the situation was concerned. She'd laid her son into the hands of God, to let Him worry—she trusted someday Ethan, and Michael, would both understand.

Maybe even forgive her.

"Oh, I wanted to show you something." Jenny smiled and squeezed her arm.

"What's that?" Sarah asked.

Jenny punched a few keys across the keyboard of her laptop.

Sarah came closer and peered down at the laptop's screen.

A slow grin spread across Jenny's face as she turned the screen in Sarah's direct view. As the website loaded, Sarah's anxious heart stilled.

Word by word, Sarah read the page's title, *Silver Wind Equine Rescue*. A photo of the sign Josh constructed appeared, and as Jenny scrolled down a bit further Sarah stood speechless.

Jenny continued to grin. She clicked from page to page, displaying contact information and photographs of their current adoptee selection.

"You did all this?"

"It was Michael's idea," Jenny said.

Sarah leaned against Jenny's desk. "Michael?"

"Yeah. You don't think I could do this all on my own did you?"

Sarah shrugged. Jenny had been the one to go to college, and passed up a job working at the CPA firm with her father in order to move in with Sarah.

But Michael? She shook her head, peering again at the website.

"How did you ever get all this done?"

"I provided the photographs. The company that put the clinic website together provided the layout. They're linked—see?" Jenny clicked again on a link in the sidebar and a page for Wolfe's Equine Clinic appeared.

Sarah looked down the hallway at the sound of Ellie's bark. She spied movement down the hall and heard Ethan's voice.

So this was what Michael had been up to. One more attempt to seal the deal of their partnership.

That was ... if Michael hadn't changed his mind.

"He probably figured it was okay to link the clinic with the rescue after all he's done to help keep the place going and all. You did say he wanted to join forces—and it's okay, right?"

Sarah blinked. "Help with the rescue?"

"If it wasn't for Michael we'd still have a leaky roof and the horses ..."

"Roof?" Sarah nearly choked on the word.

She heard the Dalmatian bark, the sound echoed in her mind like a drafty hallway. *Michael fixed the roof?* She clamped on to the edge of Jenny's desk as the room spun in slow swirling circles. She closed her eyes as she fought against the urge to be ill.

Michael?

She gripped her stomach unsure which made her more ill—knowing Michael had been the one to do all those things or the fact that Josh hadn't ever denied her assumptions.

"I guess you didn't know, huh?" Jenny placed her hand on Sarah's arm. Sarah looked up, feeling as queasy as Jenny's expression.

Sarah shook her head.

"Are you going to be okay?" Jenny asked, eyes filled with compassion.

After exhaling, Sarah said, "I thought it was Josh."

"Josh?" Jenny snorted and laughed. "Haven't you realized by now that while my twin brother's heart may be in the right place, he's not exactly Mr. Reliable?"

"But the feed bills …"

Jenny lifted an eyebrow.

Sarah's heart sank. Twice now, she'd wronged Michael. She felt herself go weak in the knees. *Oh Lord, how will he ever forgive me?*

Jenny nudged her. "Here he comes."

Sarah pulled herself together and forced herself to smile despite the sinking feeling in the pit of her stomach. "You knew this all along and never told me."

"Like I told Michael, it wasn't my place to interfere." Jenny slid the laptop back in front of her on the desk and closed down the website.

Before Sarah could question Jenny about her remark, Ellie bounded down the hall with tongue wagging and ears flopping. She spotted Ethan as he stooped down to wrestle the chubby pup into his arms. Ellie licked and whimpered in greeting.

"Hey, Mom!" Ethan held up his hand to shield his face from any more of the pup's lapping tongue lashes.

"Ready to go?" she asked, anxious to leave.

Michael walked up behind Ethan and ruffled his hair.

Ethan gazed up at him and heaved the dog higher in his arms.

"She missed me."

"So I see." But Michael wasn't looking at the pup. Instead, his gaze was on Sarah. For a split second, her heart skipped a beat. His eyes cast upon her as if he stared at stranger.

She held her head high and glared back. She wouldn't allow him to make her feel insignificant with Ethan present. He let his hand slip away from the boy. "I'll see you tomorrow," he told Ethan.

"Tomorrow?" Sarah asked.

"Michael's gonna go to church with us," Ethan said.

"Oh." She bit her bottom lip and glanced over at Jenny.

"I invited him," Ethan said.

"How nice." Sarah wrapped her arm around Ethan's shoulder.

Jenny smiled as sweet as molasses pie.

"We better get going so Michael can work," Sarah said.

"I'll see you tomorrow, Sport." Michael patted him on the shoulder and brushed past Sarah to grab the chart from Jenny's desk.

Jenny's green eyes rounded on him after Sarah and Ethan departed. She waited until his next appointment was in the exam room. Michael reached out his hand for a folder, but Jenny stood and stared at him.

"What?" he asked.

Jenny shook her head and tossed the folder at him.

Sarah blew a piece of hair away from her face and bent at her task. The thick wisp of hair tumbled back down. She leaned the rake against the wall. She reached back to adjust her ponytail. She checked her watch. It would be another hour until Jenny came to help with the barn work. Josh ran off to haul another man's horse, but she had to admit his cash donations had dwindled.

She tried each month to spread her finances further, but the monthly sum she received from her inheritance barely got them by without providing for the horses. Her parents meant well, setting up the trust and disbursing it in monthly sums until she was twenty-five. Otherwise, she would have bought every horse she came by after Gran died.

Without Michael, her anonymous contributor, she wouldn't have made it this far.

"Like this, Mom?" Ethan called.

Sarah looked up from inside the stall. Ethan tugged the large rope-handled tub of sawdust in her direction. For some reason, Josh borrowed the wheelbarrow for his ventures the past few days.

"Yep, here let me help." She dusted off her jeans. A small rip frayed across one knee and each stress point at her hips showed white against dull blue.

"Here, let me."

Sarah's head jerked in the direction of the voice. "Mr. Kingsley." Suddenly her stomach turned queasy. What was *he* doing here?

"Harold." The lines of his face wrinkled with a smile.

"Mom?" Ethan looked at her questioningly.

"It's alright. Mr. Kingsley, Harold, is Michael's father." Sarah watched the expression on Ethan's face transform from bewilderment to a large smile spread across his face.

"Here, Boy, you grab one end and I'll grab the other." He reached for the rope handle, working with Ethan to carry the sawdust.

"Where do you want this?" he turned his attention towards Sarah.

"Oh." Sarah blinked. "Um, right here." She pointed inside the stall behind her, and stared at him in his dark blue denim jeans and pointy-toed black boots. A black Stetson rested on his head. She stepped back and bumped into the rake. It flew up, hitting her in the back of the head with the pole end. Her hand grabbed back of her head, and she groaned. Bright specks of light blurred her vision.

"Are you all right?" Harold asked. He grabbed the rake before it fell off to the side. Sarah nodded. She couldn't find words—her brain dulled by the pain-filled haze.

"Here we go." He handed the rake over to Ethan when Sarah turned away. "You better spread this for your mom."

"Yes, Sir." Ethan pulled the rake through the remains of Sarah's work. Harold tipped the tub and dumped the sawdust before he took Sarah by the elbow and escorted her out into the walkway.

"Are you sure you're okay?"

"Yes." She sniffed back tears. "I'm going to have a headache later." She tried to smile despite the pain at the base of her head.

"If you're looking for Michael, his clinic is across the road." Sarah rubbed the back of her head and winced.

"Actually, I came to see you." He looked at her in good humor.

"Me?" Sarah squeaked. "I mean, really?"

He laughed. "Michael told me what you're doing here, and I'd like to help."

She didn't know what to say. Harold Kingsley was standing in her barn offering to help her, help the horses, and her eyes went wide. "By the looks of things, I'd say you could use some."

"That's really kind of you, Mr. Kingsley, but ..."

"Harold."

"Harold, but I think we'll be just fine. Jenny will be over soon to help, and Josh pitches in when he can. I don't see ..."

Harold laid a hand on her shoulder. "I didn't come to clean your stalls, Sarah."

She smoothed her hands down her hips. "Oh." She glanced over, watching the end of the rake poke out the stall entrance as Ethan spread sawdust.

"As I said, I'd like to help you. I have connections; you never know if a few phone calls here and there could be helpful." He reached in his back pocket to pull out a check. "I hope it's tax-deductible." He held out the check to her.

Sarah eyed the check. "Why are you doing this?" she looked

up from the check in his hand.

"I noticed the name of the farm as I came in, Silver Wind. Your mother's horse. She would have liked that." Sarah gulped down the lump of grief rising in her throat at the mention of her mother.

"I sold your father that horse as a foal, did you know that?"

Sarah shook her head.

"I did. When your father gave your mother the horse as a wedding gift, I was there standing right beside him as best man. When Hannah rode for the first time at Lexington, I was there, too." His eyes grew watery. "We were best friends, your father and I."

Sarah remembered the beautiful dapple gray thoroughbred her mother cherished, and it brought a smile to her face. That horse and her mother reached levels of profound recognition all over the nation. At one time, her father hired a German trainer to come and work with her mom. The same year Sarah learned to ride. She dried her tears on the sleeve of her worn chambray shirt.

"They never mentioned it," she said.

"No, I suppose they wouldn't." He frowned—pensive. "We were young then, about your age."

"What happened?" Sarah wanted to know.

"Let's just say our lives went in different directions. My family raised race horses."

"And my family jumped fences."

"We became mere acquaintances in public. Each year your family was invited to the annual gala, but only a few times did Robert and Hannah accept. I think deep down Robert wanted to remain friends as I did, but then I'd gotten married and until you showed up on the estate, I hadn't heard from your family since."

"My grandmother called you, didn't she?"

"We'd been friends since our first day at church camp." He grinned. "I'd have done anything for Robert and Hannah, including taking you in after their deaths."

Sarah's chest tightened. "So that's why she sold the horses ..." Sarah muttered. "She wasn't planning on me coming back."

Sarah felt her arms chill. If Mrs. Kingsley would have never sent her away ... would she have stayed?

"We only agreed on that summer, Sarah." Harold laid his hand on her shoulder. "You were all she had left."

Like Ethan. She felt her hands tremble. Only now she had Jenny and Josh, and perhaps for a time she'd even had Michael. They'd become her family. God hadn't left her alone, after all. *Thank You, Father God, for watching over me and blessing me with a family of Your making. Even while my heart was filled with yesterday's sorrows, You found a way to call me home.*

"Here, take the check." Harold reached out and placed the check in her hand. He closed her fingers around it, holding her hand with both of his.

"What now?" Ethan came out of the stall trailing the rake behind him.

"Oh, um," Sarah scanned quickly in her mind a list of things her son could do to keep him occupied. She looked from Ethan to the check enclosed in her hand and back at Harold.

"How about filling the tub back up again for me? Then come tell me so I can help you with it." She took the rake from him with her free hand.

"No problem." Ethan raced to the stall. A moment later, he dragged the dark green tub down the walkway towards the entrance.

"That's a fine boy you've got there." Harold kept his hand over hers.

"You're very kind."

"Does Michael know?" Harold tilted his head and watched her.

"Yes," the words came out like a hiss, and she pulled back her hand.

"Michael's a good man, Sarah. He'll do the right thing. I didn't bring him up to do otherwise." Harold followed as she walked towards the entrance.

"I believe he's doing that," she said. The stone, which was her heart, sank. The tension between her and Michael grew heavier each time she encountered him. At church he was polite, but she noticed how he slid to the opposite end of the pew during service with Ethan tucked beside him.

"Things don't always turn out the way we want them, do they?" Harold looked straight out the doorway.

"No, they don't, but who are we to decide the future?" She blanched. The old Sarah would never have said it, or believed it. But now Sarah knew she could put her trust in God to direct her towards the right path. She prayed for Michael to find the same, even if it involved her in his life as nothing more than the mother of his son.

"There's a Bible verse." Harold stopped at the doorway and stared out at the farm's landscape. "Trust in the Lord with all your heart and lean not on your own understanding; in all your ways acknowledge him, and he will make your paths straight."

He cleared his throat. "Well, I'd best be heading out now." He tipped his hat as he walked out into the lazy light of the autumn sun, in the direction of a white Cadillac parked in her driveway.

Sarah looked down at the check folded in her hand. Carefully she unfolded it. Her head shot up, but he was already driving across the old stone bridge.

CHAPTER 26

Pain trickled down between his shoulder blades. Michael rolled back his shoulders, inclined his neck to the left, and winced. He touched the small of his back and groaned. He couldn't seem to escape the pain of having tossed and turned sleeplessly throughout the night.

Laptop under his arm he trudged inside the clinic. The bell rang loud in his ears. He wondered now if installing it had been a good idea. He sighed. The waiting area was empty. Jenny walked down the hallway and rubbed her hands together. Her fingernails were pearl white, and her shaggy orange hair tapered down from its usual jag. She noticed him and grinned as she pulled down the hem of her white blouse.

"Hey Boss, you're back early." She held out her hands, palm up, and extended them towards him. He dumped the laptop into her arms with a grunt.

"Miller left an hour ago." She moved to her desk. "He won't be in tomorrow." She sat the laptop down and proceeded to boot up the machine. "Davis called; his cow had twins last night."

Michael rolled back his shoulders. "Is that all?"

Jenny sat back in her chair. "I've got your schedule set up for tomorrow, and I routed your trip for Tuesday like you asked."

Michael nodded. "Fine." He waved his hand and headed towards the hallway.

Jenny called out, "Oh, yeah, I almost forgot. You've got company upstairs."

He turned around to look at her and Jenny's grin split wide open.

Michael climbed the stairs to his apartment. Great! All he needed right now was company to add to his discomfort. What he wanted was a few hours of peace and quiet, but as long as Sarah appeared in his thoughts, he wouldn't find any.

He could only think of one person who'd be upstairs.

She wasn't there.

His father looked up from reading the morning paper at the kitchen table. Pulling open the fridge, Michael grabbed a bottle of water, but his father held up his hand at the offer.

"Nice place you got here." Harold folded up the paper in neat sections, as Michael rummaged through a cabinet by the sink.

"Rough day?" Harold asked, and Michael's shoulders slumped. His hair was mussed from random finger combing, and a dull pain spread in his left eye. He felt it twitch.

"Since six," Michael admitted with a grimace.

"Clinic looks good."

Michael twisted off the top of the bottle of aspirin.

"You've seen it already?"

"You could say I helped myself to a tour." Harold leaned forward on his elbows, as Michael tapped out a few pills and swallowed them with a gulp of water.

"Secretary seems like a real nice girl."

Michael turned and leaned against the counter. "Carrot top." He winced. "Jenny. Yeah she's really something."

"Lives over with Sarah." His father laughed at his expression. "Girl's a chatterbox."

Michael reached back over to open the fridge. "How about supper?"

"What are you offering?"

"Some of Mrs. Grayson's homemade vegetable soup." Michael

pulled out the jar and held it up for inspection.

"Is that what you feed the boy when he's over?"

Michael fumbled with the jar on the counter. "You've seen him?"

"He's a fine-looking boy. Got your eyes."

Michael pulled out two bowls from under the cupboard. "So, Mother told you?"

"It would take a fool not to see the resemblance."

Michael jerked. "When? When did you see him?" The bowls clattered in his hands.

"Oh, when you weren't here. I moseyed over to the rescue. A little run down from what I remember the place, but looks like the girl's trying real hard to put things together. I can see now why you offered to help."

Michael filled the two bowls and put them inside the microwave on the counter, then pressed a few buttons for the soup to heat.

"She doesn't want my help." Michael looked his father straight in the eye. "She lied to me."

"Did she?" Harold turned towards Michael. "Or was it because she didn't come out and tell you the truth right away?"

Michael sighed. "She probably tried, more than once, but I was too wrapped up in seeing her again and getting the clinic started that I didn't pay more attention."

"You've been dealing with a lot lately." His father leaned back in his chair and crossed his legs.

"Stupid of me, I know, but why did it have to be a *letter*? Why couldn't she *tell* me?" Michael slammed his fist on the counter.

"I'm sure she had her reasons for doing what she did. Putting her heart out on her sleeve is harder in writing, don't you think?" He stood beside Michael.

"You almost sound as if you're on her side."

"You love this girl," Harold said. "There are no 'sides' in matters of the heart, only truth."

"I would have accepted him even not knowing he was mine. When I got that letter …" Michael looked at his father. "I don't know what's worse, knowing I'll forgive her or feeling like I should go crawling on hands and knees and asking her to do the same."

Harold put his hand on Michael's shoulder. "I think you already know what you need to do, Son." He headed for the door.

"You're leaving?" Michael frowned.

"Eat your soup, get some rest. You look beat."

Michael watched his father walk out the door, and the microwave buzzed as the door closed.

After a long trip to Lexington, Michael was relieved to be back at his clinic. He met with several ranchers and horse farmers to schedule arrivals at the new equine part of the clinic. By the end of fall, he, too, would have his barn filled. That accomplishment put a bounce in his step this morning. Sarah wasn't the only one on a mission.

The day ahead of him filled with routine visits. October brought more demand than usual for vaccinations at larger farms. So he packed his gear into the truck, hoping to stay on schedule.

He caught a glimpse of Sarah across the road. He walked a few feet from his truck and squinted. He couldn't make out what she carried. As he drove down the road, he spotted Ethan curled up in his mother's arms. Michael frowned.

Normally, Sarah got up at the break of dawn, tended the horses and left Ethan to sleep in the house with Jenny. Sarah must have gotten him up, since Jenny was gone for the weekend. It was odd for her to head towards the barn this late. Now that he thought about it, the horses' feed pans were empty when he went for his morning ride.

He shrugged off the feeling of insecurity. What did *he* care if Sarah went to the barn at five in the morning or at ten? What he didn't care about, however, was giving Jenny the day off to visit her mother and to help with their church bake sale. He swore Jenny was like the wind these days. She only stayed planted at the clinic for office hours, and when the clock struck the appointed hour of her departure, she was gone. Old Doc Miller even commented on her lack of concentration. He would need to speak to her about it, maybe one day this week.

The distraction of the work crew disappeared when the barn was finished, but Jenny's attention span evaporated with the crew. Not that her boy, Brad, had anything to do with it. Michael flipped open his laptop, keeping the wheel steady with one hand. Jenny mapped out his farm visits in order from the farthest stop to the closest en route to the clinic, with no backtracks or loops. The girl was a genius when it came to computers. She saved him a few hours of travel time and frustration each morning. At least, she remembered to do that before she took off for the day.

If he made it back early, he could take on some of the chores in the barn to help Sarah. Or maybe he would take Ethan over to his place and spend time getting to know his son better. His felt as if his hands were tied around Sarah, each finger tangled in everything she touched—including the rescue.

Many of the horses improved health-wise, but with only Sarah to nurture them, it would take longer for them to settle and train. Her right-hand man, Josh, seemed high on fuel and low on octane these days, but Josh wasn't the only one crawling through the holes of Sarah's web.

It didn't take long for her to trap him.

Michael didn't like seeing the pain in Sarah's eyes when she came to pick up Ethan in the morning, and his gut reaction was to reach out to her. He got irate every time he thought of her letter. It was a moment like this which caused him to doubt his faith. Though he knew God's love would never leave him, Sarah's deception stung him.

He could forgive Sarah. It wasn't easy to forget she hid his son from him all these years. He'd missed first moments in his son's life. The scrapbook she left at his house—proof of all the growth-points he missed. He poured over the pictures of Ethan as a squalling infant, a chubby toddler, even as he is today, standing tall beside his mother—a bond he couldn't break. He didn't actually want to break it, but his heart ached. He regretted not being a part of each step—yearned to have been a family.

He didn't know which frustrated him more, knowing Jenny was right, or having his father confirm it. One of these days that girl would be wrong, and heaven help him, he didn't want to be the one to clue her in on it. He'd let God handle it.

For many nights, he lay awake wrestling with his feelings—pinned down in a cold sweat. After becoming wrapped up in a tangled mess of blankets and sheets, he finally gave in.

No matter how hard he tried, his thoughts always returned to Sarah. No matter where he went, he saw her face. It was funny how God used people to send His message when His children weren't listening.

Michael's morning appointments passed swiftly. At lunch he stopped in town at the Café on Main Street, and by afternoon found himself at the Calhoun's. Their prize racehorse wasn't eating and continued to lose weight. He gave them the name of an equine dentist before he got called away to an emergency at another farm.

It was past dark before he parked the truck at the clinic. A few lights shone over at Sarah's place. He gazed up his own front steps, and trudged up them one by one. He shut the door in the upstairs apartment and found the sofa. He closed his eyes as soon as his head hit the cushion.

Sarah hummed while she rocked; her arms cradled the large bundle wrapped in a small quilt. Ethan's head lay hot against her shoulder, and the puppy lay by her feet. She kissed Ethan's forehead. Warm to the touch, Ethan moaned in her arms. All day he'd wanted to be held or cuddled. He was getting almost too big to do so with ease, but she managed.

She continued to hum and rock. Ethan's eyes fluttered open and watched her. Sarah held him tighter. It's a fever. They always get worse at night, but that didn't reassure her.

Ethan was burning up, hotter than before.

At some point, she'd fallen asleep. Then at a quarter past midnight, she awoke to Ethan's whimpering cries. The vomit came next. She checked his temperature, and didn't need to call the pediatrician to know it was time to take him to the hospital.

Her heart took off, beating like a set of butterfly wings.

Sarah gathered him in her arms and grabbed her bag. She stumbled off the front porch and carried him to the car.

Comfortably situated in his seat, Ethan clutched his blanket. Sarah shoved the key in the ignition. She listened as the car groaned coming to life. She peered into her mirror to check on Ethan. His head slumped forward.

"Hang on, Ethan. We'll get there."

Halfway down the road between her lane and Michael's clinic she heard a "clink" and "clank," before the engine groaned one last time and left her stuck in the middle of the road.

"Not now!" She tried to start it again. "I don't have time for this!" She looked back at Ethan. His breathing became labored.

She slammed the car into neutral.

"Hold tight," she told Ethan as she got out of the car. With one hand on the steering wheel and the other holding her car door open, she pushed it off to the side of the road.

Leaving the headlights on, she unfastened the seatbelt across Ethan's lap and lifted him into her arms.

He wrapped his arms around her neck and she pressed his head to her shoulder. She ran her hand over his hair. "It's okay. Everything is going to be okay."

She turned around in the middle of the road, judged the distance back to the house and to Michael's clinic. Michael was closer. She readjusted Ethan in her arms and headed for the clinic.

Ethan whimpered while she carried him. Her arms burned with the effort to carry his weight by the time she reached the clinic's parking lot.

She spotted Michael's truck parked under a light pole. She shifted Ethan in her arms and kept walking. *Just a little further.*

Ethan groaned and she felt the warmth of vomit spill down her back. She gritted her teeth and sat Ethan down at the bottom of the stairs.

She wiped his face with the hem of her shirt. His face felt damp and his hairline was soaked. She peered up the length of the stairs.

“I’ll be right back.”

Ethan clung to her. “Don’t go.”

Sarah hunched down to reassure him, and noticed his eyes appeared glazed. What if his fever continued to rise?

“I’ll be right back, I promise.” She caressed the side of his face with her hand. “Stay right here.”

Ethan grabbed his blanket and nodded.

Sarah raced up the stairs and pounded on the door. Her heart fluttered. She pounded again. She glanced down at Ethan at the bottom of the stairs. “Michael! Michael!”

A tremor ran up her spine and her arms prickled. She jiggled the doorknob and turned it. She gasped as the door opened and she pushed her way inside.

Groping in the dark, she flicked on the light as Michael sat up on the sofa.

“Sarah?” He rubbed his eyes.

“Where are your keys?” she demanded.

“Keys?”

“Yes, keys, as in your car or your truck, I don’t care which!” Sarah searched the countertop in his kitchen.

“What?” He yawned. “What are you doing?”

“Give me your keys!” she shouted.

Michael blinked. “What’s wrong? Where’s Ethan?”

He swung his legs off the couch and stood.

“My car broke down, and I need to get Ethan to the hospital.”

“Where is he?” Michael rushed towards her.

“He’s at the bottom of the stairs. I need your keys *now*!” Sarah glanced back at the open doorway.

“I’ll take you.”

“Are you even awake?” she asked.

“Of course I am.”

“Fine.” Sarah rushed out the door.

CHAPTER 27

Michael watched the wide glass doors of the hospital's emergency ward slide open. The white marble tiles appeared dull against the maroon chairs lined against the walls. The room's white walls made the area seem larger than it actually was.

The front desk curved out from the wall, a band of maroon. A dark-haired woman sat with her head bent as her fingers glided across a keyboard. Tap, tap, tap.

Her keystrokes were interrupted by a cough from a man hunched over in the corner of the emergency waiting room.

Silence resumed. Michael held Ethan huddled in his arms while he sat beside Sarah. How long had they sat here? A minute? Or two? Not that he could keep track without a clock anywhere in sight.

Sarah tugged at her shirt.

"I can get you another one," he said.

"I don't need another one."

"You'd be more comfortable." He watched as her crossed-leg bounced with nervous energy.

Sarah rolled back her shoulders. "I'm fine."

"You've got puke in your hair."

Her eyes grew large and she reached up to the back of her

hair. She grimaced. “I’ll have to wash it later.”

“Did I mention that it stinks?” He wrinkled his nose.

Sarah’s lips thinned into a straight line.

A short man in green scrubs walked out into the waiting area. He glanced down at a clipboard. “Edith Jenson.”

An elderly woman slumped in a wheelchair rolled by, and the woman escorting her halted the chair to pull the hem of the woolen blanket clear of the wheels. There were no legs beneath the blanket, just two uneven stubs.

“There’s a shirt in the truck.” He watched the woman wheel past them.

Sarah reached over and ran her hand over Ethan’s forehead. “Maybe later.”

“The truck is right outside the doors. It wouldn’t take you more than a minute.”

Her eyes narrowed. “I need to be there when he goes in. I’m his mother.”

“I didn’t say you weren’t. I merely offered for you to be more comfortable.”

The doors slid open. The sounds from the keyboard paused. No one came in. Tap, tap, tap.

“How would you like to have puke down your back?”

“I’d change my shirt.”

She scowled at him and crossed her arms. “I’m sure this happens to you all the time.”

“I’ve dealt with worse.” Ethan lifted his head to look at Sarah. “It’s okay, Sport. We’ll be in to see the doctor soon.”

Ethan laid his head back down.

“For an emergency room, no one around here is in a hurry,” Sarah said.

“You could change your shirt and be back here before the doctor comes,” Michael offered.

Sarah glared at him. “Fine!”

Michael shifted Ethan and turned slightly away from her.

Sarah marched out of the hospital and out to the parking lot. He watched her march back inside and thrust her hand out.

He pulled his truck keys out of his pocket and handed them to her. Ethan turned his head to watch her go.

A few moments later, the sliding doors opened and Sarah came back inside. She disappeared down the hallway and returned a short while later wearing one of Michael's old shirts, and the puke gone from her hair.

She sat back down beside him, stuffed the shirt in her bag, and crossed her legs.

He tucked the blanket around Ethan. Seconds ticked by into minutes.

The man in scrubs returned. "Bart Adams."

Another man held his arm bent at a right angle against his chest stepped forward.

Sarah reached over and placed her hand on Ethan's brow.

"Feel better now?"

The sounds of a siren grew louder, and an ambulance pulled up. Red lights flashed in sequence. A young man was pushed into the lobby on a stretcher. Immediately, medical personnel swarmed around him. Sarah made a sound in her throat. His sentiments, exactly.

Sarah brushed away a fallen lock of hair from Ethan's flushed face.

Twice Sarah shifted her weight in the plastic chair. Her eyes darted over at Michael. A wet hacking cough rippled through the man in the corner, and a nurse came out shortly to cart the man off in the direction of a doctor.

"Michael Colvert," the man in the green scrubs called from the door. Sarah snatched Ethan's limp form from Michael and headed for the nurse. Michael picked up Sarah's forgotten bag as he followed. Later, he would rejoice in the knowledge of his son's proper name.

Sarah fussed over Ethan as the pediatric doctor on call, an overworked dark-skinned man, examined Ethan. Michael stood back, out of everyone's way, and watched.

"It's influenza," the doctor explained. "Children's fevers tend to spike during the night. Take him home; give him plenty of fluids and rest. I'd probably keep him home from school for a few days."

A rattle-filled sigh came up from her chest. It all made sense. She felt a tickle of laughter arise in her throat. How many nights, as an infant, had she held him and rocked him with fevers? Perhaps she might have over reacted.

However, this one had been the worst.

A nurse came in the room with a sheet of instructions, and stickers for Ethan. Michael leaned against the far wall. He thanked the doctor on the man's way out.

Silence filled the car as Michael drove them back to Sarah's. Ethan, with his head flopped to the side, slept in his seat. Through the darkness, Sarah glanced at Michael, who kept his gaze on the road. Her hands twisted on her lap, but she couldn't quite bring herself to say a word, despite the urge she felt to explain herself to Michael. Maybe, just maybe he'd understand.

Inside the house, with Ethan in his arms, Sarah led Michael to Ethan's room. She stepped back out of the way and watched as Michael laid their son down and tucked Ethan into bed. A tight hold squeezed at her throat and she forced herself to swallow it down as Michael turned and walked out of the room. Taking one final glance at her son, she followed Michael down the hall.

At the bottom of the stairs, Michael reached for the doorknob.

"Thanks for the shirt. I'll see that you get it back."

"Keep it. I've got lots of them." He turned the knob.

"Coffee?" Sarah blurted and gripped the bottom rail.

Michael faced the door. "It's been a long night."

"It's almost morning." She bit her lip.

"I guess a cup of coffee would help." Michael turned and motioned for her to lead him down the hallway to the kitchen. Sarah flicked on the switch on the coffeepot, thankful Jenny always prepped it to brew come dawn. As Sarah pushed back the curtain to view the flooded pinks and soft hues of yellow spreading in the gray twilight of morning, she felt her hand twitch and her heart beat with the drip of the coffee into the pot.

Michael took a seat at the table. "You don't have to do this, you know."

"It wasn't me who gave you the letter." Sarah leaned back against the counter and hugged her arms around herself.

Michael rested his elbows on the table. "Yet, you wrote it."

"I should have told you long ago." She took a deep breath and slowly exhaled. "I wrote that letter with childlike dreams of having you come back and take me away from this empty place, but then I stood on the doorstep of your parents' estate and knew it was never going to happen."

Behind her, the coffee continued to percolate and Michael remained silent.

"My grandmother told me if your family found out about the baby, they'd make me get rid of him—and I couldn't do that. All I had left when I came home that summer was our child growing beneath my heart."

Michael covered his face in his hands.

"You have to understand, Ethan was, until now, the only hope I've had in my life."

Michael held up his hand. "I do."

"You do?" She felt a sudden rush of panic and relief at the same time.

Michael sighed and stood up. "Your grandmother's reasoning may have held some truth, but we'll never know."

"I promised her I'd never be with any man again and I kept my promise." Sarah felt the heat of the coffeepot at her back and stepped towards Michael.

"Is that why you've held Josh at arm's length all this time?" Michael questioned.

"I've never loved Josh, not the way I loved you." She looked towards the coffeepot, watching the dark liquid drip.

Michael's hand lifted her by the chin and when she raised her gaze to his she felt a sharp pain in her chest.

"Loved, or still do?"

Sarah took a shaky breath. Her knees felt weak and unstable. "I do. I always have. Even when Gran told me I was foolish. I loved you then, and I love you now."

Her nose burned and her eyes drew pools of tears at the lashes. He muttered something about his mother and brushed his thumb across her cheek. "I know you were only trying to protect Ethan."

"I've lost almost everything that I loved in my life." Her voice trembled.

"I wouldn't take him from you, Sarah. If only you had trusted me."

She saw the grief flicker in his eyes. "It wasn't you I didn't trust, Michael—it was God. That's why, if you never say you love me and never want me to be a part of your life, I can accept that." But, even as she said those words, she felt the deep ache in her heart.

"But *now*, do you trust God?"

"With all that I am, and all that I'll ever be," Sarah whispered.

"I failed you when you needed me most."

"How could you? You didn't know."

"I've lost the last five years with my son. I want you and Ethan in my life, permanently."

Her lips parted, but she didn't know what to say. Did Michael say what she thought he said? *Oh Lord, does this mean what I think it means*?

Sliding down to one knee in her kitchen, Michael pulled a small box from the front pocket of his jeans. It was still there from his trip. He'd almost forgotten it until now.

Sarah gulped back the lump in her throat.

"Will you marry me, Sarah Colvert?"

Large tears trailed down her cheeks. She'd dreamed of this day. How many times had she awakened in the middle of the night before she could answer him? Now Michael looked at her with those love-filled blue eyes that made her heart about to explode. This time it was for real.

She caught the sobs behind her hands and nodded her head in a definite yes-motion. Michael grinned, straightened himself, and took her hand. Inside the small box sparkled an aquamarine stone on a silver band.

"I feel like Jacob." Michael slid the ring on her finger. "It took him seven years to pay for Rachel before they could be wed, but his love for her was strong and unwavering—as mine is for you, Sarah."

As Michael's lips touched hers, Sarah rose up on her toes and answered his kiss with one of her own. He wrapped his arms around her, drawing her closer. She clung to him for what felt like the length of time they'd lost. When he tore apart from her, she was breathless.

"How much longer shall I have to wait before you're my wife?"

"Is tomorrow soon enough?"

Sarah was sure he would have kissed her again, but then they heard the sounds of someone coming down the stairs. Together they turned to greet their future, as the past dissolved behind them.

EPILOGUE

Ethan rushed down the hall in front of Sarah. He skidded to a halt, stopping himself before he ran into Jenny's desk. "Come on, Aunt Jenny! We've got to go!"

Jenny glanced at Ethan and smiled, but continued to sort papers into folders.

Sarah checked her watch. Where was Michael? She glanced down the hallway and then at the glass pane door. Her image reflected in the glass, and she pushed the last tendril of her hair back into place. She tugged on the hem of her shirt and turned sideways.

"You look fine," Jenny said, setting the folders aside. Michael had told her the same thing as she helped him straighten up one of the exam rooms.

"Aunt Jenny!" Ethan wailed again. "We're gonna be late!"

Jenny closed her laptop. "I need a minute."

Ethan stuck his elbows on the desk and rested his chin in his hands. "I knew it. We're going to be late." He sighed.

Sarah tussled his hair. She smiled at him trying to force the queasiness down. She hadn't felt this way since the last time she'd entered a horse show.

"Coming?" Ethan asked.

"We'll get there soon enough," Sarah said.

Jenny checked to make sure the answering machine was on for any calls they'd miss while they were out.

"Almost ready," Jenny said, as Michael walked down the hallway, tossed his lab coat on a hook, and swept Ethan up in his arms.

"Ready, gang?" he asked.

"Almost," Ethan wrapped his arms around Michael's neck. "Aunt Jenny, are you done yet?"

Sarah laughed. "You boys go along and we'll catch up."

"Let's go, Dad."

Sarah pushed back that same tendril of hair again that fell beside her cheek. Michael leaned close to her. "Relax."

With Ethan in his arms, Michael went out the door.

"Ready?" Jenny asked as Sarah held open the door for them.

Sarah nodded.

"Let's go," said Jenny.

Scissors! Quickly, Sarah turned back toward Jenny's desk. "Can't forget these!" Sarah held up a pair of black-handled shears.

Parked cars lined both sides of the road and lane that entered Silver Wind Equine Rescue. Large groups of people milled across the front lawn. From where Sarah stood, it appeared as if half the state came for this day.

Nearby, horses stood twitching their tails in the pastures. Not one horse seemed to mind the conversations floating through the air. Outside the stables, a wide red ribbon hung low across the entrance.

Sarah felt like jumping the fence and stirring up the horses to race across the fields.

"See them anywhere?" Jenny asked, her hand shading her eyes.

"There," Sarah pointed to Michael and Ethan standing in the food line. Tables laden with red and white checkered tablecloths were set up across the lawn. People helped themselves to large vats of chili, bowls of potato salad, and platters of fried chicken and hamburgers.

Sarah brushed away tears of joy.

Jenny tugged Sarah's sleeve. "Look, there's Josh."

Sarah hesitated.

"Oh, don't tell me you two still haven't made up."

Sarah glanced at Jenny; she tried hard to put on her best smile. Yet, she didn't blame Josh for not showing up at the wedding, or for avoiding her these past few months. She should be thanking him for what he'd done. But why was this so hard? Hadn't she forgiven him? She and Michael had decided it didn't matter who gave him the letter, only that the truth was finally out.

"I need to thank him," Sarah said.

"Thank Josh? For what?" Jenny's eyebrows shot up.

"For giving Michael the letter."

Jenny's cheeks turned as red as the roots of her hair. "Ah ... well ... you see ... ah ..."

Jenny speechless? How could Sarah have been so naive not to have seen it? She nearly laughed. It was Jenny. She had, after all, threatened to tell Michael. Yet, with all the opportunities she had, why did she wait to give him the letter? And ...

"How did you know where to find it?" Sarah asked.

A smile curved on Jenny's lips. "Josh tells me everything. We are twins after all."

She should have known, not that it mattered now. She spotted Michael waving at her, and Ethan stuffing a hotdog in his mouth. People gathered in front of the stables awaiting the announcement.

"One of these days ..."

She remembered the scissors in her hand.

"I know." Jenny held up her hand. "But there is no trouble in today, and yesterday has already passed."

Sarah wished she could have more time talking with Jenny, but Ethan ran toward her. Michael stood at the front of the stables, and out of the corner of her eye she spotted Josh moseying his way along with the crowd.

"And tomorrow we'll still be best friends." Sarah parted from Jenny to join her son. Ethan pulled her by the hand as they wove their way through the crowd to the front of the stables.

Josh stood at the corner of the barn not far from them, and Jenny slipped through the crowd to stand by her twin. His hat pulled down low so the brim shaded his face from Sarah's view. With a tug from Ethan, she turned her focus on Michael—her husband.

"Ladies and gentleman, friends and family, thank you for gathering here today as we officially open the Silver Wind Equine Rescue and Clinic," Michael shouted. Applause rippled through the crowd. When it became quiet again, he said, "Before we get started, I'd like to take this moment and have Pastor Olson lead us in prayer."

Michael slid one arm around Sarah and the other around Ethan. The white-haired minister stepped forward, and Sarah felt her throat tighten. She tried to swallow back the small sob. "If only my parents could be here to witness this moment."

Michael pulled her closer. "They're here, too, Sarah, watching over us."

She swiped at her tears. Ethan hugged her waist, while the pastor prayed. It reminded her of her wedding day, with Michael at her side and Ethan standing between them, holding out their rings in his small hand. Pastor Olson had prayed over them that day too.

She heard the crowd echo, "Amen," and looked up in a blur of tear-drenched lashes. Handing Ethan the scissors, the heaviness in her heart lifted as together they cut the ribbon.

People hugged them, shook their hands, and patted their backs as they did outside the church those few months ago at their wedding.

When the last person passed through the line, Ethan pulled Michael back toward the food tables. Sarah knew she couldn't put it off any longer.

She needed to talk to Josh.

She found him sitting on the front porch steps of the old farmhouse. He forked another bite of potato salad into his mouth. Breathing a quick prayer, she sat down beside him. Expecting him to get up or flinch, she sighed with relief that he did neither.

Sarah fought hard to hold her quivering smile in place. "I'm sorry, Josh."

"We all make mistakes." He gazed towards the stables.

"I don't suppose you could forgive me?" Sarah stopped trying to force her smile, and focused on the people milling about the front lawn.

Josh put down his plate and washed his potato salad down with a gulp of soda. Finally, he looked at her. "Isn't that what friends are for?"

"You're one of the best friends I could ever have, Josh. You and Jenny will always be family."

"I know." Josh ducked his head. A moment passed then a grin spread across his face. "I suppose this means I'll have to get myself a hot date now that you're married."

She nudged him. "Blonde, right?"

"Can't say for sure. I've always been a little partial to brunettes," he said.

She froze.

Josh laughed.

Then she laughed with him. *Good ole Josh.*

"Uh-oh, trouble coming." He nodded toward Ethan and Michael walking their way.

"So I see. And it looks like they're up to something," Sarah said.

"Hey, Mom, can I have a pony?"

"Pony?" Hadn't she and Michael discussed this only a few days ago? Her gaze moved to her husband.

Michael, with a broad grin, shrugged. "It was either a pony or a baby brother."

"Can I Mom?"

Sarah went into Michael's arms and whispered in his ear.

"Should we tell him?"

"Let's start with the pony," Michael said.

"Then I suppose," Sarah said to Ethan, "it'll have to be a pony, for now."

"Yes!" Ethan pulled a fist down in the air. "Did you hear that Uncle Josh? I'm getting a pony!"

"Sure did, Squirt." Josh eased himself off the stair. Ethan ran off into the clusters of people.

"He'll never find Jenny without my help." Josh ambled after Ethan.

"You know I'll always love you," she said.

He slid his arms around her waist and drew her near. "What price do you think we should pay this time around?"

As she reached up and brought his face down to meet her tender kiss, she remembered the price of hope she'd paid for one horse's life that brought her a new family and taught her to trust in God's faith.

Somewhere in the heavens, she pictured her mother and father rejoicing, happy she and Michael had found their way back to one another.

DEAR FRIEND,

Hundreds of horses each year are saved by local rescues. Without the heart and financial support of others, these horses would most likely end up in slaughter houses.

The condition of these horses is rarely good. However, given a second chance, many of them learn to trust again and go on to spend the rest of their days in loving homes.

When I first heard about horse rescues, I knew that is exactly the right place for Sarah's story to take place. The inclusion of Sarah purchasing a horse for seven dollars comes from a true story about a horse that was sold at auction for seven dollars and wasn't able to be saved.

In memory of my former horse, Shamrock, a portion of the sales proceeds from this book series will be donated to a horse rescue.

Thank you for taking this ride with me. Saddle up dear friends, the Silver Wind Trilogy has only begun. Please be sure to join Jenny on her road of faith in *Unbridled*. You all are the very best!

Susan

READING GROUP GUIDE

1. Which character did you most relate to and why?
2. Sarah and Jenny are best friends, yet they approach their faith in different ways. Why do you think that is? Have you experienced anything similar with your best friend?
3. How did Michael's past experience in his childhood affect his ability to forgive Sarah?
4. Sometimes Jenny tried to manipulate Sarah into confessing the truth. Why do you think such tactics are usually ineffective despite the best of intentions?
5. In what ways was Bonnie, Sarah's seven dollar horse, symbolic in this story?
6. Throughout the book, we shift from Sarah and Michael's past to the present. How does their past shape who they are?
7. Sarah's loss of her parents and past with Michael caused her to develop a fear of loneliness. Have you ever clung to a false belief? How did you discover it was false, and what did you do to overcome it?

8. Jenny confronted Sarah about her reluctance to tell Michael about Ethan. What does the Bible say about confronting each other? Do you think Jenny handled it well? Should she have persisted in confrontations?
9. Sarah had a child when she was a teenager. How does that relate with our perceptions of young parenthood today? How is Sarah different?
10. At what point do you think Sarah realized that the hope she had for the abandoned horses was the same hope God had for her, Michael, and Ethan?

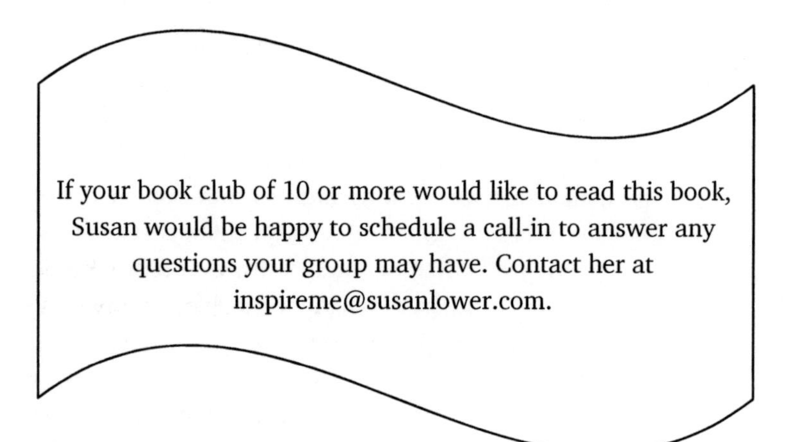

ACKNOWLEDGEMENTS

Writing a book is a team effort, and I couldn't have done this without the support of the West Branch Christian Writers and Saint Davids Christian Writers.

A special thanks to my editor, Kathy Carlton Willis, who believed in this project and had a heart for this story as much as I did. I'm forever grateful to my father, who bought me my first horse and put me back on when I fell off.

Author Eileen Berger was my first reader. Thank you, friend, for the wisdom and patience you shared with me as a writer. I will treasure it always.

I'm grateful for Amy Weigle and Susie Baldassari, my beta readers whose feedback has proven invaluable to me.

Thanks to my Facebook friends at 'Susan Lower, Author' and Twitter friends, who helped me pick the cover design for this book and name a few of the horses. Thank you for all your valuable input!

To my family: Chad, Isabella, Malachi, and Alessandra. I love each one of you so much! Thank you for the cups of tea, helping around the house, and believing in me.

Lastly, thank you, friend, for letting me share this story with you. I couldn't do this if it wasn't for you. I enjoy connecting with readers like you through my Facebook group and on Twitter. Visit my website at www.SusanLower.com or just drop me a note at inspireme@susanlower.com I'd love to hear from you.

AN EXCERPT FROM *UNBRIDLED*

"Come on Jen, don't be that way."

Jenny Anderson stared at the man who'd taken her out to dinner, sat beside her in church every Sunday this year, and just confessed he was a family man.

Only his wife and children lived in Indiana.

For a moment, she didn't think she'd heard him right. Nevertheless, by the look on his face, he was dead serious. She took a deep breath, her heart rattling in her chest.

All the while he'd been here working for the construction company in Shelbyville, Kentucky, he'd been courting her. Three days after his company started building the equine clinic where she worked, he had asked her out to dinner.

Her cheeks turned cold as the blood drained from her face. Unable to speak, she turned on her heel and strode out of the clinic. In the parking lot, she reached for the door handle of a red diesel truck.

"Didn't you hear what I said?" He followed her.

Oh, she'd him heard all right. In fact, she was certain everyone inside the clinic had stopped to stretch an ear toward their conversation.

He grabbed her by the arm.

Jenny's gaze fell to his hand. How many times had she held that hand so lovingly, just this past week? She looked up at him, holding her breath as if it would hold back the dam of tears building behind her eyes.

"If you don't mind." It took every ounce of her will power to hold steady. "I have a rescue that needs picked up."

"Then I'll go with you."

Jenny shook her head, biting her lip against any further words.

"So this is how it's going to be?"

This was the way it *had* to be. Opening the truck door and climbing inside the driver seat, she pried a set of keys from her jeans pocket. Avoiding taking one last look at the man who shattered her dreams of becoming his wife, she placed the key in the ignition. Why else would he have come at noon bearing gifts and wearing his best clothes?

"You're nothing but a Bible thumper!" he yelled.

She turned the key and the roar of the truck's engine drowned out whatever words he said next. It was probably better this way.

She glanced in the rearview mirror, relieved that at least the trailer was hitched. As she steered the truck out of the clinic's parking lot, her chest became heavy, and each breath more difficult.

She watched from her side-view mirror as he tossed down his hat and balled his fist as she drove away.

Jenny inhaled deeply through her nose and exhaled through her mouth, but it was no use.

She pulled out onto the main road. Her heart torn by one man's misleading love and her love and fear for Christ.

"Thou shall not commit adultery," she whispered. Was she guilty of such a sin even now? She prayed a silent prayer of forgiveness.

How could he? Her knuckles turned white as she gripped the steering wheel. *All these months*! They'd even sat in church together!

A lump formed in her throat. She turned left at the crossroads, following the signs toward the highway.

Her nose stung. She tried to concentrate on the rescue she needed to pick up. Since she, her twin brother Josh, and her best friend Sarah, started Silver Wind Equine Rescue over a year ago, they'd received regular calls to pick up surrendered horses.

Right now, however, Jenny felt she were the one needing rescued.

It wasn't fair! Why couldn't she be happy like Sarah was with Michael? Hadn't God brought them back together after they'd been separated for all these years?

Good things come to those who wait, she smirked. She wasn't a teenager anymore. No, it was her friend, Sarah, who'd gotten herself in trouble during their teenage years. Jenny spent her time ministering through the I'm Worth Waiting For program.

Now who would wait for her? All of the nice guys at church were either married or older and still living with their mothers.

She choked back a sob.

She'd been so certain, when he approached her at the clinic, that Brad had finally come to propose. *Oh Lord, why did you let this go on for so long?*

As she merged onto the highway, an eighteen-wheeler whizzed past. She braced the steering wheel, feeling the trailer sway behind her. The truck became a blur of black going down the highway, or perhaps it was her vision that blurred as her cheeks grew damp. She swiped at the tears rolling down her cheeks.

Suddenly, the truck gained a burst of energy. Jenny frowned. From her side view mirror, she spotted the sun glinting off the aluminum trailer.

Her heart sank into her stomach. She watched as the trailer crossed two lanes, clipped the back wheel of a motorcycle, and veered into the grassy dike between the opposing highways.

Immediately, she slammed on the brakes.

Cade Sheridan's whole life seemed to go by in slow motion. His motorcycle tilted into a sixty miles-per-hour slide down the outer lane of the highway. It was like riding the spinner at the carnival when he was young. So fast, yet everything became slow and made him dizzy. He rode the shiny side of his motorcycle with the sound of metal against pavement roaring in his ears. As the motorbike slowed down, he heard, "*Move fast when you stop*."

He leapt from his motorcycle and scrambled off the highway rolling and crawling on his belly. An instant later, metal met metal as an eighteen-wheeler zoomed by and ran over his motorcycle like it was yesterday's road kill.

He heard the high piercing squeal as the eighteen-wheeler hit its brakes and came to a screaming halt.

Cade sat up at the edge of the highway. He patted his chest and his arms. His leather jacket was torn. Yet, to his relief, his arms were still in the sleeves.

Unsteadily, he got to his feet.

Several cars slowed and pulled over. A red truck pulled up behind him.

He gazed out at the metal massacre. His motorcycle lay scattered in dozens of bits across the highway. He reached up and tried to unbuckle his helmet. His fingers fumbled with the metal D-ring.

"You alright?" The owner of the eighteen-wheeler jumped out of his truck and ran towards him. "I've called it in; help's on the way."

He couldn't get the visor on his helmet to lift. Its cracked hinge prevented it from moving upwards. He stared across at the shattered pieces of his motorcycle and stumbled back.

"Here, let me help you."

Cade turned; a red-haired woman stood before him with tears streaking down her face. She appeared out of nowhere, just like the voice he'd heard moments before. Was he in shock? He became weak in the knees. He needed to sit down before he crumbled to the side of the road.

"Help is on the way," he heard the truck driver yell again.

"I'm so sorry," she cried. "Are you okay?"

He shook his head, unsure if the rattle he heard came from his motorcycle or a piece of his brain. Slowly, he looked at her.

Her green eyes glistened in their watery state. Mesmerized by those eyes, he kept his focus on her as he reached again for the strap of his helmet. She brushed his fingers away and tugged on the straps.

Sirens sounded in the distance.

"Don't go to sleep on me now, stay awake," she said.

He'd closed his eyes at the sheer relief of her loosening his chinstrap. He tried, but opening his eyes even to squint at her became a struggle.

The pavement had been hard. His motorcycle had been hard. His life had been hard. But now, he felt everything lifting away from him, except for those eyes.

He felt a final tug on the strap, and it fell away from his chin.

"Better not take that off till the paramedics get here," someone said.

"I'm so sorry," she cried.

Sorry for what?

Then his world went black.

The story continues in *Unbridled* by Susan Lower.